The Soul Gene

Lynn Demarest

ISBN: 1478364971
ISBN-13: 978-1478364979

To Diana, my dove, who never stopped
encouraging me to write this story.

CONTENTS

Prologue: Déjà vu   1

1 Bayner Genetics   5

2 Rare as Rhenium   21

3 Chez Paris   33

4 A Prayer Answered   41

5 Lolly and Little Lila   50

6 Buddhism and Bailey   60

7 Rocco Makes it Hurt   68

8 Junk DNA   78

9 Father Jim's Boys   87

10 Reincarnation   95

11 Dalai Lama DNA   106

12 Max Dubois Hits it Big   117

13 Tickets to Tibet   126

14 Abstract Peace   134

15 Barbie in Love   145

16 Potala Palace   153

17 Too Lucrative to Cure   165

18 Zhenbang in Beijing   178

19 Nine Cherries   189

20 Repentance   203

21 Suze's Soul   215

22 Bailey Burns the Evidence   221

23 Little Dot   228

24 Let It Be   240

ACKNOWLEDGMENTS

This book could not have been written without the Internet, so first I'd like to thank Sir Timothy John Berners-Lee, the beneficent inventor of HTML, which I count as the greatest gift to mankind since Jonas Salk's polio vaccine. Thanks also is due the many unknown people who have filled the Internet with information about everything from the Dalai Lama to God of War. If you've posted pictures or videos of your vacation to Lhasa, Tibet, I've probably seen them. Thank you! Finally, I'd like to thank the friends and family who helped me proof the book and encouraged me to publish it: Barbara Worth, Sandy Ball, Chauncey Mabe, Joanne Fanizza, Adele Israel, Randall Cherry, Jim Hanford, Marie Coyne, and Francine DiGiacamo.

PROLOGUE :
DÉJÀ VU

Bailey Foster is at the beach again. She's lying facedown on a big blue towel in a strapless white bikini with the top untied to prevent tan lines. It's July in South Florida, high noon, and hot as hell.

Bailey feels her back start to burn. She reaches around and deftly reties the top, then flips over in place like a freshly landed fish. The brightness from above forces her eyes shut. From inside the lids, she sees the fluorescent red-orange glow of her own blood.

A light ocean breeze carries the squawks of seabirds and the squeals of children playing in the surf, but it does little to sooth her searing skin.

Bailey Foster knows the Sun's danger well, knows she's playing with the fire of all fires. Still, she can't resist. She loves the Sun. She loves the way it makes her hair blonder and her eyes bluer. She loves the cosmic glow it leaves humming inside her.

Her eyes still closed, Bailey feels around on the towel beside her head, finds her ear buds, and pushes them in. A strange song is playing. She's never heard it before. The singing is angelic.

We have all been here before.
This is not our first time ashore.
We have lived and lived some more.
For we have all been here before!

Bailey imagines a single photon as it screams out of the Sun and barrels toward Earth. After an eight-minute trip, the tiny particle of light zooms into a bead of sweat on her flat abdomen. The convex droplet refracts the photon into one of her sizzling skin cells, where it collides with a molecule of DNA – deoxyribonucleic acid – and blasts a hole in it like a bowling ball hurled against a ladder made of matchsticks.

Luckily, she thinks, she's still young, only twenty-six. She imagines her battered cell's repair molecules leaping into action. Evolved to fix her damaged double helix with an elegance indicative of a clever creator, the littlest paramedics put Bailey Foster's DNA back together again.

She knows she won't be able to abuse herself like this forever. As she grows old, the microscopic medics will grow old, too, and lose their knack for healing. The result could be skin cancer. Melanoma.

Maybe one day, Bailey thinks, she herself will find a cure for the deadly cancer, but she'll have to do it somewhere other than Bayner Genetics, where she works as a DNA researcher. Ever since the founders left the company to their quirky daughter a dozen years ago, Bayner Genetics research teams have studied only the rarest of diseases. Many of them Bailey had never even heard of before being assigned to hunt for their cures, which even if found would typically save only a relative handful of lives.

I have to find a new job, she thinks for the thousandth time.

You have all been here before.
This is not your first time ashore.
You have lived and lived some more.
For you have all been here before!

Bailey presses her palms against the lumpy sand beneath her beach towel and feels the awesome mass of the Earth. She imagines herself stuck to sunlit side of the gigantic blue ball as it glides around a dent in space-time created by the even more gargantuan Sun, a sphere so huge it could hold a million puny Earths.

Oh! That incredible Sun! Even from ninety-three million miles away, its nuclear heat makes her feel lightheaded. Her eyes, seeking refuge from the light, roll back in their sockets. The red-orange

glow fades to black. Her thoughts begin to drift.

She's daydreaming.

Bailey Foster sees a small wooden house sitting alone in an endless grassland. There are chickens meandering about. As they wander, they scratch at the dirt with their long toes, then step back quickly to inspect the place they've just disturbed, hoping to find an unearthed seed or the tail end of a fleeing worm.

To the left of the little house there's a pen holding a family of goats. The adult goats stand as still as statues and appear not to notice as the kids bound about as if on springs.

Nearby, in a separate pen, two pigs are luxuriating in what's left of a mud hole. A few yards from the pigs, a stoic milk cow stands in the shade of a solitary tree no taller than the peak of the little house. A big brass bell is tied around the cow's neck with a red ribbon.

To the right of the house is an immaculate vegetable garden about the size of two tennis courts, its rows manicured and straight as laser beams. Beside it, a steel windmill squeaks as it turns.

A girl comes out of the house. She looks to be maybe five. Her feet are bare. She has long blonde hair and is wearing overalls with the legs rolled up. She's holding a rope handle attached to a wooden bucket. She swings the bucket as she skips toward the windmill. Once there, she places the bucket on a worn wooden platform, reaches up, grabs a pump handle with both hands and pulls it down with all her might.

Water begins to flow into the bucket. She gives the handle three strong pumps, then lifts the bucket and puts it back down. She considers for a moment, then adds two more small pulls of water. She grabs the rope handle with both hands and lifts the bucket away. As she carries it back toward the little house, the bucket's new weight forces her to stop every few steps to rest and improve her grip.

One of the pigs grunts. The girl looks toward the sound and notices that the mud hole has almost dried up. She sighs, lugs the bucket over to the pen and, with more than a little difficulty, lifts it up onto a sturdy fencepost. The pigs grunt and jockey for position beneath the bucket. The girl pours the water onto them. They lap happily at the cool waterfall and, when it's done, settle back down

into the new mud.

The girl takes the empty bucket back to the pump, refills it, and carries it to the house. She must have put in a little less water this time. The bucket is easier to carry.

Finally, she's at the door. Before she reenters the house, she lowers the bucket carefully on the doorstep, turns, shades her eyes, and looks up at the Sun. She pulls a red cloth from a back pocket and wipes her face. Then she lowers her gaze and looks straight at Bailey. She has blue eyes.

We have all been here before...
We have all been here before...

1
BAYNER GENETICS

Abraham Bayner met Megan McConnell in Boston, Massachusetts, after the end of their first semester at Harvard Medical School. It was Friday, December 15, 1967 – ten days before Christmas and the day after Arthur Kornberg announced that he had created DNA molecules in a test tube exactly like those found in a common virus.

Kornberg's precise statement the day before had specifically warned against describing his accomplishment as "creating life," but President Lyndon Baines Johnson, a drawling ex-schoolteacher from Texas, wandered off script.

"Some geniuses at Stanford University have created life in the test tube!" the president crowed, and news outlets around the world repeated his error.

Making DNA from scratch was big news, but Kornberg's spectacular feat that day was made possible by a less dramatic but far more important discovery that had gone virtually unnoticed outside of scientific circles, maybe because its importance was more difficult to explain, more probably because no fewer than five scientists (including Kornberg himself) had discovered it more or less simultaneously.

DNA ligase, it was called, and it would be as important to the future of genetics as the solid rocket booster would be to space travel. DNA ligase was the chemical glue that geneticists would use down the road to paste a gene from one species of life into another. This precise form of cross-breeding would help scientists fix

nature's flaws, letting them design plants immune to disease and unappetizing to insects. Just as important, it would enable them to transform bacteria into tiny factories capable of manufacturing everything from insulin to diesel fuel.

You could keep Red Sox slugger Carl Yastrzemski. When Abraham Bayner and Megan McConnell thought *hero*, they thought Arthur Kornberg.

They met in the afternoon at Antonio's Pizza, on the corner of Huntington and Francis, just across the street from the Peter Bent Brigham Hospital, whose name gave Abe a cheap chuckle the first time he saw it.

Meg was there first. She had almost finished her slices when Abe walked in. He was tall, maybe six-foot-four, and had a curly mop of light brown hair that reminded Meg of Bob Dylan's frizzy do on the cover of *Blonde on Blonde*. He wore hiking boots and jeans and, under his open winter coat, the first dashiki Meg had ever seen, a colorful cotton pullover printed with a psychedelic design that looked distinctly African.

Abe bought a Coke and two slices of Antonio's cheap pizza, then looked around for a place to sit. All of the tables were taken. He considered eating at the counter, then saw Meg raise an eyebrow and point to the other side of the booth she'd taken, a cramped cubbyhole made of plywood and two-by-fours.

Abe carried his Coke and the thin paper plate holding his two slices over to the booth and set them on the table.

"Antonio's is always packed!" he said.

"Cheap pizza in a college town. Who'd a thought?" Meg said. "Have a seat. I'm just about finished."

She was a twenty-two-year-old Irish-Catholic lass with china-doll skin, flaming red hair as straight as piano wire, and emerald eyes so green they looked alien.

Abe slid into the cramped booth and felt his knees bump into Meg's.

"Sorry," he said.

"The pizza's cheap," Meg said. "The booths are cheaper."

"Thanks for sharing," Abe said. "I'm Abraham Bayner. I hate the name, so please call me Abe."

"OK, Abe. I'm Megan McConnell. I like Megan, but you can

call me Meg if you like. Most people do."

Abe folded a slice of pizza, took a big bite from its greasy point and locked onto Meg's eyes.

"What are you staring at?" Meg asked, although he was hardly the first guy attracted to her unusual eyes.

"I've never seen anything like them," he said. "They look artificial."

"I assure you they're real. They were a gift from my maternal grandmother."

"They're captivating."

"So I've been told."

"Any of your brothers and sisters have eyes like that?"

"I'm an only child."

"No kidding? Me too."

Abe took another bite of pizza. It might be cheap, he thought, but it filled the hole.

"So," he said, "what brings you to Boston?"

"I'm a medical student at Harvard."

"Me too," Abe said. "I wasn't sure what I was going to do after I got my graduate degree in Chemistry. I tinkered with the idea of getting a doctorate and just becoming a professor, but that seemed lame, you know? I want to *do* something. Then I got a call from Dean Ebert, who just about begged me to come to Harvard Med. On full scholarship, no less. How could I turn Robert Ebert down?"

"I turned him down."

"He offered you a scholarship too?"

"Yeah."

Meg took a small sip of the Coke she was nursing.

"And you turned him down? I thought you said you were a Harvard Med student."

"I turned him down at first," Meg said. "Then he offered me a new car."

"A car! I didn't get a car!"

"You accepted his offer too soon, maybe," Meg said. "I strung Dean Ebert along for a month and he sweetened the deal with a cute little Mustang. Any color I wanted. I told him I still needed to think about it. A month later he called to tell me he'd found a little house to set me up in. At that point, even I couldn't say no."

"A house! You devil! I'm living in a studio."

Meg smiled.

"My dad says when someone makes you a great offer right off the bat, you should always feign disinterest. The offer will always get better, because no one ever gives you their best offer up front. Why would they? Of course, if the Bobster had bottom-lined me, I would have said OK. But he didn't."

"We're talking about Harvard Medical School here, not Crazy Eddie's Used Car Lot."

"What's the difference?" Meg said. She pinched a pepperoni from Abe's untouched second slice. "Harvard knows the students they want most – the ones most likely to have prestigious careers that will enhance the school's image – are the ones every elite school wants. To attract those students, they realize they've got to go the extra mile."

"You've got some nerve, Megan McConnell."

"That I do, Jew Boy, that I do."

"How did you know I was Jewish?"

"Your name isn't exactly Catholic," Meg said. She popped the pepperoni into her mouth and added, "Hey! I thought Jews didn't eat pork! What's up with the pepperoni pizza?"

"I believe in God," Abe said. "I just don't believe He cares whether I have pepperoni on my pizza."

Abe started in on the slice just defaced by Meg's playful theft and then, with his mouth full, said, "Hey, did you hear about Arthur Kornberg creating life in a test tube?"

"I heard about it," Meg said, "but Kornberg didn't create life, he just synthesized a DNA molecule like the one in the *phi X174* virus. He didn't create the whole virus."

"President Johnson said he created life."

"Johnson's a failed high-school teacher. And a warmonger."

"Fucking Vietnam. I'm glad I'm in school. War is the dumbest thing we do."

"You got that right."

Meg tried to take another sip of Coke but got air instead. Abe heard the gurgling sound and offered his Coke to her. She poured a splash of it into her cup.

"Thanks," Meg said. She watched Abe eat for a minute, then said, "Hey, you want to see the house? It's just around the corner."

Abe touched his chin as if in thought, smiled, and said, "I wonder if this is the point at which I should feign disinterest."

"You overestimate my offer!" Meg said. She kicked playfully at Abe's left ankle with the instep of her right foot and they both laughed.

"Eat up and we'll go," she said.

Abe gulped down the rest of the second slice and finished the Coke. Then Meg walked him to the Mustang (she'd chosen Candy Apple Red) and drove him to the little house she'd wrangled out of Harvard.

The small Cape Cod looked like a giant dollhouse had been dropped onto a cozy lot on the tree-lined street. The house was covered in bright white clapboards and had sunny yellow shutters on the downstairs windows and on the two little dormers that jutted out from a gray roof. In the New England tradition, the front door was painted fire-engine red so that it could be seen from the street even in a snowstorm. A white birch stood in the small front yard, leafless and ready for winter. All of its discarded leaves had been carefully removed from the little lawn, which itself had turned a dormant tan but still looked thick and healthy and ready for its rebirth in the spring.

"You keep a nice yard," Abe said.

"Harvard takes care of it," Meg said as she unlocked the red door. "No sense making their star medical student dig around in the mud, right?"

"Perish the thought!" Abe said.

They went inside and Meg gave him a quick tour. The walls were decorated with enlarged photos of sunflowers, black-eyed Susans and African daisies. There were also several big photos of the campus, one of which was a map. The walls themselves were painted a pale yellow in the places where wood paneling hadn't been installed. The furniture was a hodgepodge of teak, aluminum and space-age plastic. It was modern, boxy and upholstered in vinyl and synthetic suede. The kitchen was small but equipped with the latest appliances. The refrigerator had an automatic ice maker and under the laminate countertop was the first built-in dishwasher Abe had ever seen.

"They gave all this to you?" Abe said.

"Just to use."

"It's beautiful. Just like you."

"Flattery will get you everywhere, Jew Boy," Meg said.

She stood on tiptoes, threw her arms around his neck, pulled his face down to hers, and kissed him deeply with lips that tasted of pepperoni.

Then she whispered in his ear: "I need to take a shower. But I hate to waste all that water on myself."

Meg saw the puzzled look on Abe's face and added, "You know what they say: 'Save water: Shower with a friend.'"

She led him into the bathroom. They undressed each other, kissing as the clothes hit the floor, then stepped into the shower and helped each other get cleaner than a nun's habit.

After a long shower they dried each other off and she led him into her bedroom, backed him up against the bed, and pushed him onto it before jumping on with him.

Meg grabbed Abe's erect penis and said, "Aren't you glad you didn't feign disinterest, Jew Boy?"

The new lovers enjoyed a few more minutes of petting and kissing before Abe made his move. Meg pushed him away.

"Do you have a condom?" she said.

"Sorry, no," Abe said. "You're not on the pill?"

"I don't think they've perfected it yet," Meg said. "They're still tweaking the estrogen levels. Anyway, I'm not so keen about screwing with my hormones."

Meg saw disappointment darken Abe's face and felt his erection begin to wane. She hopped out of bed, dug into the nightstand drawer, and pulled out a Trojan.

"No worries, Abraham Bayner!" she said, flapping the condom as if it were a packet of coffee sugar.

She brought Abe back to attention, ripped open the little package with her teeth, and rolled the condom on. They spent the rest of the afternoon and that night in bed, exhausting Meg's rubber supply.

Over the next four years, while they were still in medical school, the couple faithfully used prophylactics. The last thing they wanted to do was interrupt their studies with an unplanned pregnancy.

When they graduated in 1971, however, they decided to

celebrate.

"Just this once," Meg cooed. "I don't think I'm ovulating."

"You sure?" Abe asked.

Meg answered him by sliding his unsheathed penis into her. The sex was fantastic. Looking back on that night, Meg thought she could almost feel herself getting pregnant.

Abortion on demand was available in New York, but it wasn't an option for Meg, who was Catholic enough to be against having an abortion herself. They were quickly married, well before Meg began to show. They loved each other madly even after having been together for four years, they reasoned, so it was only a matter of time before they got married anyway.

Abe was a non-practicing Jew. With Meg being a Catholic – and a pregnant one at that – a secular civil ceremony seemed the best choice, perhaps the only choice. They were married on a rocky beach in Cape Cod. It was a short affair attended by their families and a few friends. Meg's parents flew in from Arizona. Abe's mother had died in a car crash when he was ten, but his father drove up from New Jersey. Meg's uncle Bill, who owned a gas station in Walpole and also was a notary public, officiated.

Abe and Meg wrote their own over-sweetened vows. Meg went first. She'd memorized the words, and so was able to recite them while gazing into Abe's eyes.

"Abraham Bayner, I love you as I've loved no man. My heart aches with the joy you bring me. My soul sings your praises to the angels of my good fortune. I thank God for you and I vow at this moment and with every breath yet to come to remain at your side come what may: wealth or poverty, luck or misfortune, health or infirmity. I take you to be my husband, my love, my life, until I turn to dust."

Then it was Abe's turn. He produced a small slip of paper from his pocket, glanced at it for a second, wadded it up, and threw it dramatically onto the sand.

"Megan McConnell, I love you as I have loved no woman," he said, transfixed by those green eyes. "No man – least of all the one who stands before you now with his knees knocking like a frightened schoolboy – is worthy of such a love. I would be grateful enough to call you friend. I fear my heart will be unable to hold the happiness that will overwhelm it the moment I call you wife. I

promise to strive with all my being to prove myself worthy of you. I vow to stand by you in the darkness and in the light, to hold your hand as we walk together to the end of our blissful journey and return to the eternity from which we came."

Abe glanced at Meg's uncle Bill to let him know he was finished.

"I now pronounce you man and wife," Uncle Bill said. Then he turned to Abe and said, "You may now kiss the bride."

Abe bent down and kissed his new wife. The unexpected power of it momentarily staggered him. He didn't hear the wedding party's applause. He hugged Meg close and whispered into her ear, "Hello, Mrs. Bayner. I love you." Then they kissed again.

"Hey, hey, you two!" Uncle Bill crowed. "Get a room!"

After the short ceremony, there was music and dancing and drinking. Meg nursed two glasses of wine. Abe got as drunk as Meg had ever seen him. They spent the night on the cape, then returned the next day to Meg's little Harvard house. A honeymoon would have to wait until they could save up some money.

Besides, they had a life to get on with.

Known for having raced through medical school in record time, the two easily landed jobs at local research institutes affiliated with Harvard University. The pay was good and they were awarded signing bonuses that they used to move into a new three-one ranch (yellow with green shutters) on Grove Street in Waverley. (Meg's bonus was half again as large as Abe's.)

Seven months after the wedding, Gwendolyn Bayner was born. She was a healthy baby and over the next three years grew up to be a happy and active toddler with curly red hair and preternaturally green eyes. The floor of the little home was littered with dolls and toys, and the place smelled of baby powder and petroleum jelly when it wasn't overwhelmed by the aroma of Meg's corned beef and cabbage.

Not surprisingly, given their academic acumen at Harvard, Abe and Meg excelled at work and were given hefty raises each year. After three years, Meg was even promoted from a research assistant to a full researcher.

Life was good.

Then everything changed.

It started when Abe felt the muscles in his legs start to tighten

spontaneously. He ignored it for a couple months, hoping it might go away. When it didn't, he visited a neurologist friend who did some tests and a week later diagnosed Huntington's disease, a progressive neurological disorder famous for having killed folksinger Woody Guthrie.

Guthrie had died in 1967 – the year Abe and Meg met. He'd made it to fifty-five, but the last dozen years of his life were mostly spent in a brain-dead fog that lifted less and less frequently as his time grew shorter and shorter.

A high-school dropout who compensated by reading voraciously, Guthrie was famous for having written This Land is Your Land and playing a guitar emblazoned with the phrase *This Machine Kills Fascists*. He was idolized by most folksingers in the sixties, including Bob Dylan, who played songs for him during visits to the Brooklyn mental hospital where Guthrie finally faded away. Guthrie was married three times and fathered eight children, the first of whom was named Gwendolyn. (Abe and Meg hadn't known that when they'd named their own daughter.)

Abe delivered the bad news to Meg one night in bed. They'd just made love. It was summer. The window was open, and the sheer drapes ruffled in a light breeze. The window let in just enough moonlight to make everything in the room look gray.

"Huntington's?" Meg said, staring at the ceiling. "That's genetic, right?"

"Yeah," Abe said. "My father's fifty and he's fine. You saw him at the wedding. So I didn't get it from him. It must have come from my mother. We always wondered what caused that crash. She was a good driver. A great one, in fact. Even in snow. So we figured it must have been some sort of mechanical failure. I'm thinking now that maybe it was a seizure."

"Oh," Meg said.

Still awash in the afterglow of orgasm, Meg's mind whirled with thoughts of what Huntington's would mean. What it would mean was an abbreviated life with a bleak ending for Abe, who would likely die in his forties, or his fifties, if he were as lucky as Woody Guthrie.

It also meant there was a fifty-fifty chance little Gwen had the disease.

Meg wept for a month. She tried to put on a brave face

whenever Abe was around, but her puffy red eyes always told him she'd been crying.

Abe generally accepted his death sentence with relative equanimity, but the reality of it sometimes welled up in him. One gray afternoon in mid-February, Meg found him in bed, curled into a ball and shivering as if a window had been left open. She slipped into bed with him, held him tight, ran her fingers through his curly hair and whispered in his ear, "We'll just deal with it. Whatever it takes, we'll deal. I love you."

Abe was both relieved and ashamed that Meg was there to suffer with him. He sorely needed her, but she deserved better.

"I'm sorry, Meg," he said. "I'm so sorry."

"It's not your fault," Meg told him. "It's nobody's fault. It's life."

Abe's future was indeed bleak. In the coming years, he'd begin to move more and more erratically and strike odd poses that would make people gawk at him as if he were some sort of invalid, which of course he would be. Later, he'd quite literally lose his mind the same as Woody Guthrie had, when his brain could no longer compensate for the neurons blotted out by the Huntington's.

Abe knew that one in four Huntington's victims tried to kill themselves. Far fewer actually succeeded, probably because they waited until they were too far gone to get the job done. No one knew whether they were driven to try by a blossoming insanity or by an entirely rational decision to end the suffering. In any case, Abe thought, he wouldn't be ready for several years, after the disease had been given enough time to eat through his nervous system like rust on a wheelbarrow left out in the rain. When he became a burden, he promised himself, he'd end it. He was a doctor, after all. He knew plenty of ways to do it, all of them certain, none of them particularly painful.

"Simple as turning off a light switch," he said, snapping his fingers and thinking that maybe the day he could no longer snap his fingers would be the day he would know it was time.

Abe and Meg agreed to make the best of things. What other choice did they have? Nevertheless, a dark cloud shrouded their lives. They tried not to talk about the Huntington's, especially not

the even chances that their little girl had it, but it was always there, a patient murderer hellbent on making Abe suffer for as long as possible before granting him a merciful end.

Spurred by the shared understanding that their lives together would be truncated, the young couple struggled to squeeze as much happiness as they could out of each day.

Abe laughed gamely with every chance he got, even at corny jokes that weren't funny, like the ones on Hee Haw reruns. (Redneck, standing in front of a fence: "I crossed a gopher with an elephant." Others: "What'ja get?" Redneck: "Some awful big holes in my backyard." Fence board flies up and hits Redneck in the seat of his pants.)

For her part, Meg tried to compensate for the happiness deficit with which they began each day by working hard to make things as perfect as she could. Who could blame her, then, for accusing God of being grossly unfair when it rained on a picnic or during an outing to Fenway Park? Wasn't it enough to have a husband with Huntington's and a child with even odds of having it too? How much suffering could one small life be expected to endure? How much more did He expect from her?

Then everything changed again.

This time, it was Meg. She started having difficulty walking, as if some wise guy had put tacky glue on the soles of her shoes. She saw a different neurologist, one recommended by someone at work, and was thunderstruck when she was given the same diagnosis Abe had been given.

"You must be mistaken," she told the doctor. "My husband has Huntington's, but it's not contagious, it's genetic."

"Yes it is," the doctor agreed. "Don't one of your parents have it?"

"No!" Meg said.

"They must," the doctor insisted.

"Well they don't!" Meg cried. "My mother and father are both in their fifties and strong as horses!"

Of course, Meg knew the doctor had to be correct. When she got home, she called her parents in Arizona. Her mother answered the phone.

"The neurologist says it's Huntington's, which must have come

from one of you, except that it couldn't have, because you and daddy are long past the age at which you'd be symptomatic," Meg said.

Meg's mother was silent.

"Mom?" Meg said.

"I was pregnant by another man the day your father and I were married, Meg," her mother said. "His name was Frankie...Frank Sanders. I lost track of him. I had no idea he was sick. Otherwise I would have told you. I'm sorry, Meg."

"How could you have kept this from me all these years? I am not a child!"

"Meg," her mother said. "You know Catholics simply don't discuss such things."

When Meg told Abe about her astounding diagnosis, he was in such disbelief that his first reaction was to laugh out loud. It was beyond unfair. It was cruel.

Not only did Meg's diagnosis mean that she would suffer the same disastrous future that awaited him, it meant that little Gwen's chances had just rocketed from fifty percent to at least seventy-five percent, and maybe one-hundred percent, depending on how badly malformed their DNA actually was.

To Abe, one thing seemed certain: Their astonishing misfortune wasn't a result of random chance. The odds that both he and his wife would share such a rare disease were so infinitesimal that Abe could not help thinking that it had been no accident, and who else but God had the power to manage such a horrible eventuality? Certainly He was not above such cruelty, for hadn't He once let the devil beset poor Job, and all just to prove that Job's faith in God was so strong that he would never reproach Him, not even after the devil murdered his family, killed his flock and afflicted him with leprosy?

Neither Abe nor Meg possessed the unwavering faith of Job, and so they grew angry and bitter. How could God be so monstrous? Why didn't He at least force the disease to show itself early enough so its victims would know not to have a child? It was unfair to let it lurk in the shadows as it did and let unsuspecting parents pass a death sentence on to an innocent child.

It was in this scornful state of mind that Abe and Meg decided

to move to Boca Raton, Florida, and start Bayner Genetics. They knew they were smart. People of average intelligence didn't get scholarships to Harvard Medical – especially not ones that included a car and a house – and they certainly didn't graduate with honors and with lightning speed, as both of them had. They told themselves if they worked hard enough, if they dedicated every waking moment to finding the cure, they would be successful, and God would have to find some other way to ruin their lives.

Their shared dedication to conquer the disease was fueled mostly by little Gwendolyn, who toddled around the house as if nothing at all were wrong. In their youthful hopefulness and their blind faith in the power of science, they assumed a cure would reveal itself in time – maybe not soon enough to save them, but plenty soon enough to save their little girl.

As Abe and Meg slid into the horror that is Huntington's disease, Gwendolyn grew up to be a stunning teenager. She had her mother's pale skin, her fantastic green eyes, and her red hair – although it wasn't straight like Meg's but curly like Abe's. At six-foot-one, she'd also inherited her father's height.

Abe and Meg kept their shared disease a secret from the girl for as long as they could, but as Gwendolyn grew older and started asking about their symptoms they had no choice but to confirm her suspicions. They could not, however, bring themselves to tell the carefree girl that she probably had the disease too.

They delayed delivering that dreadful message for as long as they could. They finally decided to do it one night after dinner in the summer of 1989. Gwendolyn was eighteen. She'd just graduated from high school and was preparing to head off to the University of Florida. Abe and Meg were each forty-four and well on the way to their graves.

"Your father and I … have something … to tell you," Meg said.

"I already know," Gwendolyn said. "I probably have it, too. I know I'm not smart enough to be a geneticist like you guys, but I'm still your child. I'm not stupid."

Abe and Meg looked at each other with contorted faces that Gwendolyn thought conveyed either relief or bewilderment.

"I looked it up, guys," she said. "If both your parents have Huntington's, you probably have it too. Seventy-five-percent

chance if you're lucky, one-hundred-percent chance if you're not so lucky."

"We're ... sorry ... Gwen," Abe said.

Shielded by a youthful inability to imagine her own death, Gwendolyn said, "It's OK, daddy. I'm sure you guys will find a cure. You're smart as hell."

Four years later, when Gwendolyn was twenty-two and fresh out of college (she'd majored in music), she met a handsome young investment banker from Miami. They were at a Florida Marlins game, in line to buy beer and hot dogs. He was a few cents short and Gwendolyn, who was in line behind him, offered to pay the difference. Just as Abe had fallen for Meg's spectacular green eyes, Douglas Douchay fell immediately for Gwendolyn's.

Before they started dating in earnest, Gwendolyn revealed that she likely had Huntington's disease. She would probably die in her fifties, she told him, and would descend into madness during her final decade.

A swooning Douglas Douchay, for whom twenty-years seemed close to forever, waved his hand valiantly. No sacrifice was too onerous to endure for his lady. He professed his love for her and proclaimed that twenty or thirty years with her would be worth one-hundred with another. And wouldn't she be needing a loving spouse to care for her when the disease really started to take hold? He would proudly be that loving spouse, should it come to that.

"I knew from the moment I met you that I loved you," he said. "In any case, those smart parents of yours – or maybe some other brilliant scientists – may well come up with a cure. The future is unknown. And don't forget: There's still a twenty-five percent chance that you're OK."

They were married in January 1993. Gwendolyn was pregnant before the wedding dress was in storage. There was no time to waste, not for Gwendolyn and not for her parents, who at forty-eight were sinking fast, with precious little time to enjoy being grandparents.

Because Douglas Douchay did not have Huntington's, their children would have only a fifty-fifty chance of inheriting the disease, assuming that Gwendolyn had it. Fortunately – or, some said, unfortunately, considering that the disease was incurable – a

genetic test for Huntington's disease had just been discovered. The good news was that the fetus had dodged the bullet. The bad news was that its mother hadn't.

Gwendolyn gave birth to a perfectly healthy baby girl. She named her Barbara, after her mother's mother, who had kept the identity of Meg's biological father a secret for thirty-two years.

As the years wore on, reality set in on Abe and Meg Bayner. The unwelcome truth flowered as slowly as the disease itself, which progressed in each of them with the patient implacability of a glacier. Within five years, their muscle tightness developed into the typical twitching and posturing. Ten years later, the genetic defect showed up in their speech, and five years after that it began to rob them of their intellect, which in turn killed any hope that they'd find a cure.

Finally, it became undeniably clear (during their diminishing periods of lucidity) that the cure for Huntington's was far more intractable than they'd imagined.

"This is God ... punishing us ... for having ... premarital sex," Meg said one night as the two lay in a bed trembling from their own incessant twitching. "We sinned ... and this is our penance."

"I'm sure God ... had nothing ... to do with this, Meg," Abe said. "It's just ... horribly bad luck. Two bad ... rolls of the dice."

Gwendolyn's naïve confidence in her parents notwithstanding, Abe and Meg finally realized that they could no longer reasonably run the company. Starting in the summer of 1994, they began looking for a buyer. They naturally tried to find one among the many other genetics and biotech companies around at the time, but everyone in the close-knit community was fully aware of their rapidly failing health. As a result, they were mercilessly low-balled. No one offered as much as a third of what the company was worth.

As it ended, Abe and Meg's shared remorse for having carelessly afflicted Gwendolyn with the disease – for if God were punishing them for fornicating they were not as innocent as they preferred to believe they were – won the day. They handed Bayner Genetics over to her in 1996, when they were each fifty and had begun to have fewer and fewer good days and more and more bad days. It would be up to Gwendolyn to find her own cure, if she could.

A year after they passed the company to Gwendolyn, Abe and

Meg were dead. Abe died first. Because his symptoms had not yet made him a total invalid, his death was unexpected, especially since he died on one of his good days. There were rumors he committed suicide, but they were never verified. (No one, least of all Meg, would have blamed him.)

Meg lasted three months longer. Like her husband, she had not descended into the deepest depths of Huntington's, and so people could be heard whispering that she, too, had committed suicide. Again, the rumors were never verified. (No one, least of all Gwendolyn, would have blamed her.)

Both Abe and Meg were cremated, at their own direction. Gwendolyn decided not to have funerals. Not for her father. Not for her mother.

"I've been mourning their deaths for years," she said.

2
RARE AS RHENIUM

When the announcement of Gwendolyn's ascent to the president's office at Bayner Genetics reached the company's veteran scientists, many of them quit immediately in disgust, despite the announcement's oft-repeated promise that nothing of significance would change. As a result, a few of the young geneticists found themselves in positions of unparalleled responsibility and influence. Some were promoted from research assistants to full researchers, others to research directors in charge of an entire lab. The pay and benefits were unmatchable at their experience level, and the work — at least at first — was as rewarding as it had been before Abe and Meg's unfortunate, if altogether anticipated, departure.

The feared changes did soon come to pass, although not even the jaded Bayner veterans could have predicted how Gwendolyn's increased interest in the details of the business would render the work marginal at its best and fraudulent at its worst. The one thing that was not altered was the company's fervent search for a cure for Huntington's disease. Before her ascension was announced, in fact, Gwendolyn called in the project's director of research and doubled his salary. When the announcement of Gwendolyn's appointment was made, he was one of the few veterans who decided to stay.

The first of Gwendolyn's transformative ideas came directly from the victims of exceedingly rare diseases that, because of their small numbers of victims, were ignored by for-profit drug

companies, which was to say all of them. What justification, after all, could a company possibly give its stockholders for frittering away money on a disease that afflicted only one-hundred-thousand or so people worldwide? A company could just as easily spend its limited resources on diseases that attacked tens of millions of paying customers who were every bit as desperate for a lifeline as those unlucky enough to come down with something too rare to provide a reasonable return on investment.

Government researchers did good and honorable work, but they were ordered by elected officials not to step on the potential profits of the free-market drug companies. As a result, government scientists focused on the hardscrabble research that yielded breakthrough discoveries in the basic science. These expensive discoveries were then passed on to the private sector, where they were used to springboard products so profitable there was plenty of cash left over to appropriately thank the cooperative politicians.

The government was aware, of course, that some diseases just weren't worth caring about. That's why there was an Orphan Drug Act. The law gave subsidies and tax breaks to companies who agreed to work on unprofitable maladies affecting fewer than two-hundred-thousand new victims a year. The few companies who took the risk, however, focused on the least rare of the most rare, which once again left the victims of the most rare of the most rare out in the cold.

It was in their desperate and exhausting search for someone willing to try to save them from their bizarrely uncommon fates that the victims of exceedingly rare diseases eventually made their way to Gwendolyn Bayner's door.

If they were of modest means, as most were, Gwendolyn listened politely and suggested they petition the government for help, all the while knowing it would do them little good. If the desperate visitors were rich, on the other hand, Gwendolyn's eyes welled with empathetic tears and she listened to their sad pleas intently and consumed a copious number of tissues, especially if there were a child involved. Parents were often willing to deplete their entire fortunes in the struggle to save a child.

It happened for the first time exactly one year after Gwendolyn had moved into the president's office at Bayner Genetics. Margaret

and Stanley Johnson, a despondent couple from Newfoundland, Canada, were desperate to save their preschooler from the ravages of Batten disease, a sickness that struck only about three in one-hundred-thousand children.

The disease was so rare because it was only transmitted to a child when both parents had similar defects in the CLN3 gene on chromosome 16. Both Stanley and Margaret carried the defect, yet neither suffered from the disease, which was most often the case. Only when their genetic material combined inside their son did it bloom into the brutally fatal cocktail that was Batten disease.

Little Ben had seemed completely normal until he was about four years old. Then the seizures started. Doctors prescribed a pink liquid that Ben was given a teaspoonful of several times a day. That worked for a few months, but then the boy developed vision problems that glasses were unable to correct. He started tripping over things that weren't there. The falls were shocking and dangerous enough when the path was clear – he'd broken both his wrists, one of them twice, all three times by falling the wrong way on soft carpeting – but they turned disastrous when the boy hit his head on something hard on his way down.

Finally, doctors found a defect in the CLN3 gene on chromosome 16 and told the Johnsons that they were very sorry to report that it was Batten disease.

The Johnsons researched Batten disease on the Internet and found that it would slowly atrophy their son's brain, gradually taking away his muscle coordination, his sight, his intellect, and finally his life, probably before he turned twenty or shortly thereafter. They also learned that virtually no one was looking for any kind of treatment, no less a cure.

Thus began the Johnsons' frantic search for someone – anyone – willing to give their doomed child a chance at life. By the time they darkened the doorway at Bayner Genetics, they'd been turned away so many times that they knew very well that their son's disease was not one anyone was interested in fighting. No fewer than two-hundred-thirty different medical research corporations, big and small, had felt their pain and suggested they petition the Canadian government for help.

Stanley Johnson was not accustomed to being told no. He owned a chain of hardware stores in Canada and was quite rich.

True, he couldn't compete with the billions that could be collected from the millions who suffered from more common maladies, but he could do what he could do, and he stood ready to spend his last dime to save his son.

It was this overwhelming sense of desperation that hit Gwendolyn like a sack of hundred dollar bills as the Johnsons shuffled dejectedly into her plush office. She rose from her chair, went to the beleaguered couple, shook their hands, and said, "Mr. and Mrs. Johnson! Welcome! Please come in. Thank you for coming. Please have a seat."

The couple seated themselves in the two big leather chairs that addressed Gwendolyn's desk – he on her right and she on her left. Gwendolyn handed them a box of tissues and studied the weary couple as she made her way to the other side of her desk. Looking at them, she couldn't help but think of the old nursery rhyme, the one about Jack Sprat, who could eat no fat, and his wife, who could eat no lean, for Stanley was as thin as a stick and his wife was as meaty as a Christmas turkey.

Gwendolyn noticed the woman's sizeable diamond engagement ring, which sank into her spongy finger to the point that it looked like the stone was imbedded directly in the flesh.

Gwendolyn produced another box of tissues for herself and set it on the desk.

"Now," she said, "what can we do for you?"

Mr. Johnson did the talking. The monologue came out of him effortlessly, as if he were an actor who has been playing the same part for so long that his lines are as easy to remember as the words to an old song everybody knows.

"Ms. Bayner, our son has Batten disease. As I'm sure you're aware, it will kill him if something is not done. Even so, we have not been able to find anyone to help us. You, frankly, are our last hope."

(He'd added this sentence the last five times he'd delivered the plea.)

"I know there are not enough children suffering from the disease to make a cure profitable. The many companies that have turned us away have made that abundantly clear. But I am a wealthy man, and I stand ready to pay your research costs in full, plus a generous profit, of course."

"I understand," Gwendolyn said, plucking a tissue from the box. She looked again at Margaret Johnson's diamond ring and wondered how it had not turned her finger blue from lack of circulation, or why the woman had not simply had the band enlarged.

Suddenly, Mrs. Johnson began to desperately work at the ring. She twirled it and tugged at it with such energy that Gwendolyn feared she might pull her finger off. Finally the ring came loose and Mrs. Johnson slid it across the desk toward Gwendolyn.

"Here," she said. "As a token of our sincerity."

Gwendolyn slid the ring gently back toward the pathetic woman and said, "Oh! Mrs. Johnson! It's a lovely ring, but I'm sure it has sentimental value far beyond its actual worth. Besides, I do not doubt your sincerity. Please, put it back on." Then she dabbed at her eye with the tissue and added, "We'll do everything we can to help your son."

Hearing Gwendolyn's offer of help, Stanley and Margaret Johnson instantly turned to jelly. They slid from the leather chairs and fell to their knees. Margaret Johnson clutched her husband's side and began to weep into his sleeve. Stanley Johnson pulled two tissues from the box and handed them to her.

"Ms. Bayner," he said looking up, "you can not know how long we've been waiting to hear those words. I can not tell you how grateful we are. You are a saint. The answer to our prayers. Bless you."

Still on his knees, his wife clawing at his side, Stanley Johnson struggled to find his checkbook.

"How much will it take to get started immediately?" he said, trying to steady his wife with one hand as he used the other to dig for the book.

"I suppose one hundred should do to start," Gwendolyn said. "Unless that's too much."

"One hundred dollars?" Stanley said.

Gwendolyn smiled and waited for the man to come to his senses. After a second or two, Stanley Johnson's face reddened and he said, "Oh! Of course! One hundred thousand! Yes! Well! I'll have to call my accountant to have that amount freed up. I'm sure you understand. It will be done by the end of the day."

He glanced at his watch and saw that it was after two in the

afternoon. "Or by the end of the day tomorrow at the latest."

"That's fine, Mr. Johnson," Gwendolyn said. She rose from her chair, made her way to the front of her desk and encouraged the couple to their feet. "Please see my secretary. She will give you our bank routing information."

Stanley Johnson struggled to stand, but was held down by his wife, who was clinging to his right arm as if he were rescuing her from quicksand.

"Thank you so much Ms. Bayner. Thank you! You are a saint," he said, out of breath with the effort to lift his wife.

"As you said, Mr. Johnson. But I am nothing of the sort. I am a simple businesswoman."

Stanley finally got his wife to her feet, and Gwendolyn began to gently escort the grateful couple to her door. Halfway there, she stopped suddenly and said, "Wait! Mrs. Johnson! Please wait right there."

Stanley and Margaret Johnson froze. Margaret clutched her husband's arm tighter and feared Gwendolyn would take back her offer to help her son. Stanley worried that the amount would rise from *thousand* to *million*. Together they watched as Gwendolyn scurried back to her desk, picked up the diamond ring, then scurried back to Margaret Johnson and returned it to her finger, although she could get it past only the first knuckle.

"Thank you, Ms. Bayner," Margaret said, looking at the ring. "You are a kind and considerate woman."

"Please. Call me Gwen," Gwendolyn said.

Margaret Johnson did not stop crying until they were downstairs and back in their car. The money was in Bayner's account by four that afternoon.

Once Bayner Genetics developed a reputation for working on impossibly unprofitable diseases such as Batten disease, a parade of people who were either sick themselves or, better yet, had sick children, made the pilgrimage to Gwendolyn's office.

The "Hope is Healing" program, named by Gwendolyn personally, became one of the company's biggest moneymakers.

"Even if we don't find a single cure," Gwendolyn said, "we're selling hope. And hope, it turns out, is rarer than rhenium."

The parade of people willing to pay market price for hope grew

even larger after Bayner scientists actually did discover a partially effective treatment for Marfan Syndrome – a genetic disorder that attacked connective tissue and so caused problems with everything from bones to blood vessels. It grew larger still after Gwendolyn, seeing how little the company would make by selling Marfanex, decided to give it away for what it cost to manufacture, which turned out to be three cents per pill.

To Gwendolyn's delight, the rich families of children and loved ones who sadly died of a disease before its cure could be found rewarded her beneficence by setting up foundations and trusts to honor the memories of the dead. All of the money went directly to Bayner Genetics, no questions asked. It was the least they could do, the benefactors all agreed, for the one woman on Earth who had tried to help them.

The second big change at Bayner Genetics sprang from Gwendolyn Bayner's own simple imagination. She knew enough about genetics to know that it was "the software that controlled how the body functioned and how it looked." It was the second part that initially caught her interest.

Her first idea was to develop a drug that would make all human beings look essentially the same, thereby eliminating racial discrimination.

"We can call it Race-Erase," Gwendolyn said, although everyone in the room usually groaned when she did.

She dropped the idea after three months when the researchers to which she'd assigned the bizarre project reported no progress and, worse yet, no hope for much progress. They might be able to get the skin color right, they said, but the other features were way out of their range.

Undaunted, Gwendolyn next suggested designing a pill that would cure obesity by making people who took it feel satiated after eating less than two-thousand calories a day. Take it once, and you'd be naturally thin for the rest of your life.

When word got out that Bayner Genetics was planning to make people stop eating to excess, several large agricultural corporations, grocery store chains, restaurant franchises and fitness companies contacted Gwendolyn and wound up paying her an undisclosed sum to drop the idea. Gwendolyn never let on how large the

settlement was, but six months after the deal was inked Bayner Genetics moved to a five-story building on the beach.

Gwendolyn was no scientist, but she knew a good thing when she saw it. If she announced plans to develop pills that would threaten the profits of other corporations, she imagined, the targeted companies would be willing to pay a small fortune to nip the threat in the bud. Like the agricultural corporations and the grocery retailers, they would pay even before investigating whether the threat was real, because they realized that it would be much cheaper to stop a threat before Bayner Genetics had spent millions in research and development.

It was a brilliant business strategy. The cost of the research was zero, and the revenue was instantaneous and limited only by Gwendolyn's curious imagination. Manufacturers of hair color paid to have her drop phantom plans to permanently change hair color with a single pill. Makers of tinted contact lenses paid her to drop publicized but nonexistent plans to change eye color. Companies selling tanning beds and suntan oils paid her huge sums to give up on developing a pill that would give people a permanent tan. (This was one trick Bayner Genetics actually could do, thanks to its work on Race-Erase.)

"Who knew suntan oil was even that profitable?" Gwendolyn said.

And on it went.

Under Gwendolyn's unorthodox leadership, Bayner Genetics became more profitable than it had ever been under the more traditional guidance of her parents. As a result, within four years of taking the helm, Gwendolyn had become very rich. No one knew for sure how rich, but it was clear to everyone that she spared herself no luxury.

She lived in an ocean-side mansion that was alive with chefs, maids, butlers, nurserymen, cabana boys and chauffeurs. The garage was stocked with five Bentley Continental Flying Spurs with single-letter license plates that read: C, A, T, U and G. The mansion's columned façade evoked the Parthenon. The front door was twelve feet tall and ten feet wide. It opened onto a foyer as big as a basketball court and decorated with larger-than-life statues of great composers and busts of lesser ones supported by granite

pedestals. (Mozart had a full statue.)

In the rear of the mansion, ornate half-moon balconies extended from each of the ten upstairs bedrooms, all of which had ocean views and their own bathrooms. The dining room table, large enough to comfortably seat twenty-two, was set with Royal Copenhagen china, gold flatware, and Waterford crystal. The dining room featured a picture window that looked out on a lush rose garden and, beyond it, a swimming pool that seemed to merge with the infinite Atlantic, upon which one could frequently see scuttling by the sailboats owned by the other members of the super-rich class.

Gwendolyn's lifestyle, while unabashedly extravagant, might have been easily excused by anyone who knew her eventual fate – that she was doomed to follow in her parents' footsteps. Certainly she had no qualms about it.

"I might as well live it up while I can," she said. "God didn't give me as much time as most other people."

The one person who steadfastly refused to excuse Gwendolyn's lavish lifestyle, and the one who most often expressed his opposition to it, was her husband, Douglas Douchay, whose income, while not small by any means, was dwarfed by that of his wife, who suspected that the disparity between their paychecks was the real reason for her husband's sour discontent.

Worse than Douglas's criticism of her unrestrained spending, Gwendolyn thought, was that he dared to criticize the methods by which she'd come by the money. It was bad enough, he complained, that she extorted untold millions from corporations by threatening them with phantom drug programs. Ten times as bad – a sin unforgivable in his opinion – was how she'd profited by selling hope to people who were so obviously doomed.

"You are apparently unaware of how valuable hope is," Gwendolyn told him.

After seven years, Gwendolyn decided she'd finally had enough of Douglas' self-righteous whining. After he left for work one morning, she instructed the servants to box up his belongings and place them on the curb outside the estate's wrought-iron gates. Then she handed a manila envelope to a lone servant and stationed him under a popup gazebo erected next to the small hill of boxes.

When Douglas returned home from work, the servant blocked his entrance and motioned for him to roll down his car window.

"Ms. Bayner has ordered me to prevent your entry and give you this," he said, handing Douglas the manila envelope.

"Ms. Bayner?" Douglas said. "Her name is Mrs. Douchay."

"She has ordered us all to begin addressing her by her maiden name, sir," the servant said. "I'm terribly sorry. She was quite clear."

Douglas opened the envelope to find divorce papers and a handwritten note that read simply, "Dearest Douglas, We're done. Have a nice life. Love, Gwendolyn."

"What is this about?" Douglas asked the servant.

"I know nothing but what I've told you, sir," the servant said. "I believe all of your belongings have been gathered up and placed in these boxes. Of course, if we've missed anything we'll be pleased to send it along."

"Is she inside?"

"I'm afraid I can't say, sir," the servant said.

Douglas grabbed his cell phone and dialed his own number, or what he still considered to be his own number.

"Bayner residence," answered a voice he did not recognize.

"Let me speak to Gwendolyn," Douglas said.

"Ms. Bayner is not here presently."

Douglas punched the phone off and called Bayner Genetics.

"Bayner Genetics," the receptionist said.

"Gwendolyn Bayner please."

"Who may I say is calling?"

"Her husband."

"I'm sorry, Mr. Douchay. Ms. Bayner is in a meeting. May I take a message?"

Douglas thought for a moment, then said, "Yes, tell her I think she's lost her mind."

He punched off the phone and called the Boca Waldorf Astoria.

"Boca Raton Resort and Club," a voice said.

"I need a room for the night," Douglas said, then reconsidered. "Better make that for a week."

The divorce agreement was finalized within the month, although it would take several more months to wind its way through the courts. Gwendolyn never showed her face. Douglas Douchay's

attorney, who'd been working on high-end divorces for forty years, told Douglas he'd never seen such a generous settlement. Douglas would never have to work another day in his life, would be given a comfortable home of his own choosing – as long as it was sufficiently far away from Gwendolyn's mansion – and could generally continue to enjoy his upper-class lifestyle. The only hitch, the attorney saw, was the confidential addendum that was not filed with the clerk of courts because no family court judge would approve of its harsh stipulation that Douglas not contact his daughter for any reason until she turned twenty-one, which was fourteen years away.

"That's a tough pill to swallow," Douglas complained.

"I agree," his attorney said, "but if you do not accede, your wife has promised – confidentially of course – to spend three times the amount she expects to spend on this settlement to make your life a living hell. I have no doubt she will succeed in that goal. I have seen it done before, and it is none too pretty. She will no doubt accuse you of child abuse. That alone would most likely devastate your career. No one wants to work with a pervert."

"I'm not a pervert."

"Of course you're not, but it's not the conviction that will destroy you, it's the accusation. Nobody wants to work with someone who might be a pervert."

"Give me the damn papers," Douglas said.

Thinking to himself that the divorce also freed him from having to care for a victim of Huntington's disease, he signed them all.

For his daughter's third birthday, Douglas Douchay had given Barbara a toy terrier, which the girl had named Terror. Gwendolyn didn't much care for dogs, especially small, yappy dogs, but little Barbara loved the pup so much that when it turned a year old and was as large as it was ever going to get, Gwendolyn had a jeweled collar made for it at Tiffany's. Seeing the collar, Douglas wondered aloud how many poor children in Africa could be fed with the money spent on the foolish bauble.

After the divorce – perhaps in response to Douglas' sudden disappearance – the dog developed a nervous bladder that caused him to piddle on the mansion's wooden floors, even though he had free access to the lush lawn outside. If the tiny drops of urine weren't promptly dabbed up, they ate through the finish and made

light spots on the wood.

Gwendolyn told her seven-year-old daughter that they had to get rid of the dog. It had become too much of a bother, she said. The girl objected so strenuously and with such a waterfall of tears that, instead of taking Terror to the pound, Gwendolyn assigned a maid to follow the little dog around all day with a roll of paper towels and a spray can of wood cleaner.

On the day the divorce was final, Gwendolyn took the modest engagement ring Douglas had given her seven years earlier and threaded it onto Terror's jeweled collar. Then she instructed the staff to begin feeding the dog in the dining room, at the head of the table that seated twenty-two, in the place once reserved for Mr. Douchay.

3
CHEZ PARIS

Gwendolyn Bayner was waiting for her sixteen-year-old daughter to join her at Chez Paris. The restaurant, which was purposefully overpriced in order to keep out the lower classes, sat atop a thirty-story hotel on the shoreline of Boca Raton, Florida, just down the street from Bayner Genetics. Through the picture windows that surrounded the dining room, she watched the setting sun create a pink and orange smear above the suburbs to the west and, beyond them, the sugar cane fields where dirt-poor migrant workers produced the sugar cubes favored by the rich and their horses.

Such is life, she thought.

She ordered a double Manhattan, her second, with three cherries. A piano started up in an adjacent room. Mozart, she knew immediately, his Piano Sonata No. 1, written when the master was a mere eighteen years old, just two years older than her aimless daughter, who, being a modern American teen, didn't know the difference between Mozart and macaroni and cheese.

Gwendolyn coerced her daughter, her only child, to meet her at Chez Paris every Friday night at seven o'clock. She did this the way all rich parents do: by threatening to cancel the credit card the girl used to lavish gifts on less affluent schoolmates who pretended to be her best friend forever, but usually lasted only as long as the largess held out.

Gwendolyn glanced at her diamond Rolex. It was seven-twenty. Barbie was late, as usual. Gwendolyn had threatened to cancel the

girl's Visa even for tardiness, but Barbie always had an excuse, most often car trouble. Even though she'd just started driving three months before, she'd grown tired of the small Mercedes Benz her mother had given her. She had her eye on a Lexus twice as expensive, although she was unaware of what either car cost and, being her mother's daughter, couldn't have cared less.

Finally, Gwendolyn saw Barbie making her way across the dining room. She was dressed all in black. Several months earlier she had adopted the shocking gothic style of her middle-class peers and, despite her wealth, their petty pessimism as well. She'd dyed her blonde hair jet black, then let a pale yellow stripe emerge down the center of her cranium, which her mother thought made her look like a skunk. The girl's fingernails were painted charcoal black, as were her lips and eyelids. Gwendolyn knew that Barbie had paid plenty for the look. She'd seen the Visa bills.

Barbie strolled through the busy dining room as if it were deserted. Scurrying waiters threw her scornful looks as they pirouetted around her snotty insolence with their loaded trays twirling precariously overhead. Finally, Barbie made it to the table and dropped dejectedly into a chair opposite her mother, as if she were about to be scolded.

"God!" she said. "What is that shitty music?"

"I believe it's Mozart, dear. He wrote it when he was about your age."

"That explains it, then."

Gwendolyn resisted the urge to lecture her daughter yet again on her favorite prodigy's incomparable genius and instead said, "So what's new? What did you do this week?"

"Nothing. Same old thing. School, shopping, school, shopping. It's so boring!"

"I can certainly put the shopping to an end."

Barbie glared at her mother.

"I'm here," she said. "Where's the stupid waiter?"

Just then, a lithe young man with closely cropped hair and a small diamond stud in one ear slid up as if on ice.

"I'm right here, my dove!" he said, addressing Barbie but giving a sideways glance to Gwendolyn. "You are looking fabulous tonight, peanut. I myself never tire of black!" He bent at the waist as if to sniff her. "And what is that perfume? *Eu du merde?*

Delightful!"

"It's BO, douche bag."

"Barbara!" Gwendolyn said. "Remember what I told you! Never fuck with people who make your food!"

"That is so correct, madam, although I would never put it so brusquely! She's an adorable little imp, is she not?"

"Charming," Gwendolyn said.

The waiter turned back to Barbie. "And what will the little dear be dining on this evening? The usual chicken fingers? Or shall we choose something from the big girl's menu tonight?"

"You haven't given me a menu yet, Sir Douche-a-Lot."

"Oh! You are so right *mon pétunia peu!* Here you are."

He handed the girl a heavy leather-bound menu. Barbie glanced at it briefly, then tossed it onto the table, knocking over her water glass. The waiter quickly righted the glass, pulled a cloth from his back pocket, and began mopping up the mess.

Barbie ignored him and said, "Bring me a salad. No dressing, no tomato, no onion, no carrot, no fucking croutons."

"Oui, ma belle!" the waiter said, dabbing at the wet tablecloth. He turned to Gwendolyn. "And for the madam?"

"I'll have a filet mignon, please. Rare. Steamed vegetables. Mushroom risotto, extra creamy."

"Very good, madam. And another Manhattan?"

"Please. A double. Three cherries. And bring your best bottle of *Chateauneuf du Pape.*"

"Excellent! I'll send the sommelier right over!"

The waiter dropped the soaked rag into Barbie's water glass. She glared at him.

"Hey!" she said.

The waiter lifted the water glass away. "More water, *mon bâton peu de céleri?*" he said.

"A Coke," she said, folding her arms over her chest.

"Excellent choice! It's a shame you missed the sunset, sugar pie. It was enough to make you devout. Have a lovely evening ladies."

He pivoted on one foot and left.

Gwendolyn looked at Barbie. "Honestly, Barbara, I don't know why you have to be so disagreeable. He'll probably spit in your salad."

"He wouldn't dare!" She stared at the damp tablecloth and said,

"Can I have some of your water? You're sure not going to drink it."

"Sure, sweetie, go ahead."

Barbie reached across the table, grabbed the water, took three big gulps, then set the heavy glass down dramatically in front of her and placed her hands on either side of it, palms down, as if bracing herself.

"I have something to tell you, mother," she said, "and you're not going to like it."

Gwendolyn downed what was left of her second Manhattan and wondered what was taking the third so long to arrive.

"What is it, sweetie? I'm sure it's not as bad as you think."

Barbie took a big breath, let it out, then said, "I'm gay."

Just then, the third Manhattan arrived. *Thank God,* Gwendolyn thought.

"Thank you, Georgie," she said. She took a healthy swig of the freshly-poured cocktail, fished out one of the three cherries with her manicured nails, then popped it into her mouth, leaving the red stem hanging out.

"You are not!" she mumbled.

Gwendolyn pulled at the stem with her thumb and index finger, then placed it on the table beside the six others. It was a trick Douglas Douchay had taught her to keep track of how many drinks she'd had, not that it ever stopped her from having another.

"You most certainly are not!" she repeated once she'd swallowed the cherry.

"I am so! I hate boys and I love girls. That makes me gay. Sandy said you'd be pissed!"

Gwendolyn took another sip of the Manhattan.

"Oh, sweetie! I'm not upset. I'm sure it's just a stage you're going through. What have those awful boys done to you? They can be so mean!"

"Girls can be just as mean as boys, mother dear. That's not what I'm saying! I'm saying I hate to kiss them. They stink, and they're always jamming my hand into their pants. Girls are nicer. They're softer. They smell nice, and they know how to kiss!"

"I'm sure this is just a little phase, dear. An experimentation. Quite normal," was all Gwendolyn could think to say. "It's fine. You'll get over it. Let's talk about something else. How's the car running? Is it giving you trouble again? Is that why you were late

tonight?"

"Don't change the subject, mother! You're always changing the subject! Deal with it! I'm gay! A lesbian! A carpet muncher! I like to eat pussy!"

At that point, the other patrons at Chez Paris interrupted their own conversations and directed their attention toward the commotion at the table by the window. Most of them were aware of Gwendolyn's feral daughter. They tried to be discreet, hiding their smiles behind raised napkins and suppressing their snickers, but Gwendolyn's ears burned and she could feel their eyes on her neck.

"Barbara! For Christ's sake!" she whispered. "We're in a restaurant! We'll talk about this at home!"

"I'm not coming home tonight. I'm sleeping over at Sandy's house. She's my girlfriend. I love her."

The sommelier arrived with a bottle of Chateauneuf du Pape swaddled in a thick white napkin and held it out for Gwendolyn's inspection. Gwendolyn nodded without looking at it.

"I'm going to the bathroom," Barbie said. She got up and left.

"A lovely Chateau La Nerthe, madam. Nineteen-ninety-two. Our last bottle. I'm sure it will please you."

The sommelier produced a compact cork puller from his vest pocket and removed the cork with a single strong pull. It made a satisfying pop. Without suggesting that Gwendolyn inspect the cork, he decanted the deep purple liquid into a crystal carafe, swirled it artistically, put his educated nose to it, then poured a splash into her wine glass.

"Such a big wine needs ten or fifteen minutes to breathe," he said.

Gwendolyn lifted the glass to her nose. "Thank you, Jacques, it smells lovely."

"Madam."

The sommelier bowed subtly, spun on his heels, and left.

Barbie returned. She was holding hands with another girl who looked to be about her age. The girl was thin, pretty, and wore a flouncy smock printed with sand dollars and sea horses. On her petite feet she wore sandals decorated with sea shells. Her naturally blonde hair had been brushed with care and her lips and fingernails were painted a girly pink.

The girl let loose of Barbie's hand. Barbie fell into her chair. Then the girl extended her left hand to Gwendolyn and gave a small curtsy.

"Mrs. Bayner, it is a pleasure to finally meet you," she said.

Gwendolyn took the girl's manicured hand and looked at Barbie, who was digging for an ice cube in the water glass.

"Bayner is my maiden name, dear. So it's Ms. Bayner or Miss Bayner, whichever you prefer. My married name…well, I guess I've just forgotten what my married name was! It was so long ago!"

Barbie made a tsk sound and looked up at the girl.

"Douchay," she said. "My dad's name was Douglas Douchay. My mom threw all his crap out into the street one day and that's the last I saw of him. I assume she paid a boatload to have him disappear."

The girl quickly released Gwendolyn's hand, took a step back and looked at Barbie, horrified. Barbie laughed and said, "I don't mean she had him killed, silly! What kind of people do you think we are? I mean she just pays him to stay away from me. You know, the same way she threatens me with the Visa. If he ever had lunch with me or anything, he'd lose his allowance, that's all. Whatever. If he agreed to abandon me for any amount of money, he is a douche bag."

"Barbie Douchay," the girl said with a giggle.

Barbie was not amused. "My name is Barbie Bayner," she said.

The girl stepped back to Gwendolyn and retook her hand.

"I have a funny name, too, Ms. Bayner. I'm Sandy Shore." She curtsied again, this time with a flourish.

"What a lovely name," Gwendolyn said. "Your parents must have a wonderful sense of humor."

"Not really. They named me Sandra, or *Sawndra* as they say it. I changed it to Sandy a couple years ago. Everybody loves a fun day at the beach, so everybody loves me! Isn't that cool?"

"Very," Gwendolyn said. She plucked the second cherry from her third Manhattan, ripped the artificially colored fruit from its stem, and placed the stem beside the seven others.

"Have you eaten, dear?" she said. "You're welcome to join us."

"Oh, no thank you, ma'am. A girl's got to watch her figure, you know."

"Humph! Those boys are so demanding, aren't they? You look

as though you'd blow away in a light breeze. Please join us anyway."

Gwendolyn gestured at the chair beside Barbie. The girl sat.

"I'm glad I chose a table for four tonight, Barbie. You didn't tell me you were bringing a guest!"

"This is no guest, mother. This is my lover."

"Is that so!" Gwendolyn said.

The Manhattans had taken effect. Gwendolyn was feeling a little slow.

"She..." Gwendolyn looked at Sandy Shore. "You certainly don't look gay!"

"No ma'am," Sandy Shore said.

"She's the girl, mother. I'm the boy."

"I see," Gwendolyn said. "I'm afraid I'm not very well versed in the ways of ... gay people."

"It's OK, Mrs. Bayner," Sandy Shore said. "You can call us lesbians. We're good with it."

"Oh, that's fine, Sandra. You seem like a lovely girl. But remember: it's Ms. Bayner."

"Yes, Ms. Bayner."

A waiter brought the orders. Seeing and smelling the food, Sandy Shore had a change of heart and ordered a shrimp cocktail and a Coke. As Gwendolyn ate, Sandy Shore did most of the talking. She was an only child, she said, like Barbie. Her mother was a homemaker, although the nanny and the maid actually did most of the homemaking. Her father was a financial analyst.

"I don't really know what that means," Sandy Shore said. "But I know that's what he is."

Barbie ate two bites of unadorned lettuce that were better suited for a rabbit, then accepted three thumb-sized shrimp from Sandy Shore, who made Barbie playfully beg for them. As soon as the shrimp and the Cokes were gone, Barbie announced that she and Sandy had a busy schedule the next day and so had to leave.

"But it's Saturday tomorrow, dear," Gwendolyn said.

"We want to get up early so we can see the sun rise on the beach," Barbie said. "Sandy lives on the beach, too."

"How poetic," Gwendolyn said.

She bade the girls goodbye and they left.

Just as Gwendolyn finished her third Manhattan, the waiter arrived and refilled her wine glass from the carafe.

"Quite a lovely young girl, madam. Your niece, perhaps?"

"Just a friend of my daughter's," Gwendolyn answered.

She lifted the wine to her lips.

"If I didn't know better, I'd say they were young lovers."

"How nosy of you to notice," Gwendolyn said. "I think they're just playing."

"If I may, madam, I would encourage you to handle the situation with kindness and delicacy. When I first announced myself to my parents, they wouldn't talk to me for a year. My father took two years, in fact. It was just awful – more for him than for me. I pray you'll not make a similar error."

"Mind your own business, faggot," Gwendolyn said. She saw nine cherry stems lying on the table. "Bring me another Manhattan. A double. Three cherries."

"Yes, madam. As you wish, madam."

Gwendolyn gazed out the window. The sun had set and the city lights were throwing a soft glow into the night sky. What was it, she wondered, that made a woman want to lie with another woman instead of being normal? Maybe it was her fault. Maybe it was because she'd thrown Douglas out of the house too soon and so deprived Barbie of a strong male figure. Or maybe, she thought, maybe it was something more, something deeper, something ingrained. Something genetic.

4
A PRAYER ANSWERED

The Monday after Barbie told Gwendolyn she was a lesbian, Bailey Foster arrived at Bayner Genetics to find a yellow Post-It note stuck to her computer monitor. "See me" was all it said, but Bailey knew it was from Gwendolyn Bayner. Only Gwendolyn would have written a note that so presumptuously assumed the recipient would know its author.

Bailey went to her lab partner's desk and found a note identical to her own. In her fashion, Susan Griffin was late. As the smartest geneticist in the company, it was her prerogative. She was two years younger than Bailey, only twenty-five, but she seemed to have twice the intelligence. Other employees were always coming to her with questions, and she could usually answer them off the top of her head. She'd entered the Massachusetts Institute of Technology at sixteen on full scholarship. Five years later, she'd not only graduated with a doctorate in bioengineering and genetics but also had managed to earn a bachelor's degree in computer science.

Susan Griffin owed her success to a horrid childhood. She'd kept secret the details of just how horrid it had been until one night when it all just burst out of her like a festering boil finally erupting. Susan Griffin was not one to easily share her feelings.

As Bailey waited for Suze to arrive, her thoughts returned to that night.

They were at the CATUG Pub, celebrating Suze's promotion. They were seated in a secluded booth in a dark corner at the rear of the joint, which sold deep fried food and three hundred different

brands of beer. Suze had had too many Newcastles. The table was littered with bottles. Suddenly, for no apparent reason, she had begun to cry...

"Oh, sweetie!" Bailey said. "Don't cry! We're celebrating!"

She moved to Suze's side of the booth in an effort to comfort her.

"It was awful, Foster."

"Tell me, Suze."

And then Susan Griffin told her story, the whole awful mess of it. It was the first and last time she would ever speak of it, but it came out of her then like water from a open hydrant.

"Even before I began menstruating, my father – that cocksucker! – started to abuse me. The first time was when I was barely ten. I'd forgotten to get a towel before taking a shower one night, so I called out to my mom. This fuck comes in with a Barney towel and holds it out to me like he's my boyfriend at the beach. I can see that towel now, the big purple dinosaur dancing and smiling under the words 'I love you, you love me, we're a happy family...'"

"Jesus," Bailey whispered.

"I was so embarrassed! I tried to grab it from him, but he wouldn't let it go. He said he wanted to help me dry off like when I was a little girl. I told him no and stayed behind the shower curtain, but he got mad and ripped the curtain down, exposing me.

"He'd been drinking, of course. They were always drinking. I could smell the bourbon on his breath. He screamed at me, 'You don't say no to your father!' Then he pulled me by the arm and wrapped the towel around me like a mummy and hugged me tight so I couldn't move. I screamed for my mother, but he said, 'She's passed out, sweetie. It's after eight o'clock.' He was always calling me sweetie, but it was more a threat than anything else.

"I started crying so hard I could barely breathe, but I didn't fight him. He probably would have hurt me if I had. As it turned out, he merely petted me. My nonexistent breasts, my little snatch, my butt. He told me I was beautiful and then grabbed my hand and made me touch his crotch. He was wearing pajama bottoms with no underwear. He was always walking around the house half naked. I could feel his penis start to grow as he forced my hand to touch it. Then all of a sudden he left, saying, 'If you tell your mother, I swear to God I'll strangle you dead like a stray cat.'

"After that, he started sneaking into my bedroom after my mother passed out for the night. He would finger me and then stick his finger in his mouth and make an *mmmm* sound. When he first starting doing it, I didn't lubricate. I was too young. So he would jerk off next to me on the bed and shoot his semen into a paper towel. It was so my mom wouldn't find his semen on my sheets I guess, although she never would. I did my own laundry as soon as I was able to. It was either that or walk around in dirty clothes all the time.

"When I was twelve or so, I started to get wet. I swear to God I didn't want to! It just happened! And that's when he started raping me. It was right then that I vowed to do well in school so I could graduate early and get a scholarship and get the hell away to college. That's why I'm so smart, Foster. I had to be smart."

"Didn't your mother know what was going on? Why didn't she tell him to stop?" Bailey said.

"I think she knew, but she was just as afraid of him as I was. Her answer was to save herself, to just keep drinking until she passed out and the pain was gone."

"Oh, Suze, I'm so sorry!"

Now they were both crying.

"I'm not done," Suze said.

She took a gulp of the brown ale.

"Once he started raping me he couldn't stop. He usually did it four or five times a week. If I was bleeding, he raped me anally. Usually he used a rubber, but sometimes he didn't. So of course I wound up pregnant. I was fifteen. I told him I'd stopped bleeding and he gave me some money to go have an abortion. I took the money and told him I would, but I never did. I was a good Catholic girl, and I was afraid of making God angry. So instead I just started eating like a pig. I was so hungry anyway. I got really fat to hide the bump. He never knew. Can you believe that? Fucking drunk asshole never knew he was raping his pregnant daughter.

"Anyway, I read a lot about having babies and put together a gym bag full of supplies for when the time came. Towels, string, sharp scissors, stuff like that. And some bus tokens. I carried that gym bag everywhere. As it turned out, my water broke late one night after both of them were passed out drunk. Thank God. I climbed out of my bedroom window and waddled to the park near

our house. There was a baseball field there. It had concrete dugouts with wooden benches, metal roofs, and cement floors. I laid a towel out on the floor of one of the dugouts and had my baby right there. Christ I was scared! But it didn't hurt as bad as I thought it would. I think I might have passed out once or twice.

"I cleaned up its little face by spitting on a facecloth and sticking Q-Tips up its tiny nostrils. Then I tied some string around the cord and snipped it. I was not crying at all. I was focused on my plan. It was quite a mess, as you can imagine. Right away the baby started nursing and after a few minutes it fell fast asleep, and I did too.

"When I woke up, it was raining. The drops were beating so loud on the metal roof at first I thought someone was beating on it with a bat. The baby just kept sleeping, though. I wrapped him in a towel and put him in the gym bag and zipped it up halfway so he could breathe. I looked around and saw the mess on the towel and the concrete. I gathered it up and threw the whole thing in an old trash barrel. Then the rain really started coming down hard and blowing sideways, right into the dugout. It was washing the blood away, which was good, but it was also soaking me and the baby."

Now Bailey was sobbing and saying "Oh Suze, oh Suze..." She kept hugging her friend, but she needed it more than Suze. Suze was on a roll.

"I took the baby in the gym bag and walked to a bus stop, as I had planned. There was a shelter there that kept us out of the rain. The bus showed up pretty fast anyway, and I got on. I went to the back of the bus, left the gym bag with the baby still inside it on the floor, and got off at the next stop. I used the back doors so the bus driver wouldn't notice I'd forgotten the bag."

"Do you know what happened to the baby?" Bailey asked.

"Yeah. The next day I saw a story in the newspaper. It said some people who got on the bus after me found the baby when it woke up and started to cry. As it turned out, the bus driver and his wife had been trying to have a baby for years, but couldn't. The woman's gyno had told her she was barren, so they'd begun praying for a baby. They thought my baby was an answer to their prayers."

"Wow."

"Yeah. I actually keep a copy of the newspaper story in my purse. You want to see it?"

"Sure."

Suze slipped a hand into her purse and pulled out a newspaper story that had been laminated in plastic. She handed it to Bailey, who pulled a couple candles together so there would be enough light to read by.

City Bus Driver's Prayer for Child Answered
by Philip Carey, Sentinel Staff Writer

The prayers of an Orlando couple who learned three years ago they could not bear children were answered Tuesday morning.

William Chambers, 37, a city bus driver for the past 10 years, said a male baby was discovered inside a zip-up gym bag on the floor at the back of his bus at about 6:30 AM by passengers who heard the newborn begin to cry.

One of the passengers was Shirley Banks, 67, who usually sits in the back of the bus on her way to her job as a daycare worker at St. John's Christian Center.

"We saw that old bag and thought someone had just left it behind accidentally like they sometimes do," Banks said. "Then we heard that little precious start to wail. He must have been asleep, I guess, and woke up hungry. Tiny as he was, he sure could scream! I lifted him out of the bag and noticed the child was only a few hours old. He still had a lot of the cheese on him and the cord was still attached and fresh."

Chambers and his wife, Loretta, 35, were told in 1997 that they could not have children. Since then, Chambers said, they've been going to church every Sunday and praying that God would somehow give them a child.

"We're not wealthy people," Chambers said. "We could not afford to adopt. So we turned to the Lord. We left it in His hands."

Banks, a grandmother of six, said after she discovered the infant she immediately brought it to the front of the bus and told Chambers to stop somewhere to get something to feed the newborn.

"Willie was speechless, I'll tell you that," Banks said. "He just did what I said without saying a word."

Chambers pulled the big bus into the parking lot of a drug store. The store was not yet open, but when the insistent Banks kept banging on the glass doors a manager opened up and, after hearing the story, donated a bottle kit, several cans of formula, diapers and other supplies.

"It's not too often you get to participate in a miracle," said the manager, John Harrington, 54. "I was honored to do it. I feel like the Lord sent that bus to my Walgreens for a reason. There was no way I was going to turn them away."

Banks carried the bag full of supplies back to the bus, took a seat at the front and began to feed the child.

"He drank about half a bottle and then was fast asleep again," she said.

Determined to get his regular passengers to work as usual, Chambers drove the bus until 10 AM with Banks cradling the baby in the first-row seat.

"I had to keep telling him to keep his eyes on the road," Banks laughed. "Even so, I'm not sure he could see so well. He was crying and thanking Jesus and singing hymns the whole way. He's a tender man, Mr. Chambers is. A good Christian man."

Officials with the Florida Department of Health and Rehabilitative Services said an effort would be made to find the child's mother. If she can not be found, the baby will be given to Chambers, they said. Chambers said he does not know who might have left the baby behind.

"I think I remember a young girl who got on the bus at about 6 AM. She was my very first passenger, and soaking wet. But she got off almost as soon as she got on. I don't remember if she was carrying anything."

Chambers said he is sure the baby is an answer to his prayers.

"I have a deep feeling in my soul that this child is a gift from God. Some kind soul was led to leave her baby on my bus by the very hand of the Lord."

Orlando Police urged the baby's mother to contact them as soon as possible if she wants the child returned to her.

"We have young mothers leave their babies at fire stations about a dozen times a year, because they've heard that's what they should do," said Captain William Coyne. "I guess this young mother was led to do something else."

Bailey Foster snapped out of her daydream. She wiped a tear from her eye and poured a cup of coffee. She took the coffee to the third-floor window of the lab and gazed out at the parking lot entrance below. Finally, she saw her partner's sky blue Toyota Prius pull into the lot. She glanced at her watch. Thirty minutes late. Early, for Suze.

After a few minutes, Suze Griffin strolled into the lab. She wore a simple white tee-shirt, jeans and blocky Dr. Martens on her feet. Her hair was jet black and cut in an Audrey Hepburn pixie.

"Hey Foster," Suze said, dropping her backpack on the floor and slipping on a white lab coat. "Happy fuckin' Monday."

Bailey handed her one of the Post-It notes.

"Gwendolyn?" Suze asked.

"Who else?"

"Motherfucker!" Suze said. "Any idea what she wants?"

"None."

"OK, let's go. Making her wait isn't going to make her less crazy."

Bailey grabbed a legal pad in case she needed to take notes. Then she and Suze made their way up to Gwendolyn's office on the top floor.

The secretary announced them and they immediately went in. Gwendolyn had been waiting for them. Her office was kept remarkably cold. The bookcases lining the walls were full of technical books and journals, many of them left behind by her dead

parents. Bailey and Suze were sure Gwendolyn had never opened them, and even if she had wouldn't have understood a word. On the plush beige carpet lay a stuffed alligator that had been given to Gwendolyn by a customer grateful to have someone work on their child's rare disease. It had huge yellowed teeth and looked remarkably real, as if it might come to life at any moment and eat them all.

Gwendolyn's desk was the size of a large door. On one corner of it, to Gwendolyn's left as she sat behind it, stood a three-foot-tall model of DNA. The desk was otherwise a perfectly empty sea of walnut.

"Good morning girls!" Gwendolyn said. "Please make yourselves comfortable."

She gestured to the two leather chairs that faced her desk – the same chairs in which the appreciative Stanley and Margaret Johnson had turned to jelly eleven years earlier. (Despite Stanley Johnson's consistent contributions of nearly two million American dollars a year, little progress had been made on the Batten Disease project. Their son, Ben, was now a fifteen-year-old invalid whose care alone consumed more than one-hundred-thousand dollars a year.)

Bailey took the chair to Gwendolyn's right. She sat demurely with the legal pad in her lap. Suze slouched in the other chair, hooking her left knee over its arm. Gwendolyn bristled at the obvious disrespect, but her experience with her daughter helped her conceal her objection.

"First," Gwendolyn began, "I want to tell you both that I think you are doing a fantastic job. I hear nothing but good things about you. So I want to give you both ten-percent raises, effective immediately."

Suze adjusted her position so that she was sitting properly in the chair. Neither she nor Bailey looked at one another, but they could tell what the other was thinking, which was: What the hell is she up to?

"Thank you, Ms. Bayner," Bailey said. "That's very generous of you."

"Not at all, Ms. Foster. You deserve it. I only wish it could be more. And that's the reason I've asked to see you this morning."

Now Suze was sitting on the edge of the leather chair.

"Word around the office says the two of you are gay,"

Gwendolyn said.

"That shouldn't..." Bailey began, but Suze interrupted.

"Let the woman talk, honey! She obviously doesn't care. She just gave us raises!"

"Quite right, Ms. Griffin. I do not care about your personal lives except so far as they make you uniquely suited for a special project I have in mind."

Oh, Jesus, Suze thought. *Don't tell me she wants us to find a cure for being gay.*

Gwendolyn continued.

"First, let me say I am prepared to devote a healthy slice of Bayner's assets to this project. A very healthy slice. A slice so large you will undoubtedly be able to use whatever resources you need."

Suze said, "This must be very important to you, Ms. Bayner."

"It is. But before I tell you what it is, I want to stress that I have nothing against gay people. Some of my best friends are gay people. The waiters at Chez Paris are all gay, and they're all delightful! But I wonder about the poor people who discover that they're gay and are not OK with it. Maybe they're already married and have a gaggle of children running around. You know? Can you imagine?"

"I guess that could be a problem," Suze said, although she wasn't really sure why it might be.

Bailey shot her lab partner an astonished look as Gwendolyn continued.

"Anyway, I'd like to see if we can figure out a way to help these folks, you know, make them normal again, so to speak, so they won't have these unnatural desires to wrestle with. I'm particularly interested in helping lesbians who have perhaps not lost their natural desire to become mothers but can't bring themselves to have sex with a man. I find that to be a dreadful shame, since the primary purpose of a woman is to be a mother."

Finally, Bailey had heard enough.

"Ms. Bayner, with all due respect, we work on diseases. I do not consider being a lesbian a disease. It is a natural state of being."

Suze spoke up before Gwendolyn could respond.

"But Foster, I think you'd have to agree that it's unnatural for a living creature not to have offspring. The primary purpose of all organisms is to propagate the species."

Bailey looked at Suze with amazement and said, "Homosexuality

is common in the animal kingdom. You know that! Fifteen hundred different species practice it: Lions, whales, dolphins, crabs. Even worms. And a very close relative of humans: dwarf chimpanzees."

"Simply a random mutation," Suze said, "and one that will never catch on in earnest since it would drive the species to extinction."

"How, then, do you explain black-headed gulls?" Bailey countered. "They're lesbians, but they get males to fertilize their eggs. There's even evidence that they're better parents than heterosexual gulls."

Gwendolyn interrupted the debate.

"Girls! Girls! I'm sure all of this is very interesting, but here's the bottom line. I am willing to spend whatever it takes to discover what makes a woman a lesbian and then reverse it. Whatever it takes. Are you in? If you're not, I'll happily ask someone else."

Suze stood up and reached across the large desk to shake Gwendolyn's heavily jeweled hand, which was soft as bread dough.

"We'll be happy to do it, Ms. Bayner. Thank you for the opportunity. Come along, Foster."

Suze grabbed Bailey by the arm and led her out of Gwendolyn's office. On their way back to the lab, Bailey scolded her. "Why would you agree to such a stupid project?" she said.

"It's no more stupid than anything else we've worked on, Foster. And did you hear what she said? We can have whatever it takes."

"Yeah, but a lesbian gene? Be serious! You're the lesbian, not me! Why do you not find this nonsense as objectionable as I do?"

"I have no intention of looking for a lesbian gene, Foster." Suze said.

"What are we going to do then?"

"You'll see," Suze said. "You'll see."

5
LOLLY AND LITTLE LILA

Without Lolly Webster's firm hand to guide them, the three-dozen girls under his control would surely stray from the straight and narrow. They would eat too much Chickin' Lickin' and get fat as sows, or else they'd get mixed up with that goddamn meth and grow scary skinny – and no man wanted to dip his wick in a sunken-eyed corpse with bad teeth. Well, not most men anyway.

And here was the main thing: Without Lolly's business sense, the girls surely wouldn't make as much money as they did. They made truckloads of money, which is why they worked for him and not at the Chickin' Lickin', where they wouldn't make enough to pay the rent, no less buy all those shoes. None of Lolly's thirty-six girls wanted for anything in this world.

Lolly Webster was the brains behind Pop Lolly's Peek-a-Boo, a low-class but well-run strip joint tucked in the back of a warehouse district in downtown Miami, between a small-engine repair shop and a manufacturer of PVC-pipe patio furniture. The entire front of the club was labia pink. A big pink awning shaded the entrance. Above it was an even bigger neon sign that alternately flashed "Pop Lolly's Peek-a-Boo" with a pair of obviously female legs, first crossed, then opened wide.

Lolly wasn't like some club owners. He told his girls they could just dance if they wanted to. Of course, he also let them know that the real money was in giving quick blowjobs in the private rooms in the back, which were dark as caves and smelled of sex, perfume,

and overturned cocktails.

A girl would have to work a whole hour dancing to make maybe fifty bucks in one-dollar garter tips – and that was on a busy Friday or Saturday night. On the other hand, even if the place was dead she could lead a customer into one of the private rooms and make fifty in ten minutes at the most, five minutes if she really knew what she was doing. Cops were an exception. All of the girls knew whatever the cops wanted was always free, from booze to blowjobs.

Lolly's girls worked hard. There was no denying that. But so did he. Being a club owner and a pimp wasn't as glamorous as it seemed at first glance. Pimps were constantly called on to do distasteful things, things no good man enjoys doing. Unholy things.

More than that, a pimp had to be a serious mind reader. Any pimp who couldn't tell what a girl was thinking didn't last long. The thing was, even if you didn't know for sure a girl was lying, you went with your gut, because usually you were right, and even if you weren't, it wasn't bad if word got around that you were crazy and apt to go ape-shit at the slightest provocation.

"A lot of bitches ain't too honest," Lolly would say to his friend, Joey Loco, who ran a club on the other side of town. "They look you in the eye and tell you they made two-hundred when they made three. That really makes me sad, and not because of the money. It ain't the money. I got plenty of money. It's the disrespect."

"You got that right, Lolly," Joey Loco would always say.

Lolly wasn't happy about what he had to do when a girl disrespected him, but you couldn't have a club full of girls and not let them know who was boss. If they got the idea they could disrespect you, before long they'd all be disrespecting you, and you might as well go get a job behind the fryer at the Chickin' Lickin'.

The first time a girl disrespected him, he'd cut her take for a week. The second time, he cut her take and beat her sorry ass. Not enough to damage the merchandise, you understand, just enough to warm her up and let her know she'd been a bad girl. The third time, he'd cut the take of all the other girls. That usually did the trick, except that sometimes the other girls were so mad about losing money they beat the disrespectful girl's ass so bad that she flew the coop. That just made things worse, because then Lolly had to send

security out to track the girl down and bring her back, and they weren't necessarily gentle about it because Lolly didn't pay them anything extra.

Every pimp tattooed his own girls like a rancher brands his cattle. The first thing you did when some skinny-assed girl said she wanted to work for you was to tell her to strip, not just so you could check out the merchandise, but so you could look for a competitor's tattoo. If she was already taken, you were honor-bound to have your security staff return her to her rightful owner, the same as a rancher would return a runaway steer.

The worst thing that could happen was when the parents of a girl tried to take her back. That usually didn't happen, because a girl usually became one of Lolly's girls in the first place because her parents didn't give a fuck or, worse yet, abused her. But sometimes it did happen, and that's when Lolly hated being a pimp most of all.

She said her name was Little Lila, no last name, which was fine with Lolly. She said she was eighteen, but didn't have any proof, so Lolly, being a trusting sort, took her word on it. He knew just looking at her that she'd make a ton of cash. She looked to be about fifteen. She was nice and thin, but had an ass on her and cute little breasts with nipples that pointed up like little birds waiting for their mother to drop in a worm. Better still, she could blow like a pro. Lolly knew this before he hired her because his interview process always included a skills test.

"Any girl can be a ho, but the best hos know how to blow," Lolly would say.

"You got that right, Lolly," Joey Loco would always answer.

As for Little Lila, she appeared to have no gag reflex. During her interview, she swallowed Lolly's nine-inch penis straight down until her nose pressed against his stomach. Then, bless her heart, she stuck out her little tongue and licked his balls.

"Little Lila," Lolly said, "You're fucking hired! Congratulations!"

Little Lila smiled.

"Thank you, Lollipop," she said.

"This is Pop Lolly's, sugar. I'm Lolly. Just Lolly. No Pop," Lolly said. "Got it?"

"OK!" Little Lila said. "Lolly! Just Lolly!"

"Right," Lolly said. "Now get on over to Tattoo You and get

yourself a tat. You're Lolly's girl now!"

"OK, Lolly. Do I need money?"

"You don't have any money?"

"I might have five dollars."

"That's OK. Just tell Jeanne you're with me and that you'll pay her as soon as you can. It'll cost you about a hundred. But girl, you're gonna make that in ten minutes once word gets out."

"Where do I have them put the tattoo?"

"Jeanne knows," Lolly said. "She'll put it in the right place."

"OK," Little Lila said.

She turned to leave. Lolly folded his arms and waited for her to turn back, but she didn't.

"Hey," he said as she grabbed the door knob. "Do you know where Tattoo You is?"

"No," Little Lila said, "I was going to ask one of the other girls."

"Good," Lolly said. "You do that."

All of the girls inside the club looked busy, so Little Lila walked outside and saw a woman smoking a cigarette in the shade of the big pink awning. She wore regular street clothes, but there was something about the way she carried herself that told Little Lila she was one of Lolly's girls. Little Lila walked up to her.

"Hey, where's Tattoo You?" Little Lila said.

"You a new girl?" the woman said.

"Yep," Little Lila said.

The woman threw her cigarette on the asphalt, crushed it with the toe of her pump, and gave Little Lila a hug.

"Welcome to the girls' club, honey! My name's Shirl. Lolly's a good pimp, but you don't want to even give him a hint that you're holding out on him. He'll beat you like a dirty rug."

"OK," Little Lila said. "Where's Tattoo You?"

"You know Industry Way right out front here?"

"Yeah."

"Well, walk north up Industry until you get to West Tenth. Tattoo You's right on the corner."

Then Shirl saw the tacit plea in Little Lila's eyes.

"Aw, hell," she said, "This shit hole is dead this afternoon anyway. Let me walk with you."

"OK," Little Lila said. "If you want to."

Shirl took Little Lila by the hand.

"Come on," she said, and the two new coworkers started on their way.

"You're a cute little thing," Shirl said. "Love those little titties. What brings you to this line of work?"

"I ran away from home."

"Honey, we all ran away from home. What made you want to be a ho?"

Shirl thought Little Lila looked awfully young to be a prostitute, and she knew only girls who planned to use the rooms in the back needed tattoos.

"I started out dancing at Platinum One," Little Lila said. "They wanted to see some ID, and I told them I'd get them some. I was hoping they'd forget about it, but they didn't and the truth is I don't have any, so they finally fired me."

"The fools!" Shirl said.

"One of the girls I made friends with told me about Pop Lolly's. They said Lolly wouldn't ask for ID, so I came here."

"You know you can just dance at Lolly's. You don't have to be a ho."

"Yeah, Lolly told me that, but then I gave him a BJ and he said it would be a damn shame if I wasn't a ho. He said I could make ten times the money."

"You must have a special talent, Lila."

"That's what Lolly said."

"What do your parents do?"

"My mom's a nurse. She works at Baptist Hospital. My dad's a computer programmer. He works for some insurance company."

"I don't mean to get personal, but did your dad abuse you? The reason I ask is that mine did me, and I know a lot of the other girls left home for the same reason."

"No," Little Lila said, but Shirl wasn't convinced.

Soon, they came to Tattoo You and went inside.

"Hey Jeanne," Shirl said. "This is Lila. She needs to get branded."

"Lolly's mark?" Jeanne said.

"Who else?"

Jeanne looked at Little Lila.

"That'll be one-twenty," she said.

"Lolly said to tell you I was good for it," Little Lila said.

"I can see that you are," Jeanne said. "You ever had any work done hon?"

"Work?"

"A tattoo."

"No ma'am."

"Well, I ain't gonna lie to you. It's gonna hurt a little."

"I'm used to pain," Little Lila said.

"OK, hop your cute little butt up on this table."

Little Lila hopped up on the table and Jeanne lifted her skirt up and rolled her panties down an inch or two. Then she snapped on blue latex gloves and used a fresh alcohol wipe to disinfect the area just above where Little Lila's delicate pubic hair started.

"You're an adorable little thing, honey," Jeanne said. "How old are you?"

"Eighteen," Little Lila said.

"I'm sure Lolly loved you the first time he set eyes on you," Jeanne said. She handed Little Lila a scrap of paper. "This is what we're going to do."

It was a drawing of a lollipop with swirled colors. Red, blue, yellow, green, and white.

"Cute!" Little Lila said.

"You may change your mind about that after we get started," Jeanne said.

Jeanne took about a half hour to finish the work. Shirl held Little Lila's hand the whole time and felt her squeeze once or twice, but the girl never made a sound and only grimaced once. When Jeanne was done, she handed Little Lila a mirror so she could see the work.

"It looks like it's sunburned," Little Lila said. "It feels that way, too."

"Here," Jeanne said. She gave Little Lila two pills and a glass of water. Lila took the pills without asking what they were.

"Now, listen carefully, because this is important," Jeanne said. "I'm going to put a bandage on and I want you to keep it there until tomorrow. Then change it with another bandage I'll give you, and keep that one on for another day. Do not take a bath, but you can take a hot shower. A scab is going to form. Don't soak the scab or it will fall off too soon. Keep the scab clean, but don't pick at it or scratch at it or the tat won't take. Let the scab come off by

itself."

"I'll make sure she does the right thing," Shirl said. "I have a feeling she'll be staying with me for a few days, until she can get set up on her own."

Little Lila smiled at Shirl and they got up and left.

When they got back to the industrial park, Little Lila noticed her father's car in the parking lot of Pop Lolly's Peek-a-Boo.

"Shit!" Little Lila said. "That's my dad's car!"

"Come with me, sweetie," Shirl said. She pulled Lila into the PVC pipe furniture factory. The place smelled of acetone and airplane glue. There was a man stretching vinyl fabric over the frame of a chaise lounge.

"Hey Shirl! What's going on?" the man said.

"Hey Daniel," Shirl said. "Meet one of our new girls, Little Lila."

Daniel dropped what he was doing, wiped his brow with a white handkerchief, and extended his right hand to Lila as he used his left to stuff the handkerchief into a back pocket.

"Hello, Little Lila," he said.

Lila took Daniel's hand. "Pleased to meet you," she said, lowering her gaze.

Daniel gently kissed Lila's hand.

"Lovely," he said.

"Daniel, do me a favor and look after Little Lila for a second. I'll be right back."

"With pleasure, Shirl," Daniel said.

"I'll be right back, honey," Shirl said to Lila. She kissed her on the forehead. "Sit tight."

Shirl went to see what was going on. Just as she was about to open the door and go inside, Lolly and another man who was obviously Lila's father emerged from the club and stopped for a final word beneath the big pink awning.

"If I see her, I'll let you know," Lolly said to the man. Shirl saw that Lolly was holding a photograph of Little Lila.

"Please do," the man said. "I'm very worried about her."

"You have my word, sir," Lolly said. He looked at Shirl with eyes that said *Where's the hell is Lila?* and walked Lila's father to his car. Shirl went inside.

When Little Lila's father had gone, Shirl told Lolly that Little Lila was over at Daniel's place.

"Go get her," he said.

Shirl went to fetch Little Lila and brought her back to Lolly's office.

"Here she is," Shirl said. She sat down so she'd be there to cool things down if Lolly got too hot. Lolly ignored her and stared at Little Lila, who was standing on the other side of his desk.

"Hi, Lolly," Little Lila said. She could see that he was angry.

"Tell me again how old you are," Lolly said. "And don't you disrespect me by lying to me."

Little Lila paused. She looked at Shirl, who had one eyebrow raised.

"Fifteen and a half," Little Lila said.

"You know your pops was just here."

"Yes. What did he want? How did he find me?"

"He doesn't know you're here. He's looking for you, though. I told him I would call him if I saw you. Should I call him?"

"No!"

"Why not?"

Little Lila looked at Shirl, who nodded yes and then looked at Lolly.

"I can't tell you."

"We have no secrets in this family, Lila."

"I still can't tell you."

"OK, then," Lolly said. He picked up the telephone, looked at the phone number printed on the photograph of Lila, and began dialing.

"He beats me!" Lila blurted out. She started to cry.

Lolly stopped dialing and hung up the phone. He still doubted she was telling the truth. Getting a beating was no reason to run away from home. Shit, his father had beaten him plenty of times, and his brothers, too. The old man had never laid a hand on Lolly's little sister, but that might have been because, seeing what the boys got, she never gave him reason to.

"Why?" Lolly said. "Why does he beat you?"

"One time it was for smoking pot. The last time it was because he found out I was giving BJs to my friends."

"He seemed like a nice man to me, not the kind of man who would beat his daughter. You have any marks?"

Lila walked around the desk to Lolly, turned her back to him,

lifted the hem of her dress and pulled her panties down on the right side. There, on the top of her right cheek, Lolly could see a fading bruise in the shape of a belt buckle. (He'd somehow missed it during his initial inspection.)

"He used the buckle side of his belt on you?" Lolly said.

"The last time he did, yeah. He might not have done it on purpose. He was angry. That's when I ran away."

"That doesn't sound like the man I met today."

"He's two different people. He gets angry when he gets drunk, and when my mom calls him at work and tells him I've been bad, he always comes home drunk."

"Give me some time to think about this," Lolly said. "Get outta here until I call for you."

An hour later, Lolly called Little Lila back into his office. Shirl came back, too.

"OK, here's what we're going to do," Lolly said. "I figure if I send you back to your father, you'll just run away again, and maybe you won't wind up with someone as nice as Lolly. So you can stay."

Little Lila ran to Lolly and started kissing him all over his face and crying, "Thank you! Thank you!"

"Wait, Lila. That's not all."

Lila backed off.

Lolly said, "We'll get you an ID showing that you're eighteen, so if there's any trouble I can just say you showed me proof of your age. I don't expect that there will be any trouble. We take good care of our law enforcement friends, and I'm sure plenty of them will grow to like you. Better safe than sorry, though. And you'll have to pay for the ID. I don't care what last name you use, but you gotta pick one."

"OK, Lolly," Little Lila said, wiping her tears.

"The other thing is, I want you to study so that you can get a GED. There's other girls that have done it. There's no reason you can't. The other girls can help you if you get stuck on something. They might even have some old books you can use, but you'll be responsible for buying whatever you need that they don't have. I'll have Shirl here keep track of your progress. She tells me you'll be living with her, at least for awhile. The first time she tells me you're not on track, your pop gets a call. You ain't gonna have that cute little body forever, so it won't hurt to have a brain to fall back on."

"OK, Lolly," Lila said.

Lolly spanked Little Lila on her cute butt and said, "Now get on out of here. I've got work to do."

Little Lila and Shirl left Lolly's office.

Outside, the club was just starting to get busy.

"Time to go to work, sweetie," Shirl said. "Put on your sexy."

6

BUDDHISM AND BAILEY

Compared to Susan Griffin's horrific childhood, Bailey Foster's was idyllic. She grew up with two brothers, both younger. Her parents were teetotalers, although they did smoke an occasional joint, usually in bed before sex.

While the Griffins were Catholic, the Fosters were essentially nonreligious. When asked, David and Joan Foster would say they believed in God, but He didn't play any particular role in their lives. The Fosters certainly didn't pray over things as they saw others did. They celebrated Christmas and Easter, but didn't go to church even on those special days. They'd been married at the courthouse.

It was perhaps Bailey's lack of religious training that prompted her to register for a comparative religions class to satisfy the humanities requirement in her first year of college. The professor was Jack Collins. Jack had come of age in the late sixties. He was an eyeglass-wearing hippy who tied his long hair back in a pony tail and had a peace symbol hanging from a leather lace around his neck. He respected every religion and taught them all as if he believed each of them were equally true. It was not his place to judge, he said.

"I'm a teacher," he told his students, "not a preacher."

Mr. Collins gave the same benefit of the doubt to the numerous gods and goddesses of Greek and Roman mythology as he gave to the Bha'i faith, Confucianism, Jainism, Shintoism, Sikhism, Taoism, Christianity, Judaism, Islam, Hinduism, Buddhism and even Scientology, Wiccan, Satanism, Voodoo and the sundry beliefs of

the American Indians.

While the course was nearly comprehensive with respect to the number of religions it broached, Mr. Collins' comparative religion class did not address the actual mechanisms of faith. Belief was taken as a given, as if Mr. Collins assumed everyone believed in something. The atheists and agnostics in the class – the ones who stood the most to gain from a discussion of what it meant to believe – were easily outnumbered by the faithful. So they kept their unpopular disbelief to themselves, until the day Bailey Foster asked the question, that is.

"How does belief even work, anyway?" she asked. "Do I just declare one day that I believe? How do I know? And what happens if later on I discover I don't?"

"You just do!" exclaimed one pretty co-ed still in pig tails. "I believe one-hundred-percent!"

"A hundred percent of what?" Bailey said.

"Of everything!" the girl answered.

Mr. Collins saw Bailey roll her eyes.

"Bailey," he said. "You believe in science, right?"

"Believe?" Bailey said.

"Maybe that was a bad choice of words. You respect science, right? You expect it will tell the truth about things, so far as it knows them, and it will expose flaws in itself and correct past errors when it discovers them. For you, science has integrity, and you trust it."

"Sure," Bailey said.

"OK. Do you believe…"

Mr. Collins caught himself. There was that word again.

"Do you trust in the Big Bang Theory? Do you think it's true?"

"Of course," Bailey said.

"Why?"

"Because the math says it most likely happened. It's still a theory, you know, so it's not presented as a fact."

"That's true," Mr. Collins said. "But it's also not an idle theory. Most scientists are so sure the Big Bang will one day be proved true that they treat it as if it's already happened. They do the same thing with gravity, which as I'm sure you know is also just a theory. I think we can agree that gravity and the Big Bang, while technically theories, are so mature and so widely accepted that they are ninety-

nine-percent of their way to becoming full-fledged facts. But let's leave that aside for now."

Mr. Collins turned to Bailey. "Ms. Foster: Do you personally understand the mathematics that led to the Big Bang Theory?"

"Well, the universe is expanding," Bailey said. "So it must have started at a central point."

"Reasonable people might disagree about that – especially when you throw in a supernatural God who may have worked some magic in order to make the universe appear any way He pleases. But let me ask the question a different way."

He turned and wrote on the blackboard:

$$4.6 \times 10^{26} \text{ cm} / 1 \times 10^{9} \text{ cm/sec} = 4.6 \times 10^{17} \text{ sec}$$

"Do you recognize this equation?"

"I'm afraid I don't," Bailey said.

"It simple," a boy sitting next to Bailey said. "Distance divided by velocity equals time."

"Exactly," Mr. Collins said. "This equation is central to the Big Bang Theory. It shows how long, more or less, every other galaxy in the universe has been travelling away from our own. In other words, every other galaxy in the universe has been moving away for about the same amount of time. The implication of this is the Big Bang Theory, which guesses that the universe started at a single point which itself was no larger than a single atom, a little less than fourteen billion years ago, or four-point-six times ten to the seventeenth seconds."

"Cool!" Bailey said. "I guess I never knew the details. That makes me believe it even more!"

"Here's the thing though, Ms. Foster: You believed the Big Bang Theory first because it made sense to you and second because scientists you respect and trust said it was true, right?"

"I guess that's right," Bailey said.

"But listen to how crazy what I just said sounds: Every piece of matter that exists in the entire universe started out taking up no more room than a single atom. I mean, how freaking crazy is that? You realize how big the universe is, right? And yet you believe it."

Bailey had to admit that the Big Bang was a truly crazy idea. In fact, ideas like the Big Bang were what she liked best about science.

They proved that truth is always stranger than fiction.

Mr. Collins went on.

"OK, now let's move to religion. When you're a kid, the people who you trust most in the world, your parents, start out by telling you that God exists. They're persistent about it. They pray, and not just before meals and after sneezes. They pray before taking a driving test. They pray before having a baby. They even pray before going to bat at the church softball game, and after they get to first base. It seems to you they're always praying. They certainly behave as though God is watching them and listening to them. Looking out for them, even. You start believing that they believe with unflagging certainty and before long you start believing, too. You believe because they're your parents. You think they couldn't be wrong, and they certainly wouldn't mislead you. Not about something so important.

"Your belief grows more certain after you get older and meet other people who are just as certain as your parents are that God exists. You meet with them every week and hear the perspective of someone who believes so completely in God that he has devoted his entire life to it. His *life*. On top of that, you know that some of these men of the cloth have made extreme sacrifices in the name of their belief, particularly the ones who take vows of celibacy."

Laughter filled the room, then died down almost immediately. The students wanted to hear what Mr. Collins would say next.

"You find it impossible to believe that so many people would waste their entire lives espousing something they do not believe themselves, so you figure they must believe. This further strengthens your certainty.

"As a member of your congregation, you can not possibly spend as much time studying God as your minister does. He has devoted his life to it, after all. So, just as Ms. Foster trusts scientists when they tell her that the entire universe once fit into a space smaller than a single atom, you believe your minister when he tells you there's a God."

Someone started to applaud, and within seconds Mr. Collins was enjoying a rousing ovation.

"Well!" he said, blushing. "Thank you. Thank you very much. And thank you for the question, Ms. Foster. I'll have to add the discussion to my syllabus!"

The day Jack Collins devoted the class to Buddhism, he strode into the room wearing a pair of Groucho Marx glasses with fuzzy eyebrows and a big plastic nose. Under the nose, he'd painted on a thick, rectangular moustache with black greasepaint. He produced a plastic cigar from his pocket, stuck it in his mouth, and asked: "What did the Buddha say when they asked him, 'Buddha, is there a God?'"

"Is that a riddle Groucho?" someone asked.

The class laughed.

"Sounds like one, doesn't it?" Mr. Collins said. "But no, it's not. Someone actually asked the Buddha the question. So what did he answer?"

Mr. Collins smiled when he saw the students struggling to remember if they'd read something about the Buddha being asked whether there was a God. He turned away from the class and picked up a piece of chalk from the dusty tray beneath the old black chalkboard. He could hear them whispering to one another.

"Anyone?" he said over his shoulder, not expecting an answer.

As he let the class stew, Jack Collins drew a cartoon Buddha on the board, cross-legged with a big smile and a round belly. It looked more like an obese Mr. Clean than the Buddha. Collins heard snickering.

"No one ever said I was an artist, guys. That's on the other side of campus," he said, then quickly refocused the class. "No one knows what the Buddha said when they asked him 'Buddha, is there a God?' No? OK."

He drew a big oval over the Buddha's left shoulder, drew a line from the oval to his cartoon Buddha, then wrote inside the circle: *I don't know.* The class laughed, but Bailey Foster thought, *That's the religion for me.*

Mr. Collins turned to the class and said, "The Buddha valued honestly viewing reality above everything else. He didn't know if there was a God, so that's what he said: 'I don't know.'"

As a budding scientist dedicated to provable truths, Bailey Foster wasn't as open-minded as Jack Collins, who seemed to believe in every religion, or at least to respect them all. Nonetheless, she found herself being drawn to Buddhism's focus on developing a dispassionate view of reality. How different was that from science, after all? She also saw the benefit of the Buddha's

pragmatic goal of simple happiness, which while she figured was not really simple at all seemed to her to be the best possible purpose anyone's life could have.

The thing that excited Bailey most about Buddhism was its give-or-take attitude toward a supernatural deity. Belief wasn't necessary. Buddhism apparently would work for you whether or not you could manage to buy into the whole God thing.

Bailey had always yearned to experience the bliss her religious friends seemed to enjoy, but, as a devotee of the scientific method, she had no earthly idea how she was going to believe something for which there was no proof. The fact that lots of other people believed something actually worked to repel her, especially after she'd read Irving Janus' *Victims of Groupthink* and then learned about the dangers of doublethink in George Orwell's *1984*. Even her own father had warned her, "Fishermen love a feeding frenzy."

To Bailey Foster, it was wise not to swallow something blindly before first having a good close look. This fit perfectly with Buddhism, which also encouraged careful inspection and taught its adherents not to accept anything on face value.

After Mr. Collins' lesson on Buddhism, Bailey began visiting the campus Buddhist Centre on Saturday nights. She discovered to her relief that God was, indeed, never mentioned. The soft-spoken monks – some of whom had names just as American as "Foster" – took turns teaching on different Saturdays, but every one of them focused on meditation techniques and other methods purported to help one see reality clearly and accept it for what it was, a sobering skill they saw as essential to a happy life.

Mr. Collins had put it this way: "You know just from looking around that the shit is probably going to hit the fan sooner or later, so why be surprised when it does? The Buddha says whether life gives you sorrow or joy, always react with equanimity and say, 'Ah! I've been expecting you!'"

The teachers at the Buddhist Centre taught the Buddha's Four Noble Truths and his Eight-Fold Noble Path, which they argued were the way to happiness.

During the Introduction to Buddhism lesson, Bailey made these notes:

The Four Noble Truths:

1. Life means suffering.
Into everyone's life a little rain must fall.

2. The origin of suffering is attachment.
All things must pass. Becoming attached to temporary things causes suffering.

3. The cessation of suffering is attainable.
You can do something about it!

4. Suffering is ended by following the Eight-Fold Noble Path.

The Eight-Fold Noble Path, as given by Siddhartha Gautama, the Buddha:

1. Right view
See things as they are. Start by accepting that all beings are subject to suffering. Go from there. Don't lie to yourself. It is what it is.

2. Right intention
Resist desire, eschew anger and develop compassion and understanding.

3. Right speech (The first ethical principal)
Do not lie or slander others. Don't use words that offend others. Avoid small talk and gossip.

4. Right Action (The second ethical principal)
Do not kill or harm others. Don't steal. Abstain from sexual misconduct.

5. Right Livelihood
Obtain wealth legally & peacefully. No dealing in weapons or living beings of any kind. No cattle ranching! If you work for a company, make sure the company isn't polluting a river.

6. Right Effort
Suppress bad emotions. Abandon them if they've already arisen. Encourage good emotions and cultivate them once they appear.

7. Right Mindfulness
You can control how you interpret the events of your life. Cultivate that power so that you are able to likewise control your thoughts and emotions.

8. Right Concentration

Stay focused on wholesome thoughts through the practice of meditation.

The monks at the Buddhist Centre spent an entire hour-long lesson on each "truth" and each "step." Even then, Bailey was not sure she understood very clearly. The Buddha's rules appeared at first to say simply, "Be a good person and behave yourself." She thought there must be more to it, and the monks assured her that there was. They also said she would understand in time and should not worry about the end of the journey. She should focus instead on her current understanding and be satisfied well enough with it. "Dwell on the path beneath your feet," they said.

However long it took her to understand the Eight-Fold Noble Path, Bailey thought it would be easier than believing in something out of thin air. To her delight, Bailey quickly experienced for herself the practical benefits of meditation. She found it easier to concentrate when she'd meditated in the morning and harder when she hadn't. The days she skipped, small annoyances distracted her. After a while, she became accustomed to starting each day with thirty minutes of focusing all of her attention on her breathing and her breathing alone. It was a revelation. It wasn't always as easy as it sounded, of course. She often had trouble staying focused, which she'd heard was normal.

One morning, she struggled to focus on her breathing but instead began imagining a complex castle built into the side of a mountain peak that was itself dwarfed by two other mountain ranges to the north and the south. The castle was so complex it was hard to judge how large it was or how many rooms it might have. There was gold ornamentation everywhere. Golden statues of every sort were stationed along eaves, at the entrances to stairways, in great rooms, on roof tops. Stuck here and there on the tessellated structure were golden spires of every size jutting into a blue sky. There were stone stairways leading up, over, and then up again.

Bailey heard the clock radio go off. Her thirty minutes were up. The old Beatles tune, the weird Tomorrow Never Knows, was just starting up, with its staggered beat and George's droning sitar.

Bailey slapped the radio off and started getting ready for class.

7
ROCCO MAKES IT HURT

The boss took a big bite of a sandwich piled high with corned beef.

"God damn this is good!" he said with his mouth full. He held the sandwich up so Rocco could see the three-inch-high mound of meat.

"Look at that!" the boss mumbled. "Where'd Bobby say he got it from? Carmine's?"

"Harold's, I think he said, boss," Rocco said. "Or maybe Fred and Murray's."

"How the fuck could you get Harold's mixed up with Fred and Murray's, Rocco? They're not even close for Christ's sake. Sometimes I don't know about you."

Then the boss took another big bite and, with his mouth again full of corned beef, said, "Hey Rocco, how many poor schmucks you think you've done for me?"

"About three-hundred, boss," Rocco said.

The boss was always asking Rocco how many poor schmucks he'd done, and Rocco had been answering "about three-hundred" for a couple years now, so now he thought maybe he should up the count.

"Or maybe five-hundred," Rocco added.

"Jesus Christ on a cannoli, Rocco," the boss said. "Harold's. Fred and Murray's. Three-hundred. Five-Hundred. Are you not paying attention?"

"Sure I am, boss."

"Whatever. Whether it's Harold's or Fred and Murray's or three-hundred or five-hundred, this is a goddamn good sandwich and you must be gettin' pretty fuckin' good at doing guys."

"I guess so, boss."

Rocco Magnano was good at it. For one thing, he never used a gun. Guns could be traced, even stolen guns. They left bullets behind, and casings. Rocco never left anything behind, except maybe a body. His philosophy was the simpler, the better. The human body was fragile. You didn't need anything too fancy to shut it down. If he was forced to, he'd do a guy with his bare hands. He'd grab the guy's coconut and either bash it against a sidewalk or just twist it until he felt that familiar snap. Or else he would just cut off the poor schmuck's air. It was amazing how fast a guy died when you cut off his air. Rocco considered it a design flaw. Whales could go for hours underwater without breathing. But a man? A man could only last a few minutes at most.

Usually Rocco used a baseball bat, a Louisville Slugger. There were a zillion baseball bats out there, all of them pretty much the same. So if some cop came looking for who had bashed in some guy's head with a baseball bat, you could always just say, hey, it's a fucking baseball bat. I use it to hit balls to the kids on weekends. What about it?

Rocco didn't know most of the people he did, and those he did know he knew only a little, like to raise a hand to them on the street. Rocco wasn't the kind of man who had a lot of friends. Most of the boss's crew knew Rocco's business and steered clear of him, like cops avoided internal affairs detectives.

Another reason Rocco didn't have many friends is that the more friends he had, the better chance there was that the boss would tell him to do one of them. Rocco always did whoever the boss told him to do, no questions asked. Not just because it paid well, but because anyone who wanted to live past the end of the week did not cross the boss. Rocco knew he wasn't the only guy the boss used to get rid of problems.

Sometimes the boss even told Rocco to do someone on the inside, one of the boss's own guys, usually a snitch or a guy whose marbles just got to big for his sack. Sometimes the crazy bastard didn't even wait until the guy was out of the room. He would raise his right eyebrow and glance at the poor schmuck, or glance at him

and give a slight cough – something subtle like that.

Then Rocco would raise his own bushy eyebrows as if to say, "You want me to do him, boss?"

Sometimes the boss would just point to his throat and say "peppercorn" and then reach for something to wash it down. Other times, he'd say nothing. Nothing meant yes.

Not that Rocco gave a half a damn, but the boss seemed to him overly anxious to do guys. The boss had ordered Rocco do so many guys over the years that it had become second-nature. He carried out the jobs with the same lackadaisical dispassion as a farmer who wrings a chicken's neck for Sunday dinner.

Even if the boss had other hit men, Rocco knew he was the boss's favorite. At least that's what he told Rocco. Maybe the boss liked him best because he was so philosophical about it, Rocco thought.

One day the boss had asked him, "How you dealing with doing so many poor schmucks, Rocco? You OK with it?"

"Life is temporary for everyone," Rocco had answered. "There's no telling when it's gonna end. Any one of those poor schmucks could have been hit by a bus the next day after I did them, so what did I take from them? Less than twenty-four hours, maybe."

Also, Rocco knew that if he didn't do it the boss would find someone else who would. Maybe somebody not so philosophical as Rocco.

"What about God, Rocco?" the boss asked.

"I ain't all that worried about God, boss," Rocco said. "For one thing, He doesn't seem to be all that against killing, no matter what the commandments say. He himself is constantly offing poor schmucks. Like in a tsunami. He takes out hundreds of thousands at a shot, even babies and old people. As far as doing guys goes, I ain't got nothing on the Lord God Almighty. He's the real expert."

"So what if God's pissed that you're stepping on his turf?" the boss said.

"Too late now, boss," Rocco said. "Once you do one guy, you might as well do a thousand. You're already fucked. And God can only send you to hell once."

Rocco had even done a couple dogs. He liked dogs, had a couple bulldogs himself. But an order was an order. The dogs'

owner apparently hadn't quite pissed off the boss enough to get himself or his family killed, but he'd done enough. Rocco wasn't sure what. It didn't matter.

Rocco did the dogs on a clear night with a full moon. He waited until three in the morning, then jumped the poor schmuck's fence, thinking how funny it was that people thought fences protected them.

The guy's two Rottweiler dogs attacked just as Rocco knew they would. They were beautiful, black and tan, and silent as an owl bearing down on a barn mouse.

Rocco, who weighed three-hundred pounds or so, stood his ground and let the dogs come. The first one to get to him got his skull crushed in mid-air with Rocco's thirty-two-ounce Louisville Slugger. *Skutsch!* The second dog got hold of Rocco's leg. Rocco reached down and crushed the dogs windpipe with one hand. The dog let loose and Rocco bashed its head in with the bat.

When he was back in his car, Rocco poured hydrogen peroxide on the puncture wounds in his leg, then went to an all-night diner for a quick bite.

None of Rocco's victims suffered unless the boss put in a special order. On those occasions, the boss simply said, "Make it hurt."

Rocco wasn't only good at killing, he was good at making it hurt. In the end, the poor bastards prayed to God to die. At that point, Rocco figured whacking them on the head with the Louisville Slugger was doing them a favor.

Like that guy Sal What's-His-Name. Cocky motherfucker, he was, stupid as a second coat of paint. He had the bad sense to kill the boss's brother. It was really the boss's half-brother, but Sal didn't know that, so the boss retaliated as if it were his full brother. He ordered Sal's whole family done. That time, the boss handed Rocco a slip of paper with Sal's home address on it. Beneath the address the boss had written "MAKE IT HURT" and underlined it twice.

Rocco spent most of that night in Sal's basement with Sal, his wife and their boy and girl, ten and eight, cute little kids. The family had just moved into the house, so the basement wasn't finished. There were just a couple of bare bulbs lighting the place. The walls

were bare concrete block and there was a lot of junk piled into the corners, stuff that looked like it belonged in a backyard shed, or maybe upstairs in the three-car garage.

After escorting the family down into the basement at gunpoint, Rocco bound and gagged them, then blindfolded everyone but Sal, who he hung from a joist by his bound wrists. Watching was part of the hurting – not the worst part by any means, but still unpleasant. Rocco didn't make the family suffer any more than he'd made the dogs suffer. It wasn't their fault Sal was such a dumb ass, after all, and Rocco was no monster.

He took care of Sal's family from the youngest to the oldest – first the girl, then the boy, then the wife. He used his bare hands on the kids. It was the most humane way, just a quick twist of the head and off they went, as if a switch had been flicked. Even though the family was blindfolded, they knew something bad was happening because Sal growled through his gag like a mad dog.

When the kids were gone, Rocco sat on the floor behind Sal's hyperventilating wife, pulled her against his chest as if they were in a toboggan, then wrapped a beefy arm around her neck. She was not a small woman, so it took a couple minutes, and she thrashed around like a landed marlin, but before long she was gone and then there was only Sal.

Rocco arranged the two kids and the wife against the basement wall so Sal could see them sitting there with their heads slumped over like rag dolls. Then he cut Sal's clothes off with a razor-sharp Bowie knife. He found a full-length dressing mirror under the basement stairs and leaned it against the wall between the two kids and the wife so Sal could watch as Rocco made it hurt.

If ever a message was sent to anyone, this message was about to be sent to Sal What's-His-Name: Thou shalt not fuck with the boss.

Before turning his attention to Sal, Rocco lifted a large canvas duffle bag onto an old piano bench and unzipped it. He reached into the bag and pulled out a hospital-green surgical mask and tied it onto his face. Then he slipped on a pair of white Tyvek hooded overalls with matching booties. He pulled on a pair of thick Latex gloves, tucked them under the elastic wristbands of the overalls, then put on a pair of clear plastic safety glasses held firmly in place by an elastic band that stretched around the back of his head.

"Safety first," Rocco said, adjusting the big plastic glasses.

Sal watched Rocco's careful preparations with horror. His naked body, hanging by the wrists like an unrepentant heretic in a Dark Ages dungeon, writhed with the anticipation of what it was about to suffer.

Rocco snapped rubber-tube tourniquets around Sal's thighs and biceps.

"Here we go, Sal," he said. "I ain't gonna lie to you. This is gonna hurt."

He grabbed a pair of bolt cutters from the canvas duffle bag and snipped off the baby toe on Sal's left foot as if he were trimming a rose bush. The little toe bounced onto the concrete floor. Sal screamed through his gag and struggled and snorted like a pig being gutted.

"Jesus, Sal! Save your energy," Rocco said. "We're just getting started."

Rocco saw four fishing poles leaning against a corner of the basement. He removed a reel from one of them, cut off a length of nylon line, then used the line to hang the baby toe from a water pipe so that it hung in front of Sal's sweating face.

"One down, nine to go," Rocco said.

Sal whimpered through his gag and struggled to get free.

"Stop moving, Sally," Rocco said.

Sal stopped moving, but when he felt the bolt cutters touch the next toe in, he starting kicking again.

"You know something, Sally? The boss was right," Rocco said. "You are a fucking dumbass."

Rocco pulled his Louisville Slugger from the duffle bag and took his place beside Sal, slightly to his right so that the poor schmuck's ribcage was squarely in the strike zone. He lifted the bat as if preparing for a pitch. Sal looked at him with his eyes opened wide, eyes that begged for mercy, eyes that said please just kill me and get this over with.

Rocco ignored Sal's tacit plea and began to announce a fantasy ball game.

"It's the bottom of the ninth, ladies and gentlemen, with two outs and a man on first. Ruth has already taken two fastballs for strikes."

Rocco scratched his right Tyvek bootie at the concrete floor as if digging into red clay and leaned over to tap the heavy barrel of

the bat against the floor.

"The Red Sox infield is playing deep. They need only one more out to win."

Sal whimpered through his gag.

"Here's the pitch!" Rocco said.

Sal closed his eyes and held his breath in preparation to have his ribs broken, but Rocco just tapped his side with the bat.

"It's a bunt!" he howled. "The ball rolls down the third base line and the Babe waddles to first. He's safe!"

Sal exhaled.

"Who the fuck ever heard of Babe Ruth bunting? And with two strikes!" Rocco said from beneath the green surgical mask. "Sally, you are one lucky sum-o-bitch! Now stay still!"

Rocco dropped the bat and positioned the bolt cutters around the second toe. Sal kicked again.

"God damn you, Sal," Rocco said. "How fucking stupid can you be?"

Rocco picked up the bat and swung it quickly into Sal's side, hard enough to crack a couple ribs and take Sal's breath away.

After that, Sal stayed still.

Rocco snipped off Sal's toes one-by-one with the bolt cutters, pausing between each toe to add it to the gruesome toe-mobile he was building in front of Sal's face. Then he took all ten fingers the same way.

Sal closed his eyes so he wouldn't have to look at the horrifying spectacle growing before him. Rocco took a small C-clamp from his bag and tightened it firmly onto Sal's right testicle. This made Sal's eyes open wide. By the time Rocco would get around to snipping off Sal's balls – which wouldn't be for hours – they'd be big as Grade A eggs. If you wanted a guy to hurt, you didn't cut his balls off until the very end. A guy would do almost anything to keep his balls from being crushed like rubber pecans.

With ten toes and ten fingers hanging from the water pipe, Rocco noticed that Sal was starting to go into shock. His eyes were closing and his head slumped to one side. Rocco reached into his canvas bag, pulled out a syringe, jammed it into Sal's hip, and gave the plunger a little push. Sal woke up and started whimpering again.

Next, Rocco went after the ankles. He used the carefully sharpened Bowie knife to carve through the skin and Achilles

tendon, then sliced through the cartilage holding the knot of ankle bones together.

The feet were too heavy for the little water pipe, and Rocco didn't want to flood the place while he was working, so he hammered a big gray nail he found into one of the joists and hung the toeless feet from it, winding the taut fishing line around the nail and knotting it off.

"I'd tell you never to piss off the boss again, Sally," Rocco said, "but that would be fucking stupid, wouldn't it? You're never going to piss off anybody again."

Rocco took a rag from his canvas bag, slipped off the safety glasses, wiped the sweat from his brow, and laughed a little. Sal didn't laugh at all. Rocco noticed that Sal had closed his eyes again. Rocco jabbed him in the stomach with the baseball bat and said, "Looky, looky, Sal."

Sal opened his eyes.

"How many do you see, Sally?" Rocco said, replacing his safety glasses.

Sal struggled to count the body parts hanging in front of him.

"Uh-wuh-wuh!" Sal cried through his gag. "Uh! Weh-weh-woo!"

"Excellent Sally!" Rocco said. "Twenty two! Ten fingers, ten toes and two feet. Wonderful. Stay awake. You don't want to miss this."

The Bowie knife sliced easily through the tendons at the back of the knees, but the kneecaps were another matter, so Rocco took a hack saw to them. Sal came in and out of consciousness several times while the calves were being removed, but hardly squeaked.

When the meaty calves were suspended from their own nails in the joists, Rocco said, "I guess I can cut you down now, Sally. Where you gonna go, eh?"

Rocco laughed. Again, Sal failed to see the humor.

Rocco gave Sal's torso a bear hug and cut him down, careful not to slip on the bloody floor. Then he gently lowered Sal's butchered body to the floor so the poor schmuck wouldn't hit his head and be knocked unconscious.

When Sal looked up and saw the body parts dangling above him and dripping red, he started beating his own head against the concrete.

"Tsk, tsk," Rocco said.

He applied a second C-clamp to Sal's left testicle and tightened it a full turn more than the one on his right. Sal whimpered.

"Try to stay awake, Sally. You'll miss the fun."

Next, Rocco found a short length of two-by-four lumber left behind by the builders. Then he found another one of the big gray nails and used it to affix Sal's left palm to the board. Then he hacked through the wrist with two heavy swings of a sharpened hatchet, which on the second and final swing sank decisively into the pine.

He used the same technique on the other wrist and then cut through both elbow joints with the Bowie knife. He suspended all the parts above where Sal was lying.

He saw Sal slipping away and gave him the rest of the adrenalin. Sal came to, but Rocco could see his light was low.

"How many do we have now, Sally?" Rocco said.

Sal looked up. What was this, a dream? How many? Let's see. Ten fingers, ten toes. That's twenty, he thought. Two toeless feet, two calves. Two fingerless hands, two forearms.

"Ug-hee-ay," Sal moaned.

"Excellent," Rocco said. "Twenty-eight! You're doing great, Sal."

Next, Rocco dug out Sal's left eye with the tip of his Bowie knife and sliced through the optic nerve. Then, finally, he removed the C-clamps from Sal's testicles, slit open the scrotum, pulled out each testicle, and cut it off.

"Simple as gelding a stallion back on the farm," Rocco said, although he had never been on a farm.

Finally, for good measure, he knocked out Sal's front teeth with the handle of the baseball bat, being careful not to prematurely crush his skull.

Rocco was tired. He'd been at it for four hours. He stood up and surveyed his handiwork, the three bodies against the wall and the crudely dismembered body on the bloody floor.

"The boss said make 'em hurt," he said. "I'd say this qualifies. What do you say, Sally?"

Sal didn't answer. Rocco didn't care. He grabbed his Louisville Slugger and took aim at Sal's head.

"Goodbye, Sally," he said. "Nice knowing ya."

The barrel of the bat sank into Sal's skull with a *skutsch*! and Sal

was mercifully gone.

Rocco carried his canvas bag to the bottom of the basement stairs. He took out a rag and used it to wipe the excess blood from the Tyvek overalls. Then he used the rag to wipe off his bloody tools — the bat, the bolt cutters, the knife, the hatchet, the hacksaw, the C-clamps. He put the tools back in the canvas bag, then removed the safety glasses, the surgical mask, the overalls and the booties. He put the protective clothing into a plastic bag and jammed it into the bag. Then he added the rubber gloves.

Rocco looked at himself in the full-length mirror. He was sweat-stained, but remarkably clean for what he had just been through. He grabbed the bag, walked outside, got into his car, and drove to an all-night diner where he ordered coffee, black, and two slices of banana cream pie.

Rocco loved all pie, but banana cream pie was his favorite.

8
JUNK DNA

After Gwendolyn Bayner set Suze and Bailey off on what she assumed was the search to cure lesbianism, Suze began right away to work feverishly on her secret project. She started arriving at the lab early, staying late, and working weekends. More than once, Gwendolyn discovered Suze fast asleep at her desk at seven in the morning. Impressed with the effort, she insisted on giving Suze another ten-percent raise.

"I'd like to keep this between just the two of us if you don't mind, Ms. Bayner," Suze said. "Foster might be upset by it, you know?"

"I don't see how," Gwendolyn said. "She's hardly putting in the effort you are."

"Bailey's working as hard as she can for now. Please trust me. She's doing fine. It's just that the project has entered a phase where the ball is primarily in my court," Suze said. "I designed the project that way. It's my fault Bailey isn't busier, not hers."

"If you say so, Ms. Griffin," Gwendolyn said. "We'll keep this just between us girls."

"Thank you for being so understanding, Ms. Bayner," Suze said.

"You'll tell me the moment you find anything," Gwendolyn said.

"Of course."

It was still early in the going. Even if Suze had been looking for the lesbian cure – which she was not – no reasonable person would expect her to have found it so quickly. Suze thought she probably

had six to nine months before Gwendolyn would start to insist she be given some reason to continue, some shred of hope.

As for Bailey, her relative idleness was a result not only of how Suze had structured the project, but also because of Suze's steadfast refusal to tell her what the project even was. Suze had even managed to keep her plans a secret after Bailey threatened one day to go to Gwendolyn and spill the beans, so far as she could. Certainly Gwendolyn would not be happy to hear that Suze was not sharing with her lab partner even the most general information about what she was up to – especially since whatever she was up to was clearly not what Gwendolyn thought it was. What possible reason could there be for keeping a project's details from your lab partner?

"This isn't fair, Suze, and it's certainly not good science," Bailey said. "You need to tell me what you're doing. If you don't, I'll have no other choice but to tell Ms. Bayner that you're being unnecessarily secretive. It's unproductive! Who knows? Maybe I could help you. I'm your partner, damn it!"

"You won't tell the old girl," Suze said. "I'd be fired. Besides, you trust me too much. I've already promised this will be good. Do you doubt me? I'm the smart one, remember? You're the one with the faith. It's time to show you have a little."

"I'm a Buddhist," Bailey said. "I don't know if there's a God." She put her hands on her hips defiantly. "In any case, I'm sure you're not one."

Suze looked up at the ceiling and sniffed the air.

"Still smells like bullshit to me," she said.

Suze was a devout atheist, of course. What else could she be? Any God she could ever believe in would not have allowed her to suffer such a horrifying childhood.

"This had better be good, Suze, " Bailey said.

Suze didn't hear her. She was already back at her keyboard, her eyes fixated on the esoteric code filling the computer monitor, her mind crawling back into the virtual world where she was building the software that would change the world.

In the beginning, at least, Bailey wasn't completely idle. Suze gave her a couple of specific jobs to do, and although the duties revealed nothing about what Suze was up to, Bailey searched her

heart and decided that she did, in fact, trust her lab partner. She also didn't want to be a snitch, particularly if it meant Suze would be fired. So she did what Suze told her to do, even if she had no idea why she was doing it.

First, Bailey supervised the construction of a roomful of computers configured to Suze's specifications. There were one-thousand-twenty-eight state-of-the-art servers connected together so that they worked as one giant processing machine.

Bailey also hired a team of systems administrators to keep the computers up and running, which turned out to be no small task. Extra air-conditioning was needed to keep the room cool and lessen the chances that any of the servers would fail. Nonetheless, several of the machines did malfunction and so needed to be replaced. The setup cost more than two-and-a-half million dollars. Gwendolyn Bayner hadn't blinked an eye.

"She was obviously serious about giving us whatever we needed," Suze told Bailey.

"Let's hope she doesn't regret it in the end."

"She won't," Suze said, although she harbored her own secret doubts.

Once the computers were installed and stress-tested, Suze told Bailey to begin collecting as many digital DNA sequences as she could lay her hands on and load them into the system. Bailey threw herself into the task with the enthusiasm of a five-year-old at an Easter egg hunt. The DNA sequences – which amounted to little more than long strings of A's, C's, G's, and T's – came from all over the globe.

Some came from law enforcement agencies who had created a database containing the DNA of known criminals. They used the DNA database in the same way as they used fingerprints: to nab repeat offenders. Most criminals had been arrested before, since four out of five people who went to prison wound up going back to prison.

Other agencies had collected DNA data from the families of missing persons. The DNA was used in the hope of identifying the decomposing human remains that were found all too often by hikers and nature lovers who – often at the insistent urgings of a canine companion – happened upon the shallow, leaf-covered graves of murder victims. (More often than not, the murder victims

were wrapped in old blankets or plastic tarps, as if their killers had oddly cared at least enough to prevent dirt from getting into their eyes.)

A government department called the National Newborn Screening & Genetics Resource Center routinely collected the DNA of all newborn babies in an effort to locate genetic peculiarities that indicated a predisposition for a panoply of diseases, everything from Angelman Syndrome to YY Syndrome.

There were similar programs aimed at specific diseases. The Autism Genetic Resource Exchange gathered DNA from the families of autistic children in an effort to find DNA markers that might someday predict the disorder. Similar databases existed for melanoma, schizophrenia, multiple sclerosis and a long list of other diseases thought to be caused by malformed genes.

Still more DNA samples came from genealogy companies that collected the genetic material of curious people who wanted to research their ancestry, perhaps hoping to discover that they had inherited a royal genome or, perhaps equally as thrilling, one passed down by a famous thief or social iconoclast. Bailey discovered that some exceedingly careful parents had taken DNA samples from their children and given the samples to organizations that would use them to identify the remains of the children, should they ever go missing and turn up dead.

For the same reason, police departments routinely swabbed the cheeks and gums of known prostitutes. They knew from experience that sex workers had a bad habit of turning up dead because they always neglected to run background checks on, or psychological evaluations of, their sometimes homicidal customers.

Funeral homes had collected DNA samples from their dead clientele with the expectation that it could be used later – after the science had progressed – to test whether the descendants of the deceased had a predisposition to come down with one disease or another.

Militaries around the world collected the DNA of their soldiers, to be used in case the massacred bodies were unrecognizable, which was all too often the case given the proficiency with which human beings had learned to slaughter one another.

A peculiar company that claimed to design custom perfume formulas derived from their customers' DNA provided several tens

of thousands of samples. Another company that infused pen ink with the owner's DNA, so that the signatures could later be validated without question, provided a few thousand more.

In the end, even Bailey was surprised to find that her painstaking search had collected upwards of twenty-six million different DNA samples.

When she told Suze how many samples she'd collected, Suze gave her a heartfelt hug and said, "Twenty-six million! Good God! I would have been happy to have a tenth as many! Excellent!"

Bailey did not return the hug.

"Thanks, Suze," she said, stepping away from her affectionate lab partner. "I worked very hard on it. I just hope that whatever you're up to justifies the effort."

Suze said nothing.

Then Bailey said, "What's next?"

Suze, thinking she was rewarding her partner for a job well done, said, "I think you've earned a well-deserved vacation."

"Pardon me?"

"Take a vacation, honey. You haven't had one in years, and once this train gets moving you won't be able to get off, trust me. Besides, I've got nothing more for you to do. And if you pace around here like I know you will, you'll drive me batty."

"Let me help you then."

"You know C?" Suze asked.

"What?"

"C. The programming language."

"You know I don't."

"Then you can't help. I've got to finish this software, Foster. If I don't, we're screwed and Gwendolyn just paid a cool two and a half million for nothing. So I suggest you leave me to it."

"This had better be good," Bailey said.

You ain't just shitting kittens, Suze thought.

She was worn out from endless days and nights of nothing but work. More than once, after discovering that she'd run out of clean clothes, she'd opted to buy new ones in order to delay having to spend time doing laundry. Finally, she started shoving her laundry into a pillowcase that she dropped off at the cleaners when she saw her supply of underwear getting low. Her apartment was a wreck. There was dust everywhere, and cobwebs had begun to appear in

the corners. The toilet had developed an orange ring at the water line. The kitchen sink was full of dirty dishes. Suze ignored them and started eating fast food at the office.

Worse still, her perpetual state of fatigue was making her start to question the soundness of her approach. She considered trying to explain it to Bailey. That would certainly sooth Bailey's hurt feelings, but it would also consume precious time, for Bailey would be horrified to find that she couldn't clearly explain her vague plan.

In the end, she decided to forge ahead, trust in her famous intelligence, and see where it led.

Bailey put in for two weeks vacation, effective immediately, and went home. She hoped that by the time the two weeks was up Suze would be ready to tell her what in the hell she was doing.

After Bailey left the lab, Suze visited Gwendolyn's office to explain the situation. She didn't want Gwendolyn to wonder why Bailey had stopped coming to work. Gwendolyn already had noticed, after all, that Bailey hadn't been working as hard as she had.

"Ms. Griffin, are you sure you're not putting too much on yourself? You've been doing nothing but work! I've found you twice myself in the morning asleep at your desk. Had you been working all night? Perhaps you're the one who needs a vacation."

"That's very kind of you, Ms. Bayner," Suze said, rubbing her tired eyes. "But I'm fine. I'm just so excited about this project I can't tell you. I've never been so excited about anything in my life."

Gwendolyn beamed.

"I knew you were the right one for the job!" she said. "Listen, I know it's still early, but do you have any progress to report?"

"Not yet, but I promise I'll let you know as soon as there's any sort of breakthrough. Bailey has done a great job setting up the computer system and populating it with DNA samples. Thanks again for approving the requisition. I know it was a lot of money."

"I told you I'd give you what you needed," Gwendolyn said, "and I meant it."

Then Suze remembered reading something that might encourage Gwendolyn to stick with the project, should she be secretly harboring any thoughts of abandoning it as she had so many others.

"You might also be interested to know," Suze said, "that a

South Korean geneticist, someone named Chankyu Park, has managed to convert heterosexual mice into lesbian mice by removing a gene from their genome, which is sort of encouraging."

"That is wonderful news!" Gwendolyn said. "How do you tell when a mouse is a lesbian?"

"When they don't accept the advances of the male mice, of course," Suze said. "But mice are not people, Ms. Bayner, so don't get too encouraged. But I'd have to agree that it's at least an interesting development."

"It most certainly is!" Gwendolyn said. "Carry on!"

As Suze was leaving, Gwendolyn called out to her, saying, "Don't make yourself sick, dear!" Suze gave her a dismissive wave of her hand as she disappeared through the doorway.

Ignoring her fatigue, Suze continued working and doing little else. The frustrating thing – and the main reason she had decided not to share her work with Bailey – was that she wasn't exactly sure what she was looking for. The trick she was trying to pull off was to write software that would search through the genetic samples Bailey had collected with an eye toward finding patterns in the genetic regions once known as "Junk DNA." The regions were given the derisive name because they were thought to have no reason to exist, no biological purpose. More recently, however, the regions had been renamed "non-coding DNA" after scientists discovered that some of the DNA in them did play a role after all. (It regulated the DNA in segments that were known to have a purpose.)

Strands of DNA called "genes" had been known for decades to contain the step-by-step recipes an organism followed in order to make the things it needed to exist. The recipes were written not in a human language like English, but in a much simpler code using only four symbols that took the form of molecules. For simplicity's sake, scientists abbreviated the molecules with the first letters of their chemical names: A stood for adenine, C for cytosine, G for guanine, and T for thymine.

As a computer programmer, Suze recognized that DNA was not unlike a computer program. Computers used a binary code with only two values: 0 and 1. Life, whether it be plant life or animal life, used a code with only four values: A, C, T and G.

Incredibly, the coding genes – the genes that scientists knew

were used in some way by the body – accounted for only about two percent of the total genetic material in each human being. The other ninety-eight-percent was non-coding DNA, the largely opaque realm that had intrigued Suze for years and toward which she now directed her considerable intellect, albeit unbeknownst to Gwendolyn.

What patterns to look for was the question. Virtually anything might be possible, since Suze wasn't even sure what she was searching for. What she knew she wasn't looking for was a gene. That had already been done, of course. None had been found, which was why the apparently functionless zone had been called Junk DNA in the first place.

Not sure what else to do, she started with the rather bold assumption that the endless strings of A's, C's, G's, and T's were not necessarily meant to be read sequentially, as they were in genes. In this light, she wrote her software to be as general as she could make it. Essentially, she told her software what a pattern was and left it to the complicated code to find examples that fit the definition.

One problem was that every time she ran the software against the giant database of genomes, it took several hours to finish, even with the massively parallel system she had instructed Bailey to build. Each genome, after all, contained three billion base pairs, and there were twenty-six million of them. Several times, Suze ran a test only to fall asleep while it was churning away. Then she'd wake up an hour or two after it had finished. This wasted time frustrated her further.

To solve the problem, she enhanced her software so that when it was done it would cause her computer to play a song, loudly, in order to wake her up. She let the software choose which song to play from a predefined list. After she had run about a hundred more tests, her curiosity drove her to look at the Song Count Report. This is what she saw:

Song	Artist	Times Played
Instant Karma	Lennon	43
The Art of Dying	Harrison	37

Déjà vu	CSNY	20
Moon Dance	Van Morrison	10
London Calling	The Clash	8

Suze wondered what the problem might be. The random number generator responsible for choosing the songs should have chosen them at about the same frequency, but it hadn't. She'd obviously made a mistake somehow. Why else would the computer seem to have a preference for The Beatles and Crosby, Stills, Nash and Young?

The computer's song selection was a curiosity, but which song played wasn't really important as long as one of them did, so she let the problem go and instead began reviewing the latest report that had been kicked out by her complex software.

At first, Suze wasn't sure what the report was trying to say. The screwy software seemed to have found not instances of similarities, but of differences. Certain rungs of the DNA ladder, when taken in a peculiar non-sequential sequence that jumped from chromosome to chromosome, were almost always different in each of the twenty-six million samples. The only exceptions were the DNA of dead people and newborn babies, in which the particular non-sequential sequence matched in three cases, always a dead person's DNA matching that of a newborn baby.

Then she noticed something else. While the strange sequence was unique in most of the DNA samples, it frequently was unique in only a single base pair, a single rung on the DNA's spiraling ladder. There was usually another DNA sample that contained the exact same sequence except for a single base pair, or sometimes two.

"What the hell," Suze said, scratching her head.

Then she got an idea and went back to tapping on her keyboard.

9
FATHER JIM'S BOYS

Father James O'Toole looked at himself in the bathroom mirror and considered how lucky Jesus Christ was to have died at thirty-three, while he was still young and beautiful. Father Jim had not been so fortunate. At fifty, his hairline had receded incompletely, leaving a gerbil-sized tuft of fur perched high on his head. He gazed at the ridiculous thing and considered shaving it off, but there was no time for that. The boys' choir practice started in ten minutes. He did his best to flatten the embarrassment with a handful of water.

Next, Father Jim peered at the bags of flesh that hung like melted wax below his eyes. Under the magnification of his powerful eyeglasses (the world receded into a kaleidoscopic blur without them) the furrowed sacs of skin appeared jowly and reptilian. He noticed a coarse and shockingly long hair sprouting from the tip of his nose. It was in the place where one might expect to find a witch's mole, with which, thanks be to God, he had not yet been afflicted. He wondered how long the errant hair had been there, how many people had seen it, then pinched its base between two fingernails and plucked it.

He pulled his lips back and revealed uneven teeth, yellowed from years of secretive cigar smoking and anchored tenuously in place by receding gums that had transformed his once youthful smile into something mildly grotesque.

"You've got do something about those teeth," he told his reflection.

Father Jim was choirmaster at St. Paul in Chains, a Catholic church nestled in the center of Pinewood Equestrian Estates, an affluent suburb east of Saint Petersburg, Florida, where homeowners could own two horses per acre but only three-percent of them actually did. The church campus had been built entirely with parishioners' donations with no help from the mother church. The chapel building itself, as well as the priests' quarters and the activity rooms, were constructed lavishly with imported wood, stone and stained glass.

The chapel held thirteen-hundred. On any given Sunday, luxury cars spilled out of the parking lot and onto the manicured lawn, and the collection baskets overflowed with twenties and hundreds. Everyone's teeth were perfect.

St. Paul in Chains was Father Jim's sixth assignment since he'd be ordained at twenty-five. He'd been the boys' choirmaster at all six churches. Even if his body had failed him, his voice, despite the cigar smoking, had not, and so he was deemed by all concerned at St. Paul in Chains to be an ideal choice for choirmaster.

Ordinarily, each of the three choirs – the boys', the girls' and the adults' – would have their own choirmasters. Father Jim had volunteered to take them all on by himself. Not only did this save money, he rightly argued, it also was preferred in order to achieve a certain coherence between the performances, especially when the three groups were called on to sing as one, as they would be that coming Easter.

In return for his additional choir duties, Father Jim was excused from confessional duties. That was fine with him. He had always considered confession a presumptuous intrusion on parishioners' privacy anyway.

Father Jim popped his third Oxycontin of the day and swallowed it down with a handful of tap water. He used the wet hand to once again go after the stubborn tuft, centered the white chiclet on his black collar, and sprayed two pumps of spearmint breath freshener onto his tongue.

"Off to battle," he said.

The Easter concert was in two weeks. As choirmaster, Father Jim picked the hymns. The adult choir would sing *Jesus Christ is Risen Today, Alleluia Alleluia Let the Holy Anthem,* and *O Filii Et Filiae.* The girls' choir would follow with *The Strife is O'er The Battle Done,*

Victoria, and *Regina Coeli Latare.* Then the boy's choir would sing *A Touching Place, Christ the Lord is Risen Today,* and *Regina Coeli Jubila.* Finally, the three groups would fill the altar for a grand finale of *Christ the Lord is Risen.*

The rehearsal room was spacious, acoustically refined and decorated with photographs of famous church choirs from around the world, including even the accomplished Mormon Tabernacle Choir, despite its affiliation with the offbeat sect. In one corner was a harp that no one had ever played and a baby grand piano, at which a visiting nun was running through the hymns that Father Jim had selected for the boys. Risers were built against one of the longer walls, even though there was little room for an audience. If Father Jim had said it once, he'd said it a thousand times: "Practice as you perform, perform as you practice."

Rehearsals in the final weeks before a concert were all business, and Father Jim did not abide tardiness, so the room was alive with boys well before he got there. One boy was tirelessly chasing three others who screamed as though they were being pursued by a bear. Two others were wrestling for an audience of about a dozen more who cheered on their favorite to win. Several others were flying paper airplanes or playing with pocket-sized cars they ran over impromptu ramps they'd constructed from stacks of hymnals.

When Father Jim finally entered the room, the boisterous din dissolved into a series of urgent shushes. The wrestling boys quickly untangled themselves and struggled to straighten their hair and tuck in their shirttails. The boys flying paper airplanes ran to collect them and slide them into their pockets, carefully, so as not to crush the wings. The boys playing with the pint-sized cars gathered them up. Each of the boys helped deconstruct the car ramps by grabbing one of the stacked hymnals before scrambling to their assigned place on the risers.

The nun at the baby grand noticed Father Jim enter the rehearsal room and began to play *Jesu, Dulcis Memoria.* The solemn hymn made Father Jim assume a royal gait on his way to his place addressing the center of the risers. As the nun came to the end of the first verse, he motioned for her to wrap it up, which she did with a traditional amen cadence.

"Thank you, Sister Susan," Father Jim said. "Boys, say hello to

Sister Susan McHenry, who will be accompanying us today as we rehearse for the glory of our Lord."

"HELLO SISTER SUSAN!!!" the boys called out exuberantly, if not quite in unison.

"My Goodness!" Sister Susan said. "What powerful lungs these boys have! I can not wait to hear them sing!"

"Well then let's get right to it, shall we?" Father Jim said.

He clapped his hands and rubbed the palms together as if preparing for a feast.

"I trust that we're all in good voice today? We have avoided milk, ice cream and all other phlegm-producing edibles? That is right, is it not Mr. Thornton? Mr. Rodriguez? Mr. Oliver – please tuck in your shirt."

Dicky Thornton and Jesus Rodriguez, the pudgiest kids in the group, looked at their shoes. (They had both eaten ice cream the night before.) Chuck Oliver, one of the boys who'd been wrestling, struggled to tuck in his shirt. The boy on the riser behind him helped. Father Jim continued.

"As you know, we'll be singing three hymns by ourselves this Easter. I'm sure you've not forgotten, but our three hymns are: *A Touching Place*, page forty-three, *Christ the Lord is Risen Today*, page one-twenty-two, and *Regina Coeli Jubila,* page twelve. At the end, we'll be singing the *Christ the Lord is Risen* – not to be confused with *Christ the Lord is Risen Today* – with the girls and the adults. That one's on page two-twenty-two."

Father Jim surveyed the twenty-four clean-cut youths standing at attention before him, each of them picked by his own hand, none of them older than twelve. The boys had been scrubbed in every crevice and smelled of soap and hairspray. They were clothed in identical white shirts, navy blue shorts, white socks and black shoes. Although one might criticize their tousled hair and slouching socks, Father Jim thought, one could no more resist their young perfection than one could hold a week-old puppy in his arms and not nuzzle it.

Father Jim clapped his hands together twice.

"Let's turn to *A Touching Place*," he said, and for a few seconds there was the sound of turning pages as Sister Susan and the boys found page forty-three. Then Father Jim raised both hands, looked into the eyes of the boys most apt to be daydreaming, then

mouthed the tempo silently as he beat it out with his hands –
"one…two…three…four…" The boys' tender voices filled the
room.

> Christ's is the world in which we move.
> Christ's are the folk we're summoned to love.
> Christ's is the voice which calls us to care
> and Christ is the One who meets us here.
> To the lost Christ shows his face;
> to the unloved He gives His embrace;
> to those who cry in pain or disgrace,
> Christ, makes, with His friends, a touching place.
>
> Feel for the people we most avoid.
> Strange or bereaved or never employed;
> fear that their living is all in vain.
>
> Feel for the parents who lost their child,
> feel for the woman whom men have defiled.
> Feel for the baby for whom there's no breast,
> and feel for the weary who find no rest.
>
> Feel for the lives by life confused.
> Riddled with doubt, in loving abused;
> Feel for the lonely heart, conscious of sin,
> which longs to be pure but fears to begin.

When they finished, Father Jim held his palms out to them as if
signaling a dog to stay. The boys stood in reverent silence as their
voices floated off toward heaven.

Finally, Father Jim dropped his hands and said, "Good job,
boys! Very good! You will surely all make the Lord and your
parents proud. I'm sure this year's Easter concert will bring a tear
to every eye."

With Sister Susan playing a plain but proficient accompaniment,
the boys' choir ran through the other three hymns and then sang
the four selections a second and third time before the hour had
passed and it was time to go.

It was just about then that Father Jim began to feel the full
impact of the Oxycontin.

Sister Susan excused herself and Father Jim stationed himself in
a plastic cafeteria chair at the exit of the rehearsal room. As each
boy passed to leave, he pulled them between his splayed knees and
gave them a close hug and a kiss on the forehead and praised each

between us and the Lord. The Lord would be displeased if you told anyone. Promise now…"

"I promise, Father Jim," Johnny said.

"Good boy, Johnny. You're a very good boy," Father Jim said. "A very obedient boy."

The next time Johnny stayed late, Father Jim kissed the head of his adorable penis and, seeing that Johnny did not object, proceeded to fellate the boy to orgasm. This time, there was no need for a paper towel and Father Jim, soaring on Oxycontin, felt the boy's youthful vigor enter his own body as surely as if he had quaffed a quart of the boy's blood.

One day Father Jim invited Johnny Kirkland to reciprocate by reaching into the good father's open zipper and grabbing a handful of fifty-year-old cock.

"Very good, Johnny, very good," Father Jim said. Then he lowered his pants and said, "Now do to Father Jim what Father Jim did to you."

Johnny Kirkland's small hands fumbled about a bit, but he'd had some practice on his own penis and so before long Father Jim, even high on Oxycontin, reached orgasm. Just before he did, he grabbed a nearby paper towel and used it to catch his load.

"Jesus loves you, Johnny," Father Jim said, zipping his pants and jamming the paper towel into his pocket, "and so does Father Jim."

The time after that, Father Jim taught Johnny Kirkland how to masturbate Father Jim while Father Jim masturbated him. The time after that, Father Jim smeared a finger of sexual lubricant onto Johnny Kirkland's anus and entered him from behind while he reached around and masturbated the boy's small penis. (Of course the good father used a condom. Father Jim was no fool.)

Father James O'Toole realized that what he'd been doing with Johnny Kirkland and all the other boys over the years was a sin, of course. He was an expert on sin. But weren't all men sinners? Yes, they most certainly were. The Bible said so. It was right there in Romans 5:12: "Wherefore, as by one man sin entered into the world, and death by sin; and so death passed upon all men, for that all have sinned."

All men – and was Father Jim not a man? – needed to be washed in the blood of the lamb. Jesus Christ had died on the cross for the very purpose of saving man from his uncontrollable urges.

Father Jim included.

Some men cheated in business. They thought nothing of taking advantage of single mothers and the aged, whose weakening minds made them easy marks. Some men cheated on their wives, spreading their seed about like wild dogs. Some men were drug addicts. (Father Jim did not consider himself a drug addict. The Oxycontin had been prescribed for back pain.) Some men raped. Some men murdered.

Murder. Compared to murder, Father Jim thought, his transgressions were minor, and easily forgivable.

Jesus, he was sure, would hardly have to break a sweat.

10
REINCARNATION

I
t was Tuesday. Bailey had been on vacation for twelve days. Her study of the Buddha's Eight-Fold Noble Path had made it surprisingly easy for her to enjoy the time off from the very first day. *Turn off your mind, relax, and float downstream, baby.*

She'd decided right away not to travel anywhere, because she expected Suze to call her back to work at any minute. That was Suze. Even so, her mind was as far from Bayner Genetics as it would have been had she flown to Fiji. She awoke late each day and – after her thirty minutes of meditation – spent an hour or two reading and drinking coffee in her sunlit kitchen nook.

The first three days, she consumed the *The Art of Happiness, A Handbook for Living*. In the book, an American psychiatrist asked His Holiness the Fourteenth Dalai Lama a series of big questions that all boiled down to: How can anyone be happy in the face of so much suffering and injustice? The answer was essentially the same each time: It is what it is. Happiness is a product of the mind, a thing independent of the events in one's life. With sufficient attention and awareness, you can train yourself to be happy regardless of what's happening to you. The book was, more or less, a westernized run-through of the Buddha's Eight-Fold Path.

On the fourth morning, the day after she'd finished *The Art of Happiness*, Bailey was listening to the news and heard that the fourteenth Dalai Lama was coming to Miami. The cheerful lama was the fourteenth human being identified as embodying the spirit of the first Dalai Lama, who was born 1391, one year after France

started burning witches for the umpteenth time.

Divine visions in 1937 had led Tibetan lamas charged with finding the thirteenth Dalai Lama's successor to the doorstep of a poor, four-year-old boy named Lhamo Dondrub. When little Lhamo was presented with a roomful of toys, he correctly identified the ones that had belonged to the former Dalai Lama by pointing at them and crowing "That's mine! That's mine!" That was more than enough evidence for the questing lamas, and little Lhamo was immediately given the job and renamed Tenzin Gyatso (short for Jetsun Jamphel Ngawang Lobsang Yeshe Tenzin Gyatso.)

Of course, the actual spiritual leadership of Tibet was not immediately conferred on the four-year-old. Instead, he and his family were taken to live at Potala Palace in Lhasa, where he learned how to be a Dalai Lama.

Eleven years later, when Tenzin Gyatso was fifteen years old, he took over the actual leadership duties. Shortly thereafter, China began introducing communism into the little country, which it insisted belonged to China. Many Tibetans rebelled, but the Chinese were powerful and resolute. Despite support from the Central Intelligence Agency of the United States – which went so far as to train Tibetan troops in Colorado – the resistance could not hold and the Dalai Lama was forced to flee Tibet and go into exile.

The Art of Happiness had been a quick read. It left Bailey hungering for more, so she stopped by the bookstore on her way back from the beach. With the Dalai Lama coming to town, the bookstore had a table full of his books along with many others related to Buddhism. The monks at the Buddhist Temple that Bailey attended were reticent to discuss reincarnation. Whenever she'd asked about it, they'd insisted it was unnecessary. This only piqued Bailey's curiosity, so she ended up choosing a book titled *Reincarnation: The Missing Link in Christianity.*

In the book, she read that Christians had believed in reincarnation for a few hundred years until it was squelched by church leaders who felt reincarnation (which was described as the penalty for not having achieved enlightenment) left them with too little control over who was and who was not eligible to be reborn. The book introduced Bailey to poor Giordano Bruno, who was burned at the stake in 1600 after having been found guilty of heresy

by the Roman Inquisition.

Bruno was a smart aleck. The only surprising thing about his execution was that it hadn't happened twenty years earlier. He'd been annoying church officials with his crazy and contrarian ideas since he'd been ordained at twenty-four years old. For one thing, he was a pantheist – that is, he believed God was present in all of nature and was not an anthropomorphic being. That alone would have been enough to condemn him, but Bruno also refused to renounce his belief in reincarnation, a belief that the church was determined to banish.

Bruno was sentenced to burn by Cardinal Robert Bellarmine, who was famous for having put Galileo Galilei under house arrest for daring to say, as Copernicus had before him, that the Sun was at the center of things instead of the Earth. Galileo, perhaps realizing that he was dealing with irrational anti-intellectuals, recanted the idea. He was confined to his house anyway, probably because Bellarmine doubted his sincerity.

Like Galileo, Giordano Bruno agreed with Copernicus' heliocentric solar system, but he dared to go even further. He held fast to the shocking claim that, not only did the Earth circle the Sun, the Sun itself was an unexceptional star and merely one of an infinite army of suns, each of which supported its own Earth.

The devout and confidently righteous Bellarmine saw Bruno as a more dangerous heretic than Galileo. His ideas were more offensive, and he had more of them. On top of that, instead of wisely backing off as Galileo had done, Bruno refused to disavow his beliefs. Consequently – and to the great satisfaction of no small number of priests, bishops and cardinals – the foolishly stubborn man was put to the flame.

After Bailey finished reading each morning, she went to the beach and stayed for exactly thirty minutes. Any more of the South Florida sun, she knew, and she'd burn to a crisp. As it was, she appeared to have changed races, except for her blue eyes and blonde hair, which had been made even blonder by the ultraviolet radiation. When the monks at the temple saw her, they were astonished by the transformation.

"My goodness, Bailey!" one joked. "Are you sure you're following Buddha and not Ra?"

"Just following my heart, Master." Bailey said, and then smiled a smile that beamed as if a tiny light had been embedded in each tooth.

One day, Bailey decided to drive down to Miami Beach for a change of pace. On the way, she found herself following behind a black Mercedes Benz carrying a big family. Lying in the car's back windowsill – maybe because there were no seats left – was a young girl who smiled and waved to Bailey, as children often do. Bailey smiled and waved back, but after a few miles she lost sight of the Mercedes, which apparently had sped ahead of her.

A few minutes later, Bailey passed through the Golden Glades toll booth and saw the Mercedes pulled off to the side of the road, its hood raised. She surprised even herself when she veered to the right and pulled up behind it. She knew little enough about her own car, a "mellow yellow" Volkswagen Beetle convertible she'd bought five years earlier. She knew even less about the big black Mercedes. Just the same, something inside her made her stop. She yanked up the emergency brake and stepped out of her little car.

The large family in the Mercedes had piled out of the car. Five of them – two boys, two girls and an older woman – were standing in a group on the grassy swale. The girl who had smiled and waved at Bailey was peeking around from behind the older woman's skirt. The three females all wore colorful skirts and head scarves. The four males all wore black pants and white shirts.

The oldest man and what appeared to be his eldest son were staring blankly at the engine. They said nothing, but Bailey would not have been surprised to hear that they were both silently pleading with God, asking Him to please let the damned thing start.

Shading her blue eyes with a flattened hand, Bailey approached them and said, "Having trouble?"

The man and his son looked up and stared at her without saying anything. They appeared to be Arab, or perhaps Jewish. They had strong noses, dark skin and bushy eyebrows. Bailey forgave them for staring. She supposed a blonde, blue-eyed girl with such a great tan was something to see. Or maybe the two of them just didn't think a girl could know anything about cars. (And maybe they were right.)

Then the oldest woman standing in the swale said something to

the men. She spoke in a language Bailey didn't recognize, but she was clearly distressed.

The oldest man snapped out of his stupor. "Oh, yes. Car trouble," he said, pointing to the cursed engine. "We have a plane to catch."

"Oh my!" Bailey said. "Then we'd better see what we can do. You're not out of gas, are you? I've done that before!"

The younger man rolled his eyes and said, "There is petrol."

Still worrying that she'd foolishly taken things too far, Bailey nonetheless motioned the two men aside and took their place. She pretended to inspect the engine knowingly, tugging gently at hoses and wires as if to make sure everything was well seated. After a few seconds, she'd run out of things to tug at. Not knowing what else to do, she turned to the elder man and said, "Go ahead. Get in and try it again."

Bailey felt her heart pounding in her chest and behind her eyes. She had no idea where this was leading. How would the man react if the car didn't start? That was certainly the most likely outcome. She hadn't done anything. Why would it start?

Bailey hoped the family wouldn't be too mad at her for wasting their time, but why wouldn't they? They had a plane to catch. This was just a waste of time. They'd likely be furious, once her clumsy ruse was discovered. She imagined herself fleeing to her little convertible Bug as the family attacked her, throwing rocks they'd found on the swale and spitting foreign insults that would sting even without being understood.

The older man did as Bailey asked. He sat in the driver's seat with his left foot on the pavement and his right foot on the gas. He turned the key.

No one was more surprised than Bailey when the car started right up as if she had worked some sort of magic. The man stepped on the gas, the engine roared, and Bailey gestured to the eldest son to close the hood. As he did, the rest of the family piled back into the Mercedes.

"Thank you! Thank you! Thank you!" the family sang from within the packed car. Only the little girl wasn't cheering. She had a serious look on her face, as if she'd just seen an angel, or a ghost. Bailey's smile beamed and she waved to the relieved family.

"Go on!" she called to them. "You'd better hurry! You've got a

plane to catch!"

The big black car sped away.

Walking back to her own car, Bailey thought, "Well, that was interesting."

What had just happened? Why had that car started? Those men hadn't been able to fix it. Had it just been overheated? Had one of the spark plug cables been a little loose? She'd never know.

Bailey climbed back into the Bug and found herself praying that it would start, too. It did, and she continued on her way to Miami Beach.

It was Tuesday, but school was out, so the beach was busy. Most of the imaginary plots of sand had been staked out by groups of teenagers, but also there were the usual porn stars and strippers (it was easy to spot their breast implants), waitresses and the pampered trophy wives of wealthy men who liked their women brown. (They also usually had implants.)

Bailey set her beach bag on the sand and pulled out a big orange towel. She spread the towel out on the sand by using the sand itself to tuck in the corners so they wouldn't flop over in the breeze. She plopped down on the towel butt first, shed her tee-shirt (noticing now that it had a picture of Charles Darwin on it) and smeared a thin layer of Ban de Soleil on her already brown body. She set her smart phone alarm for fifteen minutes, laid back and popped in her ear buds. It was Mingo Reese, on his *Everything is Mostly Nothing* album, a strange tune called *Artful Dying*.

Weird, she thought. *You never hear this song on the radio.*

> Keep yourself steady, my dear,
> when the door that was open closes
> and you pass alone into another room
> to start the circle again.

Bailey felt a slight chill as a thick cloud drifted in front of the Sun. Three seconds later, the cloud was gone and she again felt the Sun's energy recharging her. She smiled, then wiped the smile from her face. She didn't want to get lines.

> Day and night, night and day, the moon and its phases.
> You are the Sun. You are the Moon.

The seasons are your sisters.
Join the cosmic karmic dance!

For the first time since her vacation started, Bailey allowed herself to wonder what Suze was up to. Writing a computer program of some kind, that was for sure. The program must be designed to work on those samples she'd collected, right? But how? Maybe Suze didn't even know, which is why she wouldn't tell Bailey. Perhaps she *couldn't* tell. The damned fool was off on some wild goose chase – and with two-point-five million of Ms. Bayner's money! Oh well, lots more where that came from.

We are itinerant beggars,
Praying to find our peace.
Silly man! Silly woman!
Cross your heart and hope to die!

The odd song was interrupted by the phone ringing. Bailey flipped onto her stomach and punched at the phone to answer it. She didn't bother to look at the name. She knew who it was.

"Yup," she said.

"It's Suze, babe. Cut your vacation short, girlfriend. I think we've found something."

"Is it the lesbian gene?" Bailey asked. She was still irritated that Suze hadn't let her in on her research.

"Don't be a smartass, Bailey."

"Tell me."

"Not until you come back."

Bailey looked at her smart phone's timer.

"I have another twenty minutes, then I'll come. Also, I'm in Miami Beach, so it will take a while."

"Get here as soon as you can. Trust me, honey. This is worth it."

"Then tell me now."

"I can't explain it over the phone. In fact, I can't explain it at all. That's what I need you for."

Bailey didn't let on that she was happy to finally be needed.

"OK Suze, I'll be there as soon as I can. Play a few games of Solitaire while you wait."

"Fuck you, Foster! Get your ass in here! That's an order!"

"Since when are you the queen bee?"

Suze considered telling Bailey about her improved relationship with Ms. Bayner and her additional raise, then thought better of it.

"Sorry Foster, I'm just tired. I'm sorry. I'll wait for you. But hurry!"

"OK OK," Bailey said.

Bailey punched off the phone, then told herself she was tan enough and decided to leave the beach right away. She yanked her Darwin tee-shirt over her head, slipped into her sandals, gave her towel a quick shake, and headed for the Bug. She was dying to know what Suze had been up to for the last four months.

Initially, Bailey's plan was to drive home, catch a quick shower, and change clothes. She might as well keep Suze waiting some. But after a few minutes on the road she found herself driving straight to Bayner Genetics.

She walked into the lab wrapped in a sandy towel. Suze was on her computer, playing Solitaire. She heard Bailey come in, but didn't turn around.

"You know they made this damn game harder, don't you?" Suze said nonchalantly, as if she hadn't just been staring out the window at the parking lot below, waiting impatiently for Bailey to arrive.

"I don't have any trouble with it," Bailey said, although in truth she'd never played the game at all.

"I've played ten games and haven't won yet," Suze said. She moved the mouse pointer to a virtual card, clicked on it and dragged it from one stack to another. Suze spun around in her chair and noticed that Bailey hadn't changed clothes.

"Nice look," she said. "Darwin. One of my faves. I knew you'd come right away."

"OK, what is it?" Bailey said.

She grabbed a chair next to Suze and sat in it backwards, using its oval back to rest her arms. Then Suze started to explain.

"I wrote a program to look at all the DNA samples you collected," she started.

"Duh!" Bailey said. "I'm not that stupid, Suze."

"Shut up and just let me tell you, Einstein!"

Bailey put her hand to her lips and pretended to turn a key that locked her mouth. Suze continued.

"My focus was non-coding DNA. I've been interested in Junk

DNA for years, as you know. It's got to be there for some reason. Otherwise, it would have been discarded by evolution. My program had to be very general, because the truth is I didn't really know what I was looking for."

"I knew it!" Bailey said. "What are you, crazy? Do you realize how much money is involved here?"

Suze ignored her.

"I didn't really know what I was looking for," she repeated. "I just wanted to look for patterns of any kind. It was something to do to get started. So I wrote the software so that I could tell it what a pattern was and it would dig through all the samples to find them."

"How did you do that?"

"Fuzzy logic. Usually computers are used to do specific things. You know, specific calculations. But they can do probabilities, too. It's all just math, after all. So they can recognize things that are sort of like the thing you're searching for, but not exactly. Maybe only fifty-percent, say, or even less.

"It was the definition of what a pattern was that took so long. I kept tweaking it and running it, tweaking it and running it, but I wasn't getting anything. It wasn't general enough."

"I don't mean to interrupt, Suze, but what's that?"

Bailey pointed to a corkboard on the wall where Suze had pinned her Song Count Report.

"It's nothing. Those are the songs the software played to wake me up when it was done. I tried to get as much sleep as I could while it churned. But never mind that. It's not important. Pay attention. So, the pattern definition was the tricky part. It felt stupid to just tweak it and run it, but I had no other ideas, so that's what I did. I just kept tweaking the definition of what a pattern is and let her rip. Again and again and again.

"Finally, just before I called you this morning, the damn thing spit out something that caught my eye."

She handed Bailey a thick sheaf of papers. Bailey glanced at it, but had no clue what it meant.

"This report shows places where a certain genetic sequence is unique across the entire sample database, with very few exceptions."

"A contiguous sequence of unique base pairs?" Bailey asked. She was confused. She knew DNA from one person to another was

largely identical. Finding a specific sequence that never repeated itself over millions of samples would be very odd.

"No. Not contiguous," Suze said. "I didn't want to restrict the search that way. I figured others had already done that. I let the software look for any patterns it could find, contiguous or not. It's one of the reasons it took so long to run. The sequence found by this crazy software jumps all over the fucking place, from chromosome to chromosome. It uses all twenty-three chromosome pairs for Christ's sake, even the sex ones!"

"This doesn't make sense. It must just be some weird anomaly in your software," Bailey said.

"That's what I thought at first. But I've been looking, and I can't imagine what could be causing this. I think the software is just doing what it's told to do. So for now, bear with me, OK? If we assume there's no software bug, why else could this be happening? What could it mean?"

"Well, let's use Occam's Razor," Bailey said. "What's the simplest explanation?"

"It's an identifier of some kind, like a key in a database."

"OK. I say that's what it is."

"That's crazy. How could it be an ID?"

"Crazy? What's more crazy, that it's an ID or that all of the matter in the universe once took up a volume of space smaller than an atom?"

Bailey smiled as she remembered Mr. Collins and his comparative religion class.

"If you put it that way," Suze said, "I guess it's not that crazy. But what's it for? Why would there be a unique identifier in DNA?"

Given Bailey's interest in Buddhism and reincarnation, the answer to her seemed obvious.

"It's there to keep track of the soul."

"Excuse me?"

"Reincarnation. As a soul moves from one life to the next, whoever keeps track of karma needs some way to tie all the lives together so he can figure out how close a particular soul is to attaining nirvana, or whether it needs to be punished for past behavior. Souls keep getting reborn, of course, life after life, until they become enlightened and ascend into nirvana, never to return

to human form again."

"Of course," Suze said. "So the ID's there to help God keep score. Great. I can see the headlines now: Famed Atheist Scientist Discovers that God is Real."

"Sounds good to me," Bailey said.

"I think we're jumping to conclusions, but I'll play along. Any idea how we can test your whacky theory?"

"Well, we certainly can't call God on His smart phone and ask Him, but we might be able to find someone living who knows which body their soul last inhabited. If we fed the two DNA samples into your program, it should find that the two sequences are identical, right?"

"Yeah, but how are we going to do that? How are we going to find someone who's crazy enough to think they know where their last body is buried? I think that whack-job Shirley MacLaine thinks she's lived past lives, but I don't think she knows exactly who she was, and even if she did, how would we go about finding the dead bodies and getting DNA from them? You expect us to become grave robbers?"

"I think I have an idea how we might find someone who knows exactly where his soul's past bodies are," Bailey said.

"I gotta hear this," Suze said.

"All in due time, Suze. All in due time," Bailey said, pleased that the worm, at long last, had turned.

"Screw you, Foster. I'm going home to get some sleep. Maybe I'll be able to figure out what's going on when I've had a chance to clear my mind. That Buddhism crap has obviously addled yours."

"Maybe," Bailey said.

Suze shed her lab coat, grabbed her backpack, and stormed out of the lab, not looking back. As she left, she realized that she wasn't sure whether Bailey had meant "maybe you'll figure it out" or "maybe Buddhism has addled my mind."

Before Bailey left the lab herself, she unpinned Suze's Song Count Report from the corkboard and stuck it in her beach bag. It had not escaped her notice that the top three songs were all related.

11
DALAI LAMA DNA

His Holiness the Fourteenth Dalai Lama was coming to Miami. A concert was scheduled at which he would not only implore thousands of his admirers to be happy, but also tell them exactly how to go about doing it. It was undeniably true that the Dalai Lama seemed to be in a state of perpetual bliss. If he was willing to reveal the secret behind his supernaturally sunny demeanor, plenty of people were willing to listen.

Bailey called her Buddhist temple to see if they knew anything about the visit. They had, in fact, been contacted by a member of the Dalai Lama's advance team, a man named Thipor Dulip. They gave her Dulip's number. Bailey called it.

"Good afternoon," said a voice so calm it whispered. "This is Thipor Dulip. You have reached His Holiness the Fourteenth Dalai Lama. How may we help you today?"

"My name is Bailey Foster," Bailey said. "I am a research geneticist at Bayner Genetics."

"How lovely! You know His Holiness is a great admirer of genetics. He has studied it quite carefully. So have several of his closest advisers, some of whom left their scientific work for a higher purpose."

That's not going to be me bub, Bailey thought.

Then she said, "I have been working on a project and think I may have found evidence that reincarnation is real."

"Excuse me?"

"Reincarnation."

"Yes, I know of reincarnation. What have you found?"

"Well, it was actually mostly my partner's work. She wrote a computer program that sifted through millions of samples of DNA. We think it has found a unique identifier encoded in each sample. Occam's Razor tells us it's an ID of some kind."

"Ah! The Great and Powerful Occam!"

"Simplicity is power," Bailey heard herself say.

"You sound like a very wise young woman," Thipor Dulip said, "but I'm afraid the Dalai Lama's schedule is completely full, as usual. One can not expect to make an appointment to see His Holiness at the last minute. Maybe you can write him a letter."

"I really don't think a letter will do," Bailey insisted. "I need to see him personally. I need to get a DNA sample from him. It's not painful or anything, just a swab inside the cheek."

"And what do you propose to do with the Dalai Lama's DNA?"

"I want to compare it to the DNA of the eight Dalai Lamas who I understand are still entombed at the Potala Palace in Tibet."

"Ha ha ha!!!" The meaning of Thipor Dulip's laugh was clear. It said: Bailey Foster, you are an idiot.

Thipor Dulip said, "You expect the Chinese – the Chinese mind you – to simply let you dig up old Thubten Gyatso and the others? That, my dear, is utterly remarkable."

"My impression was that the bodies are in stupas, not buried. In any case, I was hoping the Dalai Lama would have some idea how I might get the samples. We don't need much, you know. A tiny amount will do."

"Miss…Farmer is it? You sound like a delightful young woman, and your project sounds perfectly thrilling. But although you may know a lot about genetics, you apparently are totally ignorant of the Chinese, especially with regard to their relationship with His Holiness. In any case, all of the prior Dalai Lamas are nothing but ashes. Each of them was cremated in the Buddhist tradition, so I don't think … Excuse me for a moment, won't you?"

"Sure," Bailey said.

Ashes? If that were true, her whole plan was shot. There was no way to extract DNA from cremains. She listened closely to hear what was being said away from the phone, but heard only murmuring. Thipor Dulip was away for a long minute. When he came back on the line, his tone was officious.

"His Holiness will see you tonight at nine o'clock," he said. "We're at the Biltmore in Coral Gables. We'll have someone meet you in the lobby. He'll be holding a sign with your name on it. What is it again?"

"Bailey Foster. B A I L E Y F O S T E R," Bailey answered.

"Nine is his bed time, so you won't have very long. Therefore, I advise you to be on time and meticulously prepared. However much time he gives you, you realize, you will be depriving him of sleep. He's not a young man, as I'm sure you're aware."

"Thank you!" Bailey squealed. "Yes, I will! Thank you so much!"

"No problem at all Ms. Farmer. We'll see you tonight at nine sharp."

"It's Foster. Bailey Foster."

"Got it," Thipor Dulip said. Then he was gone.

Bailey was shaking as she punched a finger at her phone to hang it up. In five short hours, she had a personal meeting with the Dalai Lama himself. What should she wear? She started tearing through her closet, destroying it, then caught herself.

"Calm down, Bailey," she thought. "He's just a man."

She went to the kitchen, made a cup of tea and honey and sat down at the table to consider how she wanted the meeting to go. It was sure to be short, so she'd better heed Thipor Dulip's advice and be prepared. Her mind raced. Why had Mr. Dulip suddenly changed his tune? Had the Dalai Lama himself been there in the room? The thought thrilled her.

She imagined the meeting. She saw herself in a navy-blue suit and a white blouse, ultra conservative. (Did she even have such a suit?) The Dalai Lama, of course, would be wearing his traditional monk's wrap, a dull rust color with a distinctive saffron swath. She imagined shaking his hand and sputtering, "Your Holiness."

And then I will just fucking faint, she thought.

She picked up a pen and wrote on a legal pad:

1. Dalai Lama 14 DNA: Bring cotton swab.
2. Dalai Lama 5,7-13 DNA: ???

How *was* she going to get the DNA of the eight dead Dalai Lamas? Well, she thought, she was close to getting some DNA from the fourteenth Dalai Lama, and she wouldn't have thought

that was possible just a few minutes ago, so maybe there was at least a chance.

Bailey had read on the Internet that the bodies of eight prior Dalai Lamas were housed inside sacred gold stupas – some sort of tomb – at Potala Palace in Lhasa, Tibet. The Chinese government had converted the palace into a museum a few years after they'd forced the current Dalai Lama to go into exile. They'd also removed most of the treasures from the palace. Had they removed the bodies as well? If it was the aim of the Chinese to diminish the importance of the Dalai Lama, they might have done just that. After all, the authorities had bulldozed the home of His Holiness the Thirteenth Dalai Lama (Thupten Gyatso) in Dharamshala. A few protests had sparked up, but the powerful Chinese had little trouble quickly restoring order.

More than a half-century had passed since they'd forced the Dalai Lama to flee his home country, land of the fabled Himalayas and Mount Everest. Even so, the Dalai Lama was still revered around the world, most of all in Tibet, which the Chinese now called the Tibet Autonomous Region, although there seemed to be little about it that was autonomous.

In the beginning there had been regular protests in Lhasa and elsewhere, with the people of Tibet calling for the Dalai Lama's return and the restoration of their freedom. In recent years, however, the protests had grown few and far between. The Chinese had mercilessly beaten and jailed anyone who appeared to be leading a protest. The nuns and monks who dared disobey orders to remain in their mountain enclaves – to stay away from the cities where they could stir up unrest, and especially Lhasa – were taken away first, usually never to be seen again. Many of them had simply fled to India. At the turn of the 21st century, monks were allowed back into Lhasa because they were valued as tourist attractions.

Bailey looked at her watch: six thirty. She had to give herself two hours to drive from Boca Raton to Coral Gables. She didn't want to give herself any chance to be late, so that meant she had to leave at seven at the latest. Thirty minutes. She ran to the bathroom, brushed her hair and her teeth, then threw on some new jeans and a white polo shirt. She dropped a Q-Tip into a small Zip-Lock bag, wrote Dalai Lama (#14) on the bag with a felt pen, dropped the

bag into her purse, and ran out the door.

Her old yellow Bug started up and took her without incident to the Biltmore Hotel in Coral Gables. She drove the whole way with the top down so she could enjoy the sunset, but it was dark by the time she pulled up to the hotel's entrance at eight-thirty. The air smelled of freshly mowed grass and fertilizer.

She put the Bug's top up, flipped her keys to the valet, took a ticket from him, and went inside.

Then she saw herself in a mirror. Christ! Her hair looked like it belonged on a blonde witch, or a victim of electrocution. She look around the lobby and saw no one holding a sign with her name on it, or "Farmer" either. Thank God. Her heart was pounding. She hoped no one would see her.

"Where's the nearest ladies room?" Bailey asked a bellhop, who smiled and pointed. She quickly followed his direction and found the lobby restroom. Inside, she realized she needed to pee and went into a stall.

When she came out, there was a piece of paper on the sink with BAILEY FOSTER written on it.

How did that get there? she thought.

As Bailey began brushing her windblown hair, a woman emerged from an adjacent stall. Had Bailey missed seeing the paper with her name written on it before going in to pee? She'd been so harried, it was a distinct possibility. Or had the woman slipped into the restroom, quiet as a mouse?

"Convertible," Bailey said to the woman, smiling uncomfortably as she worked frantically at the tangles.

"Looks like fun," the woman said.

The woman began washing her hands. This made Bailey realize she should have washed her hands before brushing her hair. Embarrassed, she put the brush on the counter and began washing her hands, too. The woman glanced at her watch, grabbed the piece of paper with Bailey's name on it and hurried out. Bailey dried her hands, then finished brushing her hair as she scolded herself in the mirror.

"Why didn't I tell her it was me?" she cried. "I hope she didn't notice that I was brushing my hair with pee hands! God!"

Already things were going badly. She looked at her watch. It was eight-forty-five. At least she wasn't late.

When she left the bathroom, Bailey didn't see the woman. She made a quick tour of the hotel lobby and then visited the pool area out back. No woman. It was eight-fifty-five. When she reentered the lobby – where she'd been asked to wait in the first place – the woman was there. Bailey walked up to her, slightly out of breath.

"I'm Bailey Foster," she said.

"The nice woman in the bathroom," the woman said. She had a British accent. "You look very much better now, Bailey Foster!"

Bailey finally noticed that the woman was wearing a navy-blue suit with a white blouse, ultra conservative.

"I hope His Holiness will not be too horrified," Bailey said. She pawed at her hair, looked down at her jeans and penny loafers with the bright new pennies in the slots, and wished she'd dressed better. The woman smiled.

"Oh, he won't care about your hair. You could shove a hot poker up that man's bum and he'd laugh about it for a week. He's incorrigible!" She looked at her watch. "We have three minutes! I assume you have some identification?"

Bailey dug into her purse, pulled out her wallet and held it open so that the woman could see her driver's license.

"Excellent! Lovely to meet you, Miss Bailey Foster. You must be very special. The Dalai Lama is usually in bed at this hour. Please follow me."

Bailey followed the woman to an elevator, which they took to the top floor. When they stepped out of the car, Bailey noticed several huge men dressed in black pants and black tee-shirts lining the entire length of the hallway. Each of them must have been taller than six-feet-three and heavier than three-hundred pounds. Each was silent and watchful.

Bailey saw the woman wink at the one nearest the elevator door. The woman glanced back at Bailey and said, "Security. They look vicious but they're all pussycats."

The bodyguard the woman had winked at looked at the ceiling and suppressed a smile. Bailey followed the woman down the hallway and into a room where two identical and comfortably upholstered chairs had been placed in the middle of the floor, facing one another.

"Please, sit," the woman said. She gestured to one of the chairs. Bailey sat. A few seconds later, at exactly nine o'clock, the Dalai

Lama entered the room. He was wearing sky blue silk pajamas covered by a white terrycloth robe and fuzzy bedroom slippers, also sky blue. He looked tired at first, but when his eyes met Bailey's he went to her with renewed energy. Before she could rise from her chair, he took her left hand in both of his and shook it vigorously while giving a little bow. He didn't seem to notice her hair or what she was wearing. He looked directly into her eyes from behind his oversized eyeglasses.

"I am pleased to make your acquaintance, Miss Foster," he said, taking his place in the other chair. Their knees were almost touching. "Sad to say, we'd better get right down to business. My babysitters get upset with me when I miss my bedtime, and then they won't let me have any cookies! Ha ha ha!"

The Dalai Lama's laughter was silly. He let his inner-child shine through without a hint of self-consciousness. In his presence, Bailey felt a warm glow that made her think of lying in the sun at the beach. If she hadn't realized how impossible it was, she would have sworn she was falling in love. The Dalai Lama whispered, concealing his moving lips with the back of his hand. "Luckily, I have my own supply!"

He looked around the room as if checking to see if anyone was spying on them. There were two body guards standing within six feet. The English woman was there, too. Nonetheless, the Dalai Lama pretended he and Bailey were alone.

"The coast is clear!" he said. Then he reached into the right pocket of his terrycloth robe and pulled out two cookies. Each cookie was individually wrapped in gold cellophane and tied with a red ribbon. He extended one of the cookies toward Bailey. She politely refused.

"Thank you, but I've already eaten," she said, but the truth was that she was worried that there was no time for cookies. Then she found herself worrying that the Dalai Lama would think she'd been such a glutton at dinner that she couldn't possibly force down even one cookie.

Undaunted by her rejection, he waved the cookie at her playfully and said, "Please! Take! Organic! Vegan! Delicious! Oatmeal and raisin!"

Bailey took the cookie. If there wasn't much time, she thought, why was the Dalai Lama wasting so much of it on cookies?

"Good," the Dalai Lama said, pleased that his gift had been accepted. "I understand you want some of my DNA." He took a big bite of cookie, brushed away a crumb from his mouth, and shrugged."Why?"

Bailey was glad to finally be getting down to business.

"My research partner and I think we've discovered a unique identifier encoded in all twenty three chromosomes, in the regions that used to be called Junk DNA."

"Ah! Junk DNA. Never did like that name." The Dalai Lama waved an index finger back and forth, as if scolding a child. "The human body is too perfect to contain junk! Don't you agree?" He held his arms out as if to display his own aged body and laughed heartily.

"Ha ha ha!"

Slightly embarrassed and still worried about the time, Bailey strove to stay on point.

"We think this ID is somehow connected to the soul. We want to test our theory by comparing your DNA to the DNA of the eight Dalai Lamas entombed at Potala Palace."

"Potala Palace! I spent my childhood there. Wonderful place for a boy. Lots of hiding places! My Chinese friends have turned it into a tourist trap. They don't know half of its secrets. Your idea is intriguing, Geneticist Bailey Foster. But what would it prove?"

"We think it will prove that reincarnation is real."

"I have doubts about that myself, you know. Despite who they claim I am. But who knows if the remains are still there? Who knows if the Chinese have removed them? They tell me they removed all the treasure and replaced it with cheap replicas. Made in China! Ha ha ha!"

This time, even Bailey laughed.

"I guess I'm willing to bet they haven't moved the bodies," she said. "I was hoping you might be able to help me find a way to get DNA samples from them."

"Bodies?" The Dalai Lama smiled cleverly. "Surely you know Buddhists usually choose to be cremated, as my friend Mr. Dulip said. No DNA in ashes! Do you think the Dalai Lamas are different?"

Bailey felt as if she'd been struck by lightning. Her arms dropped to her sides. Thipor Dulip had been right. She was an

idiot.

"I'm sorry," she said, worried anew about needlessly encroaching on the Dalai Lama's sleep. "I seem to be wasting your time. I thought … well, never mind."

She stood to leave, but the smiling Dalai Lama urged her to stay.

"Sit! Sit!" he said. "My friend Mr. Dulip thought the same thing you're thinking. But I know something you and Mr. Dulip do not know. The Dalai Lamas are not cremated!"

He popped the last bite of the oatmeal raisin cookie into his mouth, clapped his hands together joyously, then rubbed them against his terrycloth robe.

"The bodies of the Dalai Lamas are washed in perfumed water and disinfected with antiseptics. Then they are wrapped in cashmere cloth – but not the head and arms – and are placed in simple wooden boxes. So you see, Bailey Foster, all is not lost! If you could get inside the sacred stupas, you could take a bit of mummified skin. The bodies age well in the dry Lhasa air. The little wooden boxes are easily opened. I even peeked once myself. Curiosity killed the cat! Ha ha ha! But of course I haven't been to Potala since I left in 1959. That's a long time ago, but the Chinese still don't like me. I don't know how much help I could be to you. Let me think."

Bailey felt like she'd been rescued from drowning. The Dalai Lama rubbed his chin as if contemplating deeply whether there was some way he could help Bailey Foster get DNA samples from his spiritual antecedents.

"Do you think," Bailey said, "that the Chinese government would allow a scientist to enter the stupas? For purely scientific research?"

"Do you have money?"

"My company does."

"The Chinese might let you in for money, if you have enough. They call themselves communists, but they're pure capitalists, you know. They love money! So maybe you can pay an entrance fee to the tourist trap! Ha ha ha!"

Then he said, "Is there anything else I can do for you Bailey Foster?"

"Actually," Bailey said. "I do still need to get your DNA."

"Ah! I have already taken care of," the Dalai Lama said.

He pulled a small Zip-Lock bag out of the same robe pocket that had concealed the cookies. Inside the bag was a Q-Tip that Bailey assumed he'd rubbed inside his cheek. He handed it to Bailey.

"Thank you," Bailey said. "But I actually need to take the sample myself."

She dropped the Dalai Lama's Zip-Lock into her purse and produced her own, the one marked with "Dalai Lama (#14)." She removed the Q-Tip and turned to the Dalai Lama.

"Say ah, your holiness," Bailey said.

The Dalai Lama laughed and slapped his knee playfully and said, "Scientists! So mistrusting!"

He opened his mouth wide, as if for a dentist. Bailey moved closer to him with the Q-Tip and the body guards reacted instinctively. The one to her left struck as fast as a mongoose and grabbed her wrist with his powerful hand.

"Ow!" Bailey protested.

The Dalai Lama waved off the huge body guard with a laugh and pointed at his open maw.

"Uh uh," he said.

Bailey Foster rubbed her wrist, scowled at the body guard, then ran the Q-Tip inside the Dalai Lama's cheeks, under his lips and under his tongue.

"I didn't really think you would lie, Your Holiness. But I had to be sure."

"Trust but verify! Ha ha! Not very trusting!" He pointed at the body guard who'd grabbed Bailey's wrist. "Same as him!"

The Dalai Lama looked at his watch and pretended again not to want to anger his keepers. He kissed Bailey on the cheek, shook her hand again, bowed, and was gone.

The English woman led Bailey back downstairs.

"I hope you got everything you expected," she said as they entered the lobby.

"I didn't get what I expected," Bailey said. "I got more."

Waiting for the valet to fetch the Bug, Bailey felt her knees go weak. Did she really have the Dalai Lama's DNA in her purse? Yes, she did. Better than that, she was sure she did.

"Good girl!" she praised herself for insisting on her own sample. "Good scientist!"

Hopefully, the Chinese wouldn't charge too much to let her poke around in the stupas at Potala Palace.

12
MAX DUBOIS HITS IT BIG

Max Dubois kicked back in his chair and put his feet up on his desk. It had been a good month. He'd wrapped up three lucrative cases of insurance fraud, his specialty. As if that weren't good enough, he'd also finally landed a date with the lovely Miss Jane Whitmire, a vivacious State Farm agent with legs that went on forever and a bust line that she was unashamed of putting on display.

He'd asked Jane out once before, but had been forced to cancel the date after hearing at the last minute that one of his targets – a deadbeat collecting disability payments for back pain – had coincidentally reserved a tennis court for the same night. (He'd paid the court attendant to watch for the deadbeat's name on the reservation sheet.) Max couldn't miss the opportunity to catch the fraudulent fuck on camera, so he'd called Jane and cancelled.

The lovely Miss Whitmire had made it obvious how much she liked the idea of dating a private eye. She'd told him several times how exciting his job must be and then touched him on the shoulder in a way that, while outwardly platonic, nonetheless carried as much sexual electricity as if she'd been petting the inside of his thigh in a dark movie theater. Even so, Max's last-minute cancellation had made her go cold. She'd rejected two subsequent offers before accepting the third, saying, "You're not going to give up, are you, Maxie?"

"I always get my man," he'd answered.

"I'm hardly a man, honey," she'd said, sweeping his hair off his

forehead in a way not so platonic.

Clearly, the gods were shining their ever-loving light on Max Dubois.

Then the phone rang. He removed his feet from his desk and let it ring twice more while he considered ignoring the call. If he cancelled with Jane a second time, she probably would not believe whatever excuse he gave, real or not. Finally, his curiosity got the better of him and he punched the button labeled "SP-Phone."

"Dubois Investigations," he said.

"Maximilian Dubois," said the voice on the line.

"Speaking."

"Mr. Dubois, my name is Wallace Clinton, I am a vice president at Jones Industries."

Max jotted the names on a legal pad: Jones Industries, Wallace Clinton. Max had never heard of Jones Industries, but it sounded like one of those multinationals with a name so vague it allowed the conglomerate to have its fingers in several diversified pies, everything from jet engines to toilet tissue. Maybe they did some insurance, too.

"Good afternoon, Mr. Clinton. How can I help you?"

"You sound like you're on speaker. Is the room secure?"

Oh, this guy's serious, Dubois thought. Then he said, "Yes, Mr. Clinton. You may speak freely."

"Fine. A pharmaceutical company in your area, a concern called Bayner Genetics, has announced that it is working on developing a pill that will prevent tooth decay, apparently by converting saliva into some kind of antibacterial agent. One of our many subsidiaries is in the business of supplying dentists around the world with amalgams, which as I'm sure you know are the materials used to fill dental cavities. We also are in the business of selling dental equipment, much of it associated with the treatment of tooth decay. Bayner's announcement alone, which was made three weeks ago today, had an instantly negative impact on the stock prices of those two subsidiaries. You can imagine how that got our attention."

Dubois ran his tongue over his upper molars and wondered how wonderful it would be never to suffer the dentist's drill again.

"Yes, I can see how it might," he said.

"We have reason to believe, however, that the project is fraudulent, designed solely to extort our company and others who

would be harmed by such a product."

"You mean they're not really going to do it?" Max said, his dream of avoiding the drill fading away. "What would give you that idea?"

"We have information that several other large corporations have confidentially paid Bayner substantial sums of money in order to dissuade it from pursuing the development of products that would similarly damage their businesses. One was a pill that supposedly would give you a permanent tan. Tanning bed companies and suntan oil companies paid to kill that one. Then there was one that would curb the appetite. You can imagine how many companies wanted to see that one gone, all the big diet companies and the big ags, as well as the grocery chains. There were even pills to permanently change hair color and eye color. As you can see, none of these things are medicines, per se, which is the business Bayner supposedly is in."

"The anti-tooth-decay one is kind of a medicine," Max said. "Hell, I'd take it."

"I'm sure you're not alone," Wallace Clinton said. "In any case, we have discovered so many of instances of these payments that we doubt the veracity of the projects. We don't think any of them were real, and we don't think the anti-cavity pill is real, either. We think Bayner announced it with the sole purpose of extorting payments from companies with an obvious interest in seeing it quashed."

"Do you have any proof?"

"If we did, we wouldn't be calling you. We'd be letting our attorneys off their chains."

"You haven't told Bayner that you flat out refuse to make the payment then?"

"Correct. We have, however, been contacted by several of our competitors. They are ready to strike a deal and are pressuring us to join in. We have a good working relationship with many of the companies and don't want to anger them. Bayner knows that we are a large player in the tooth-decay market, with much to lose, and so they have set a price that is too high for the other players to comfortably pay without our participation."

"Clever."

"Devious is more like it. And probably illegal, too, especially if the product is a phantom. In any case, before we agree to such a

large settlement – the amount of which I am not at liberty to disclose – we want to make a diligent effort to find some evidence that the threat is actual."

"What sort of evidence – or a lack thereof – are you looking for?"

"Certainly internal Bayner documents outlining the viability of such a project would convince us that it is real. If they are like most companies in their business, they look very carefully at a proposed new drug before deciding whether to invest the money necessary to develop it. They might also investigate whether it would be marketable, although we have no doubt that an anti-cavity pill certainly would be. Nobody likes cavities."

"Have you asked Bayner directly for such documents?"

"Yes. They insist no such documents exist. That, naturally, just made us more suspicious."

"Corporate espionage is a little outside of my specialty, Mr. Clinton. I usually work on disability fraud. You know, guys who claim they have back trouble but then play eighteen holes of golf a day."

"You have come highly recommended to us, Mr. Dubois. We're sure you can do the job, and we stand ready to compensate you quite handsomely."

Now this guy Clinton had Max's full attention.

"How handsomely are we talking?"

"Thirty-thousand to get you started, plus another one-hundred-thousand if you complete your work within thirty days, one way or the other. Your expenses are your own, but if you find that you need special outside expertise, we will be happy to negotiate those costs on an individual basis as they arise."

If the gods had been shining on him before, they were now leading Max Dubois directly to the pot of gold at the end of the rainbow. He struggled to conceal his excitement.

"That sounds acceptable, Mr. Clinton. Thirty days isn't much time, though."

"That's true. Time is definitely short. Bayner's price will only increase as time wears on, since if the project is real they are spending money pursuing it even as we speak, and will want to be reimbursed for those expenses as well as for any potential profits the product might reasonably have been expected to reap."

"Sounds like we have a deal, Mr. Clinton. I'll get started on it immediately."

"That's fine, Mr. Dubois. Please give me your bank routing information so that I can have the funds transferred into your account immediately."

By four o'clock that afternoon, Max Dubois' bank account had ballooned by exactly thirty thousand dollars. He'd made plans to meet Jane Whitmire at the Outback at seven o'clock that night, but under the circumstances he decided to call Morton's, a high-end steakhouse where he was able to get a reservation for eight o'clock. He called Jane to tell her of the change of plans.

"State Farm Insurance. Jane Whitmire at your service," she answered.

"Jane, it's Max."

"Hey Maxie! You calling to cancel our date?"

"Not at all, my sweet. Just a change of plans."

"You're not going to feed me Taco Bell in the car while we stake out some guy limping around a condo tennis court, are you?"

That stung a little, but Max figured he deserved it.

"Not at all, my love. I was thinking that instead of going to the Outback we might go to Morton's. Consider it fair compensation for bailing on you the last time. I really did feel bad about that, even though it was legit and paid off for me in the end."

"Morton's? That's kind of posh, Maxie. You sure you can afford it? You know I don't put out on the first date."

"I'm just trying to do the right thing here, Jane. I have no expectations."

"OK, Maxie. I'll meet you there. Seven?"

"I couldn't get reservations for seven on such short notice, so we'll have to make it eight."

"OK, that's fine. It'll give me time to go home and get freshened up. It's been a long day here at the farm."

Max got to Morton's a half-hour early. He went to the bar, ordered a Jameson's on the rocks and sat down on a barstool with a clear view of the front door. Fifteen minutes later, he saw Jane walk in and approach the maître d. No doubt about it, she was a knockout. She was wearing a little black cocktail dress, black stilettos that made her long legs seem even longer, and a push-up

bra that Max saw was making it difficult for the maître d to maintain eye contact with her.

Finally, she glanced in Max's direction and he waved her over. Jane touched the maître d on the shoulder and started to make her way toward the bar. As she did, the maître d watched her walk away. Max couldn't help but notice the lustful look on his face.

"Hey Maxie," she said, giving him a chaste peck on the cheek and resting her little black clutch purse on the edge of the bar.

Max took her in, from her feet to the carefully coifed brown hair that cascaded over her bare shoulders.

"Jane," he said, "if you'd been a tenderloin, that maître d would have taken a bite of you. You look absolutely delectable, and you smell like love potion."

"Thanks, Maxie!" she said, touching his cheek. "You don't look too bad yourself."

"What're you drinking?"

"House chardonnay is fine."

Max tried to attract the bartender's attention as Jane surveyed the expensive restaurant.

"Hell of a place this is, Maxie. I've never been here."

"Only the best is good enough for you, Jane. Only the best."

Finally, the bartender came over.

"A chardonnay for the lady," Max said.

The bartender placed a wine glass on the bar and looked at Max as if to say, *What's a worm like you doing with a dame like that?* Max watched the bartender pour the glass half-full of wine and thought, *There goes your tip, asshole.*

Then Max heard his name called – or he heard his name called the way people usually pronounced it, dew-BOYS rather than dew-BWAH. Max threw a ten on the bar and led Jane by the arm to the maître d stand, where a young woman escorted them into the dining room.

The place was packed, and as they walked to their table the rich aroma of steaks and seafood made them both salivate. They passed by people eating bloody tenderloins the size of softballs and lobster tails as big as the barrel of a baseball bat.

"I'm starving!" Jane said as the young woman pulled out her chair, which she lowered herself into demurely.

"Then you've come to the right place," the young woman said,

handing her a menu. "Enjoy! Your waiter will be right over."

Max sat down and accepted a menu from the young woman.

"Maxie," Jane whispered to him. "My menu has no prices!"

"Doll, this is my treat. Order what you want. Price is no object."

"What happened to you today, Maxie? You rob a bank or something?"

"Better than that. I got a call from a multinational who wants me to do a little corporate espionage. And they're paying the big bucks."

"It's not going to be dangerous, is it?" Jane said, half hoping he would say yes.

"Nah. There's a company here in Boca. Bayner Genetics. The company that hired me thinks they're trying to extort them."

"No kidding? I thought you did insurance fraud."

"I do, but the money was too good to pass up. These guys are serious, and they told me they were sure I could handle the job. Someone apparently gave me a good recommendation."

"What did you say the company was?"

"Bayner Genetics. It's a drug company, I think."

"I've heard of it."

"Yeah?"

"Yeah. We insure the owner's cars. All Bentleys. Fucking five of them! For what they cost to insure each year, you could buy a new Toyota."

"Looks like extortion is quite lucrative. How much does one of those babies cost?"

"A Bentley? Upwards of a quarter mill at least, maybe more."

"Christ!"

"Yeah, and the woman who owns the company..."

"It's a woman?"

"Yes, asshole. It's a woman. Gwendolyn I think her name is."

"Like the serial killer?"

"What?"

"You don't remember? It was back in the eighties."

"Oh, honey. That was before my time. I was a mere child."

"There were these two lesbians. Both of them looked like men, real bull dykes. They worked as nurses assistants at an old folks home in Grand Rapids. Gwendolyn was the real whack job. She had her lover stand lookout as she strangled old ladies with

Alzheimer's disease."

"Gawd! That's awful!"

"Yeah. It was some kind of sick game for her. She picked victims whose initials spelled out 'murder,' like she was in some bad B movie. She even bragged about it, but no one believed her. What kind of an asshole would brag about such a thing, after all? Then the two lesbos broke up, I think because the lookout didn't want to do any killing herself. After that, the case broke wide open."

"Jesus! People are fucking crazy sometimes."

"More often than you'd expect, at least in my experience."

"Anyway, my Gwendolyn – who hasn't killed anybody so far as I know – didn't even come in to take out the policy. I've never set eyes on her. She had her chauffeur shuttle the paperwork back and forth. We don't insure cars that expensive without taking a look at them first. You know, to see if there's any damage. Rich people can be real assholes sometimes, you know? So I visited her mansion. Beautiful place, right on the beach. Looks like the goddamn Parthenon. I checked out the cars personally. They're freaking unbelievable. The chauffeur let me sit in one of them. It smelled like money."

"The rich are different from you and me," Max said. "Very different."

Finally, the waiter arrived. Jane ordered a double-cut filet mignon, rare. Max ordered a New York strip, medium-rare, and a bottle of the most expensive Cabernet Sauvignon on the wine list.

"Very good, sir," the waiter said.

When the wine came, the waiter decanted it into a carafe and poured a splash into each of their wine glasses. Max took a taste and marveled as the expensive wine thrilled his taste buds and then, after he swallowed, vanished gradually into a continuously changing kaleidoscope of flavors.

He looked at Jane and said, "I could get used to this."

"You and me both, Maxie," Jane said. "You and me both."

They followed up dinner with a couple of Bailey's Irish Creams at the bar, then Max walked Jane to her car. They were both a little tipsy. When they reached the car, she turned her back to the driver's door, leaned against it, then pulled Max against her.

"That was a wonderful dinner," she said. "I had a great time tonight."

"Likewise," Max said. He could feel the bare skin of her back through her little black dress and let his right hand slip down to where he felt the elastic of her panties biting into her flesh. Up close, her scent was intoxicating. "You sure you're OK to drive?"

"Yeah, I'm fine. How about you?"

For a second, Max thought of saying no, he was way too drunk to drive, so maybe she'd better take him home and tuck him into her bed. Then he said, "Yeah, I'm good. See you tomorrow, maybe?"

"I've got a date with the girls at the office tomorrow, sweetie," Jane said. "But don't stop trying."

"I never do," Max said, and as he did Jane kissed him deeply, letting her tongue dance with his. She still tasted like the last sip of Bailey's and Max felt his cock wake up. He pressed it gently into her thigh.

"Maxie, I told you I never put out on the first date," Jane cooed. "It's a firm rule for me. But I have no rule about the second date."

She rubbed her hand against his burgeoning crotch for an instant, then clicked her car door open and got in. Max backed away from the car with his hands in his pockets. Jane gave a little wave before driving off.

13
TICKETS TO TIBET

The day after Bailey Foster visited the Dalai Lama at the Biltmore Hotel, she delivered the two Zip-Lock bags to Suze at the lab. Her excitement over having met the Dalai Lama got the best of her and she ended up telling Suze all about her plan to compare the living Dalai Lama's DNA to that of his dead antecedents.

"That's crazy," Suze said.

"Crazy as the Big Bang?" Bailey answered, dropping the two Zip-Locks on Suze's desk. "The Q-Tip in the blank one is the sample he took himself. The other one is the one I did personally. They should be the same, but check them both and tell me what you find."

"The Dalai Lama let you stick a Q-Tip in his mouth?" Suze said, holding both bags up to the light. "That alone is a miracle."

"It was amazing!" Bailey said. "His body guards tried to stop me, but he waved them off and let me do it. I guess he trusted me. He was a very nice man. He even gave me a cookie."

Bailey pulled the oatmeal raisin cookie from her purse. It was still wrapped in its gold cellophane and red ribbon.

"How adorable," Suze said. "How does it taste?"

"Are you kidding? This is a gift from the Dalai Lama. There's no way I'm going to eat it!"

"Oh good Lord," Suze said. "Bailey Foster, you've turned into a groupie! Scientists are not groupies!"

"I have not!" Bailey said, but she secretly felt it might be true.

"Whatever. I'll take care of your grunt work," Suze said.She picked up the Zip-Locks. "I need a break from pounding on this stupid software anyway. I've looked at everything I possibly can think of, but I can't see anything that would have caused our strange sequence. I can't look any more. I'm bleary-eyed."

"Thanks Suze! I'll call you later. I'm going to go home to figure out what to do next."

"See ya," Suze said. She balanced the bags playfully on top of her head. "I'll let you know what I find."

The Dalai Lama had suggested that Bailey petition the Chinese government for access to the eight dead Dalai Lamas, but he hadn't suggested how she might go about doing such a thing. When she returned home from the lab, she searched the net for a few minutes and found a web site for the Ministry of Science and Technology of the People's Republic of China, which was led by someone named Zhenbang Zhao. "At least it's a start," she said.

She wrote a letter to Mr. Zhenbang Zhao, minister of the ministry.

```
Minister Zhenbang Zhao
Ministry of Science and Technology of the People's
Republic of China
15B Fuxing Road
Beijing, 100862, P.R. China

Dear Minister Zhenbang Zhao,
    I am in total agreement with your ministry's lofty goal
of fostering scientific cooperation between China and the
other nations of the world. It is in that spirit that I
write this letter.
    My name is Bailey Foster. I am a senior geneticist at
Bayner Genetics in Boca Raton, Florida, USA.
    Recently, I have been assigned a project to study non-
coding human DNA, which as you may know accounts for
ninety-eight percent of the DNA in humans. Its purpose is
largely a mystery, since it does not appear to code for
proteins.
    I won't bore you with the details, but we have
discovered a non-contiguous sequence of base pairs that
are essentially non-repeating in a database of twenty-six
million samples of DNA. Assuming the simplest explanation
is the most likely, we are investigating whether this
strange sequence - which incidentally uses base pairs from
all twenty-three pairs of chromosomes - might be an
identifier of some kind.
```

An identifier of what? We asked ourselves the same question, of course. Being a student of Buddhism, I was naturally led to the idea that this unique identifier may well be connected somehow to the individual human spirit or soul.

Subsequently, in considering how this theory might be supported, I came upon the idea of comparing the DNA of a dead body from which the spirit had passed with a living body into which the spirit has now set up residence, as it were. The hypothesis is that the non-contiguous sequences in these two samples will match.

I realize this is a highly irregular request, but I hope you will be curious enough about our findings to allow me to extract DNA samples from the eight Dalai Lamas known to be entombed at Potala Palace. Incidentally, I realize that the bodies of Buddhists are customarily cremated, but in that case we have developed procedures to extract DNA from cremains, so this is not a hindrance.

Bayner Genetics stands ready to remunerate China for any expenses involved, of course, and also to show our gratitude by bestowing on your ministry a direct cash payment, the exact amount to be negotiated.

For your information, I have not collected the DNA of the present Dalai Lama, who I assume will be more than happy to provide his own sample after I have the DNA of his predecessors.

I respectfully beg you to respond as soon as possible to my request.

Kindest regards,

Bailey Foster,
Bayner Genetics
987 Winston Road
Boca Raton, Florida, 33486 USA

Bailey worried about the little white lies in her letter. For one thing, the return address was her own, not that of Bayner Genetics. She didn't want Zhenbang Zhao's response, should there be one, to fall into the hands of Gwendolyn, who still thought they were looking for the lesbian gene. Also, she had of course met with the Dalai Lama. In light of the Chinese hatred for Tenzin, however, Bailey thought it best to limit her association with him. She'd also lied about having a method for extracting DNA from cremains. She didn't want to let the Chinese know that she knew the bodies of the Dalai Lamas had not been cremated, since that information was apparently something of a secret. Thipor Dulip hadn't known about

it, and he was close enough to the Dalai Lama to answer his phone.

Bailey printed the letter, stuck it in an envelope and walked it to a nearby post office to make sure she gave it enough postage.

The mail clerk weighed Bailey's letter and glanced at the destination address.

"Beijing China!" he said. "We don't get many letters going that far. We don't get many regular letters at all, except for bills and junk mail. How come you just don't send an e-mail? That's what everybody else does. Dang email! Pretty soon mailmen – sorry, mail carriers – will be just as lonely as Maytag repairmen."

"Junk mail is still business," Bailey said. "And you also have packages. You can't email a package."

"You just wait," he said. "They'll figure out a way."

"Yeah?" Bailey said. She was irritated with the clerk's negativity. "I think if you love regular letters so much maybe you should figure out a way to make regular letters popular again. You know there's nothing like getting an actual letter in the mail, especially one written by hand. It's a little piece of the person who wrote it, right? A person who is probably someone you love. There's your catch phrase: 'Every letter is a love letter.' And the TV ad would have people of all races and ages opening their real letters and smiling like each one has a hundred dollars in it."

"Hey! That's not a bad idea! I might just do that! I might just!"

When he handed Bailey the receipt, he had a big smile on his face.

"Thank you, ma'am. Have a great day."

Bailey felt good after leaving the post office, like she had changed things for the better, if only a tiny bit. She thought maybe it was an omen of good things to come, good karma in action, just like how she'd helped that family in the black Mercedes. She began to believe that China would say yes.

Six weeks later, once she'd convinced herself several times over that there was no way China would reject her generous offer, she got Mr. Zhenbang Zhao's short response.

Dear Bailey Foster,
 Thank you for your recent letter, which we read with great interest. The Ministry of Science and Technology of the People's Republic of China is always ready to cooperate with scientists from around the world in a

```
effort to foster scientific advancement.
   Your proposal is interesting, but the Ministry of
Science and Technology of the People's Republic of China
concentrates solely on scientific areas of investigation.
Because your project delves into the realm of the
spiritual, I'm afraid we can be of no help to you. China
is officially atheist, I'm sure you're aware.
   Perhaps if you shared with us your inventive software
and the method you've discovered to extract DNA from
cremains, we could look into the matter more fully.

Wishing you the best of luck in your endeavors,

Zhenbang Zhao, Minister
Ministry of Science and Technology of the People's
Republic of China
```

Bailey Foster threw the letter on her kitchen table and began to cry. She was so sure they were going to say yes! Now what was she going to do? She had lied about having a method to extract DNA from cremains, so sharing that secret with the Chinese wasn't even possible. In any case, there was no way they were going to give away Suze's software, especially not to the Chinese. They were always looking to steal American secrets.

Bailey thought she might possibly travel to Potala Palace – it was a tourist destination, after all – but she was sure the stupas encasing the dead Dalai Lamas were off limits to regular tourists. Even if she could get anywhere near them, how could she possibly obtain the samples without being seen?

She decided to call Suze.

"Griffin," Suze answered.

"Suze, it's Bailey."

Suze could tell she'd been crying.

"Aw, sweetie, what's wrong?" Suze said.

"I just got refused by the Chinese. They won't let me get samples from the dead Dalai Lamas. They say it's not science, it's religion, and they only work on science. They suggest we give them your software if we want them to consider it further."

"Fuck that!" Suze said.

"I agree," Bailey said. She fell silent and thought, *But now what?*

"By the way," Suze said. "The sequencing of the Dalai Lama's DNA just finished, and you were right. They're identical. They both contain the same ID as well, of course, and it's an ID that is

nowhere else in the database."

"So he wasn't lying," Bailey said, smiling.

"Apparently not," Suze said.

"Hang on Foster, UPS is here. Be right back. "

Bailey heard the phone drop onto the desk and then Suze thanking the UPS guy. Then Suze was back.

"You won't believe this, but there's a package here from your boyfriend. It's kind of big. Enough to hold maybe a couple dozen cookies, but it doesn't seem to weigh enough for that. It literally just arrived. Want me to open it?"

"My boyfriend?" Bailey asked.

"That's what it says, 'His Holiness the Fourteenth Dalai Lama of Tibet,' although there's no return address..."

"Holy shit!" Bailey said. She wiped her tears away.

Suze said, "Should I open it?"

"No! I'll be right there!"

Bailey raced out of her apartment and drove to the lab. When she got there, Suze was sitting in a chair with the package on her lap.

"I'm dying to eat one of those divine cookies!" she said. She held the package out to Bailey. "Open it!"

Bailey took the package and sat down on the floor next to Suze's chair. The package was wrapped in plain brown paper. Bailey opened it carefully with a pocket knife and found a plain cardboard shipping box inside. Inside the shipping box was a finer box, gold with a red top. The red lid had not been taped down. Bailey lifted it off easily and set it aside on the floor. Inside the gold box, she found clothes.

The tags on the clothes said Made in China. They appeared to be some kind of simple uniform. There was a loose-fitting shirt with flowing sleeves and a pair of baggy pants that tied at the waist. Both were made from a dull beige linen. Digging into the box further, she found a necklace. The chain was silver and hanging from it was an amulet, a disc decorated with the head of a lion.

"He sent you clothes and jewelry?" Suze asked. "He must be your boyfriend! What the hell did you wear when you went to see him, rags?"

"I wore jeans. Nice jeans. And a polo shirt, I think."

"Keep digging," Suze suggested. "We're obviously missing

something."

Bailey removed the tissue paper from the bottom of the gold box and found a folded piece of paper hidden beneath it. She smiled at Suze, unfolded the Dalai Lama's letter and started to read, trying her best to adopt the Dalai Lama's accent.

"Dear Bailey Foster," the letter began, "After further consideration and a more comprehensive check of your background (and that of Bayner Genetics) I have decided that there is something more I can do to help you further your research."

Bailey felt her pulse quicken.

Suze said, "Holy shit."

Bailey kept reading, but dropped the accent. "Inside this package you have no doubt found a suit of clothing and a necklace. The clothing is purposefully loose fitting and will no doubt fit you. Not knowing your shoe size, I have not included the appropriate sandals, but I trust that you can find a pair once you get to Lhasa."

"Lhasa!" Bailey exclaimed, "That's where the Potala Palace is!"

"Keep reading," Suze said.

"We have made all the arrangements. In an envelope attached to the red box top ..."

Bailey grabbed the red lid she'd set aside and looked under it. A gold envelope was attached to its underside. Inside it, she found an itinerary, a map, several plane tickets that would take her from Miami to Los Angeles and then to Beijing, and train tickets that would take her from Beijing to Lhasa. There was also a ticket that would get her into the Potala Palace.

She read on, waving the gold envelope at Suze.

"Inside the envelope you will find your itinerary, travel tickets and a map of Lhasa, including the Lhasa Commercial Hotel, where you will be staying."

Bailey was so excited she was short of breath, but she kept reading.

"You are expected to visit Potala Palace the morning of August fourteenth. Join the third tour of the day, which I believe begins at about eleven o'clock. Make sure to wear these clothes, especially the amulet. Leave the rest to us. Good luck on your exciting journey! Tenzin. P.S.: I have scheduled you to arrive a few days before the fourteenth to allow you to acclimate yourself to the altitude. The air is quite thin."

Bailey leapt from her place on the floor and walked in a brisk circle, the Dalai Lama's letter still in her hand.

"I'm going to Tibet, Suze!" she squealed.

She jumped up and down and spun around like a schoolgirl in love.

"Yes, yes, YES! I'm going to Tibet!"

Suze tapped her toe against the gold box on the floor.

"You sure there's no cookies in there?" she said. "I'm starving!"

14
ABSTRACT PEACE

The six-hour flight from Miami to Los Angeles itself was grueling enough, but it was nothing compared to the thirteen hours it took to get to Beijing on China Air. The capitol city was literally on the other side of the earth, so when Bailey Foster arrived she was suffering not only from travel fatigue but also from the worst jet lag possible. Her noon was China's midnight.

The good news, Bailey saw, was that the train station was immediately adjacent to Beijing International Airport. The bad news was that her itinerary said the train to Lhasa didn't leave until the following day at noon.

It already was midnight. The cheery young girl behind the desk at the Beijing Airport Hotel told her there were no vacancies. Even if it was noon back in Boca Raton, Bailey felt too tired to bother finding someplace else to stay for the night. She also was reluctant to leave the rail station, lest she somehow miss the train. It was true that the train's departure was twelve hours away, but as they say, shit happens.

She noticed there were many other travelers littering the train station floor. A lone janitor wearing ear buds languidly worked his mop between them as they slept here and there on the already spotless tiles. Bailey curled up in a corner using her two suitcases as a bed, not because it was comfortable but so that she would be awakened if anyone tried to steal her things. She had come to realize that the simple linen uniform Tenzin had given her was

somehow more than a gift. If she lost it or the amulet, the Dalai Lama's plan, whatever it was, probably would be ruined.

Bailey pulled out her smart phone and set the alarm to go off at eight o'clock the next morning. Just as she was putting the phone away, an extended Chinese family of five leaned their bags and other belongings against the wall a few feet away and sat down on the floor. Bailey smiled a tired smile at them, but they seemed not to see her.

There appeared to be three generations: An elderly couple, a younger couple and one male child of about four, who was as quiet and well-mannered as the adults. The boy glanced at Bailey and immediately diverted his gaze to the shiny floor. Then he gave a slight bow and turned away. He was nothing like the cheerful girl in the Mercedes Benz. Then again, even the girl had become shy at close range.

The middle-aged man, who was probably the boy's father, began blowing into an air mattress. In a few seconds, his face turned red and he handed the nozzle to his wife, who blew into the mattress until she, too, was red in the face. Then she handed the nozzle back to him. While the pair handed the slowly growing mattress back and forth, the boy returned his attention to Bailey. He seemed fascinated with her blonde hair and blue eyes, and even before the mattress started taking shape the boy summoned up enough courage to approach Bailey and touch her hair.

"Hong Lí!" the boy's grandmother called to him. "Hong Lí!"

Before the boy turned away, Bailey snapped a photo of him with her smart phone. This upset the grandmother further. She pointed at Bailey and squealed, "Zhàopiàn! Zhàopiàn!"

The father stopped blowing into the air mattress, pulled his son away from Bailey and said, "I'm sorry, but we prefer no photographs. May I delete?" He held out his hand, but Bailey was not about to hand her smart phone to a stranger.

"I'm sorry! I didn't realize," she said.

"One should not go around taking photographs of strangers. It's very rude."

"Here," Bailey said, "let me show you as I delete it." She rose to her knees and held the smart phone so the man could see what she was doing. Then she brought up the boy's picture.

"He's beautiful," she said. She looked at the father and saw that

he was not smiling. She deleted the photo.

"OK?" she said.

"No more photos!" the father said.

He went back to helping his wife. When the air mattress finally was inflated, the boy got on first, then the older couple, then the parents. They each used their coats as blankets and each other for pillows.

They must have been even more tired than Bailey – certainly they had a better sleeping arrangement – because before too long Bailey heard a choir of snoring. She reached for her ear buds, pushed them in, navigated to pandora.com and entered "Music to go to sleep by." A haunting tune called *Touching Calm* by a band named *Liquid Mind* began to play. Bailey drifted away on the droning.

In the morning, the Chinese family was gone by the time Bailey was awakened by her smart phone's alarm.

Bailey rubbed her eyes and saw that her two suitcases were still there. She punched off the alarm, loaded her luggage on a push cart someone had left nearby, and began looking for her train. When she'd walked from one end of the station and back again without seeing anything about Lhasa, she finally asked a woman in uniform for help.

"Where's the train to Lhasa?" Bailey asked her.

"Lhasa!" the woman said. "Beijing West."

Bailey took out her smart phone, navigated to Google Translate and converted "Where's Beijing West?" into Chinese. She held the translation out to the woman.

"I speak English," the woman said, smiling.

Bailey was embarrassed.

"I'm so sorry," she said. "Of course you do!"

"It's all right," the woman said. "Come with me. You look like you slept on the floor last night."

Bailey followed the woman to a train with an electronic sign that said something in large Chinese letters and, in smaller text beneath it, Beijing West.

"You have a ticket?" the woman asked.

Disoriented and still drowsy, Bailey gradually realized the woman was telling her she was going to have to travel to another

train station called Beijing West to pick up the train to Lhasa. She looked at her smart phone. It was ten o'clock. She wondered how far away Beijing West was. Did she have time to get there before the train left at noon? She hurriedly dug for the envelope that held her passport, visa and tickets and handed the whole thing to the helpful woman. The woman dug into the envelope and pulled out two train tickets.

"This one will take you to Beijing West," the woman said. She held up the ticket and Bailey saw now that it had Beijing West printed clearly on it. The woman held up a second ticket. "This one will take you to Lhasa. Wonderful journey!"

The woman slipped the pair of tickets into Bailey's shirt pocket, handed the envelope back to her, and disappeared into the station. Wishing she'd packed lighter, Bailey pulled her suitcases off of the push cart and lugged them onto the shuttle train. No one ever asked to see her ticket.

When she arrived at the Beijing West station less than an hour later, she easily found signs that led to the Qinghai-Tibet Railway, which had only been in operation for a few years. She handed her ticket to a smiling man stationed at the entrance to the train. The man ran the ticket under a portable scanner clipped to his belt, gave it back to her, then held out his hand and said, "Health card, please."

"Health card?" Bailey asked.

"Yes," the man said. "Health card."

Bailey gave the man her travel envelope. He dug through the documents and handed it back to her.

"No health card," he said. "Go to window."

He pointed toward the ticket counter.

"Can you watch my bags?" she asked.

The man grunted and nodded.

Bailey hurried to the ticket counter. She was third in line. As she waited, she kept an eye on her bags and the man with the scanner, who was helping other passengers board the train. Several times she heard bells and mechanical groans that made her think the train was pulling out of the station a few minutes early, without her, but was relieved to see that it did not move. She wondered how "All Aboard!" sounded in Chinese, or if they even bothered with such things here. Finally, she was at the window.

"Health card," she said to the woman behind the window.

"Ticket please," the woman said.

Bailey handed her the ticket the man with the scanner had just given back to her. The woman scanned it and a printer nearby spat out a short document. The woman pushed it through the slot and said, "Sign, please."

The document was in English. At the top, it said, "Passenger Health Registration Card." Bailey signed it quickly without reading the rest of it. (The Passenger Health Registration Card had been required since 2006, when a 75-year-old man with heart trouble died on the train after refusing to get off as the train's doctor had advised him to. The card held the Chinese harmless for any health problems passengers might suffer while on the train.)

The woman behind the window took the signed document and pushed a small card through the opening. Bailey took it and her ticket back to the man with the scanner, who scanned the card and said something in Chinese to a younger man waiting nearby. The younger man took Bailey's suitcases and led her onto the train. Bailey followed him as he struggled to carry her suitcases down a tight hallway. Finally he came to a little door. He opened the door and pushed her suitcases inside. Bailey saw a narrow bed made up with clean sheets and a wool blanket.

"Bless you, Tenzin!" she said, and stepped into the little room.

"Duìbùqǐ?" the young man said.

"Oh, never mind. Nothing." Bailey smiled. "Thank you!"

She tipped the young man with the first bill she pulled from her pocket without looking at it to see how much it was worth. Not wanting to arouse the young man's suspicion, she slowly shut the door.

Shit! she thought once the door was closed. *These people hate the Dalai Lama! They invaded his country, didn't they? What the hell were you thinking?*

She laid down on the bed. It was only about two feet wide and an inch shorter than she was tall, but the sheets smelled wonderful. She flicked the light off and listened to the other passengers as they walked by and settled into the cabins around her. She was hungry, but was too afraid to wander about the train looking for food. She dug into her purse and found some gum. She expected the door to come flinging open at any second. They would drag her out of the

nice smelling bed and off to some austere interrogation room, equally small but not as comfortable, where they would repeatedly ask her: Who is this Tenzin you speak of?

But no one ever came.

Bailey felt safer when she sensed the train pull out of the Beijing West station. Why, she wondered, had the Dalai Lama passed on China Air's service to Lhasa and put her instead on a train that took two days to reach Tibet? The train was an engineering achievement. Maybe he thought a scientist would appreciate it.

It was undeniable that the Qinghai-Tibet Railway was new and exciting, a marvel that had cost the Chinese billions and climbed mountains so high that the railcars were pressurized like airliner fuselages. The engineers also had installed machines that gleaned the oxygen from the thin air outside and pumped it into the airtight cars. The concentrators made the air inside the cars so oxygen rich that smoking was prohibited.

The Chinese were justifiably proud of the Qinghai-Tibet Railway. It was the highest train in the world, of course, since it terminated in Tibet, the roof of the world. It also meant that Lhasa and all of Tibet would be assimilated more quickly into the Han culture of China, a longtime goal of the People's Republic and one that many Tibetans opposed because they feared losing their own culture.

So why would this train appeal to the Dalai Lama? Bailey wondered again. *And two days? I'm not on vacation, I'm on a mission!*

Bailey fell asleep after having chewed only two sticks of Juicy Fruit for dinner. Her growling stomach woke her well before sunrise. She left the little cabin, which was not much larger than the bed, and found her way to a dining car. She was drinking a second cup of strong coffee and eating eggs with toast and sausage when the rising sun illuminated the Chinese countryside and made the reason for Tenzin's choice clear.

One spectacular view after another filled the window as the train sped along at one-hundred-twenty kilometers per hour. She saw herds of antelope and gazelle grazing on vast grasslands, crystal clear lakes on plateaus higher than the clouds and deep gorges that made her feel like she *was* flying.

Forty-four hours later, about four hours outside of Lhasa, she

began to see herds of grazing yaks being tended by Tibetan nomads whose traditional yak-hair tents were just visible in the distance. Then farmers tending their fields with plows pulled by beasts of burden came into view. A few minutes later, the fast train pulled into Lhasa.

After two days on the cramped train, Bailey was ready to get off. She lugged her bags off of the train and onto the platform. She was out of breath by the time she got the two suitcases to the front of the train station, where she planned to catch a cab to the Lhasa Commercial Hotel. Then she noticed a bicycle-powered rickshaw waiting at the curb. Pinned to the colorful wagon that had been rigged to the bicycle was a small sign that read *Bailey Foster*. Bailey approached the rickshaw driver with her two suitcases and dropped them on the sidewalk.

"I'm Bailey Foster!" she announced breathlessly. She tried to remember if the Dalai Lama's letter had mentioned anything about a rickshaw.

"ID please," the rickshaw driver said.

Bailey swung her long hair around to get it out of her eyes. The motion made her dizzy. She showed the rickshaw driver her passport. His eyes lighted up.

"Hello Miss Bailey Foster!" he said.

He immediately tore down the sign and piled her bags into his colorful wagon, which to Bailey looked vaguely unsafe. Then the rickshaw driver helped Bailey climb aboard and moved close enough to her that she could smell his musky odor.

"Hello, Miss Bailey Foster!" he whispered. "Personal guest of His Holiness the Fourteenth Dalai Lama! I will take you to your hotel now. And do not worry. I will keep our secret!"

He put his hand to his mouth and made a motion as if turning an invisible key. Then he jumped out of the wagon and onto the bicycle seat and they were off.

With a stamina that impressed Bailey considering how much trouble she'd had with her suitcases, the strong young man pedaled the rickshaw north on a road named Jiangsu, then west on Beijing Road. As the rickshaw driver labored, Bailey relaxed as if she were royalty. She watched the bustling little city go by.

The buildings were awash with color. The roofs that were visible where often colored red or blue, and virtually every building

sported awnings, window frames and eaves dressed in colorful fabrics that fluttered in the mountain breeze and made the structures come alive.

The bicycle-rickshaw pedaled through a Lhasa that had been modernized by the People's Republic. There was a supermarket, a convenience store, a store selling steamed bread, a hair salon, a store that sold wine and cigarettes, a building supplies store, a shop selling hot food, a kitchen supply store, a restaurant, the local Lhasa television station, a gas station, a farmer's market, a furniture row with five or six stores, a flower shop, a police station, a bakery, a bicycle shop, a movie theater, a Bank of China branch, a travel agency, a shoe store called Zuxia Shenghi, a clothing shop and an elementary school where she saw children dressed in uniforms and playing on brightly colored monkey bars.

Several times along the way, the rickshaw driver called out to people he apparently knew. The sidewalks were filled with pedestrians. Many of them were dressed as westerners or modern Chinese, but others wore the traditional attire of the Tibetans. Many of the Tibetan women wore calf-length multicolored aprons over their long skirts and wide-brimmed hats to protect themselves from the sun. Lhasa residents called their home the "sunlit city" for good reason. When it rained, it mostly rained at night.

Some of the pedestrians wearing Tibetan clothes held a polished stick with a metal wheel attached to the top. A weighted ball on a chain was attached to the side of the wheel so that when they drew a small circle in the air with the tip of the stick – usually clockwise when viewed from above – the centrifugal force of the ball spun the wheel around. The wheels were Mani Wheels. They contained slips of paper upon which prayers had been jotted. The spinning transmitted the prayers to whomever they were intended, once for each revolution, just as if they'd been uttered aloud.

Bailey also saw people prostrating themselves repeatedly amidst the throng of busy pedestrians, who avoided them as they might a blind man. These devout souls were on their way to Jokhang Temple or some other sacred site, which they intended to reach in the fashion of a giant inch-worm, one body length at a time.

The prostration, she knew from her reading, was done in order to atone for misdeeds and bolster one's karma as well as the karma of all of humanity. Standing in place, they first reached heavenward,

then crouched and dove forward into a full prone position by sliding their hands along the sidewalk until they were outstretched with their nose touching the concrete. To protect their hands, they wore thick gloves or grabbed wooden blocks that slid along the sidewalk like pallet skids. After a brief pause face down, they returned nonchalantly to a standing position and repeated the process. Over and over and over again these strange people did these spiritual squat thrusts. Even stranger, no one walking by gave them a second look. Likewise, they seemed not to notice passersby.

The rickshaw came to a red light, and the driver handed a slip of paper to Bailey. On it, she read:

The Seven Limbed Prayer

With my body, speech, and mind, humbly I prostrate.
I make offerings both set out and imagined.
I declare every unwholesome action I have ever committed.
I rejoice in the virtues of all beings.
Please stay until samsara ends,
And please turn the Wheel of Dharma for us.
I dedicate all these virtues to the great Enlightenment.

Finally, the bicycle rickshaw pulled up to the Lhasa Commercial Hotel.

"Where is Potala Palace from here?" Bailey asked the rickshaw driver as he lifted her suitcases out of the wagon.

"Potala," he said, pointing to the north. "Not far. You can walk if you can breathe OK."

Bailey offered the bicycle-rickshaw driver one-hundred-fifty yuan for the ride, but he refused.

"Tenzin took good care of me," he said. Then he pedaled off.

A colorfully dressed bellhop took Bailey's bags into the hotel. She checked in, went to her room and flopped onto the bed.

Lhasa, at last!

The next morning, Bailey pulled on a pair of jeans and a shirt, slipped on her Nikes, and went for a walk. Still not acclimated to the thin air, she found that she had to stop frequently in order to catch her breath. During one rest break, she stopped at a store that

sold wigs and hats. She went inside, thinking that a wig of straight black hair might help her blend in at the palace. The wig looked peculiar with her blonde eyebrows, but she figured she could paint them with mascara. She bought the wig.

She continued on her way to the Zuxia Shenghi shoe store – a forty-five minute walk from the hotel, not counting rest breaks – and bought a pair of sandals she thought would not only work well with the Dalai Lama's clothes but would also be easy to walk in. When the time came, she planned to walk the mile and a half to the Potala Palace. When she walked out of the shoe store, she saw the rickshaw driver that had taken her from the train station to the hotel. He saw her, too, and pulled up next to her.

"Hello Bailey Foster!" he said. "Free ride? I give you a tour of Lhasa."

Bailey tossed her shopping bags into the wagon and hopped in, surer now of its safety. The driver spun around on the bicycle seat and faced her with his feet on the edge of the wagon.

"I should introduce myself," he said, extending his hand. "I am Kamala Gyadatsang. Tibetans usually don't have second names, but I gave myself one. It means 'family of the enemy of the Chinese,' so I share it only with friends. You can call me Kama."

"OK, Kama," Bailey said as she shook his hand. "Show me Lhasa!"

First, Kama took her to Jokhang Temple, which Kama said was the most sacred temple in Tibet. Several people were prostrating themselves on the stone courtyard, most of them in places where the stone had been rubbed to a smooth polish by the repeated sliding of so many devout hands. Hanging from the front of the temple were five huge tapestries that looked like gigantic black quilts with white borders and white geometric patterns sewn into them. Kama told Bailey the people prostrating themselves focused on centers the geometric designs in order to help them meditate. At the top of the building was a dharma wheel flanked by two kneeling deer, all of it painted gold.

"It used to be called Tsuklakang, 'House of Religious Science,'" Kama said. "But now it's just Jokhang, 'House of the Buddha.' People travel many miles to come here, but even if they prostrate themselves the whole way, they don't go inside right away. First, they walk all around the building, stopping at each corner. Then

they go inside, where there are many statues, but none as important as the two which are the Buddha himself, one when he was eight and another when he was twelve. You can see inside later. It's very beautiful and elaborate."

"It's beautiful and elaborate even from out here," Bailey said.

Next, Kama pedaled to the Potala Palace. It was a huge structure on a hill and immediately reminded Bailey of the castle she had once imagined during meditation. It looked to her as though an enormous white sailing ship with a brick brown wheelhouse had been dropped into the hill's peak. On the several zigzag stairways that led up to the palace's many levels, Bailey saw women dressed in clothes that looked like the simple uniform she'd gotten from the Dalai Lama. Surely, she thought, Tenzin must have given her the clothes to help her blend in. But what about her blonde hair? All of the women she saw had straight black hair. Bailey was glad she'd bought the wig. Without it, she'd look unmistakably foreign. With it, she thought, she'd blend in easily.

Across the street from Potala Palace was the Tibet Peaceful Liberation Monument, a towering structure the Chinese had built to commemorate the triumph of the People's Republic over the Dalai Lama and his imperialist allies. Most notable among the allies were the Americans, who until President Richard Nixon normalized relations with China in 1972 had helped the Tibetan resistance, mostly monks, hold back the cultural tsunami from the east.

"It is an abstract version of Mt. Everest," Kama said, pointing at the modernistic spire. "Just like the 'peaceful liberation' is abstract. Almost one-hundred-thousand Tibetans were killed. Most of them were well-educated people who had a lot to lose and so could not be so easily overthrown."

"Doesn't sound like a very peaceful liberation to me," Bailey said.

A chill went through her. Were these the Chinese with whom she would be playing cat-and-mouse in a few days? If she were caught, she imagined she might disappear like any number of Tibetan monks before her. The seriousness of her mission finally struck her, hard.

"Take me back to the hotel, please, Kama," she said. "I've seen enough."

15
BARBIE IN LOVE

One afternoon after school let out, Barbie Bayner waited for Sandy Shore in the parking lot, as she had done every day since the girls had started dating several months earlier. The little Mercedes was running and the A/C was on. Barbie waited until the student lot was almost empty, but Sandy never showed. Barbie was used to being stood up by her other friends, but she'd thought Sandy was different. She was a nice girl, always happy, always ready to do whatever Barbie wanted to do, even if nine times out of ten it was just to go to the mall.

She reached for her cell phone and told it: "Sandy." The phone dialed Sandy Shore's number. Sandy's voice mail answered immediately.

"Hi! This is Sandy Shore! You know what to do! Toodle-oo!"

"Where the fuck are you, Sandy?" Barbie said into the phone. "I've been waiting here in this fucking parking lot for an hour. I thought maybe you had something to do after school, but what the fuck could take an hour? Call me back. I'm waiting another five minutes and then I'm outta here!"

Ten minutes later, she hit redial and got voice mail again.

"Fuck her!" Barbie said.

Barbie drove to the mall. She parked in the usual place, near the entrance to the food court. She bought a Coke at Burger King and took a wad of napkins from the dispenser. Then she went to a nearby table that was covered with half-full soda cups and burger wrappers left behind by some inconsiderate diners. She used the

wad of napkins to plow the mess off the table and onto the floor, then threw the napkins on the floor, too.

A middle-aged woman wearing a maid's uniform and teal rubber gloves appeared and glared at her.

"Why you do that?" the woman said, pointing a teal finger at the mess and then shaking it at Barbie. "You a bad girl!"

"Screw off, bitch," Barbie said. "I'm having a bad day. Anyway, it's your fault. It's your job to clean these shitty tables. If you'd been doing your job, I wouldn't have had to knock all that crap on the floor."

The woman shook her head in dismay and started to clean up the mess. "I hope you don't talk to your mother like that," she said.

"Hope all you want, lowlife," Barbie said.

She redialed Sandy's number, but got voice mail again.

As the woman in the teal rubber gloves finished mopping up the spilled sodas, three of Barbie's gothic friends swarmed up to the table and dropped into the plastic chairs as though they could not have made it a step farther. There were two boys and a girl. They were all dressed in clothes that were completely black except for the silver studs and buckles and chains that were attached here and there. They all had tiny barbells in their tongues and had randomly shaved their heads so that it looked as though a squadron of moths had attacked them. Compared to them, Barbie almost looked normal.

"Hey loser," said one of the boys. He had a ring through his left nostril that was connected to an earring in his left ear with a gently arcing chain wisely held on with small magnets, so if some moron came by and tugged on it like he was trying to stop a city bus, it would break away painlessly.

"Back at you, Spike," Barbie said. "You seen Sandy?"

"Yeah, I saw her about a half hour ago," the boy said. "She was in Saks digging through nighties and shit with Frankie Scutaro."

"The football player?" Barbie asked.

"He's not just a player, loser. He's the quarterback. He even looks like Tebow. Hey, flip me five bucks, will ya? I'm on E."

Barbie dug into a pocket and tossed a wadded twenty at the boy, who caught it in mid-air.

"Come on, guys," the boy said. "Let's hit the King. Barbie's buying."

"As usual," Barbie said.

After the ebony trio left, Barbie decided to cruise the mall. Maybe she could find Sandy and see for herself what she was up to with that stud Scutaro. When she came to *Black Is Beautiful*, her favorite goth boutique, she went inside to have a quick look. She wound up buying a studded leather bracelet (like she needed another one), a black tee-shirt that said *Go Fuck Yourself* across the front, and a tube of black lipstick, which she applied on her way out of the store.

Then she saw Sandy. She was with Frank Scutaro, all right. They were hanging all over one another. *Get a fucking room,* she thought. She slipped back into *Black Is Beautiful*. Sandy would never come in there. She was a Saks girl all the way. But then the two did start heading toward the goth store. Barbie hurried to the back of the boutique and slipped into a changing room, which had only a black curtain covering it. Once inside, she peeked through a slit in the curtain, but no longer saw the amorous couple.

Two minutes passed and she heard Sandy laughing and saying, "Not here, Frankie! Wait until we get back home! My parents are going out to dinner tonight!"

They were right outside the changing room.

Then Barbie heard Scutaro say, "Come on, Sandy! You're so hot! I can't help it!"

The next thing Barbie knew, Sandy was dragging Scutaro into the dressing room where she was hiding.

"Ahem," Barbie said.

Sandy Shore turned around and saw her.

"Barbie!" she gasped.

Barbie looked at Scutaro.

"Just so you know, asswipe, I don't do threesomes."

"Who the fuck are you?" Scutaro said.

"I'm the one who was licking her little pink twat before you starting sniffing around it, dog boy," Barbie said.

"We haven't done anything!" Sandy protested.

"Yet," Barbie said. "But what the fuck were you pulling him into this dressing room for, to check his hat size?"

"Uh," Sandy said.

"Eat shit and die, cunt," Barbie said.

She pushed her way past the two of them, then turned back and

looked at Scutaro.

"She smells good on the outside, cockmaster, but watch out for that slash. It reeks like putrid herring. I think she might have the crabs."

Barbie Bayner was as mad as she'd ever been. Madder than she'd been when her supposed friends gave her the cold shoulder after they'd gotten as much out of her as they wanted. Madder than she'd ever been at her mother. Her anger made her start crying. She just wanted to get home.

As she made her way through the throng of shoppers, she saw mothers pushing strollers and young couples aimlessly window shopping with Mrs. Field's cookies and ice cream cones. How could they all act so normal? Didn't they know how bad life sucked?

Just before she got back to the food court, she ran headlong into someone who caught her in a bear hug before she fell down. It was David Epstein, one of the smart kids at school. He was wearing Converse basketball shoes, old jeans, and a white tee-shirt decorated with a picture of someone she didn't recognize. She'd never spoken to him before, but he knew who she was.

David could see she'd been crying.

"Barbie?" he said. "What's wrong?"

"I don't want to talk about it!" Barbie said.

"OK, sorry!" David Epstein said. He held up his palms as if she were going to hit him. But then Barbie got an idea.

"You're Epstein, right?"

"Right!" he said. "David." He was pleased she knew his name. Well, half of it anyway. Barbie wiped the tears from her face and threw her arms around his neck.

"Hey, David Epstein, you want to hang out?" she asked. "You're not dating anyone, are you?"

She knew he wasn't.

"Sure," David said. "I mean, no, I don't have a girlfriend. We can hang out for a while if you want. I can't stay long, though. I just came here to pick up God of War III."

"Bitchin!" Barbie said. "That game is totally gross. I can buy it for you if you want."

"That's OK, Barbie. I've been saving money I make mowing lawns. I got it covered."

Barbie had never known anyone to outright reject her offer to buy them something. Usually, in fact, they came right out and asked her for money as Spike had done.

"OK, can I at least walk with you to the store?" she asked sweetly.

"Sure," David Epstein said. "It's just up the way here."

"Cool!" Barbie said. "Come on. I know where it is."

"Yeah, I do too. I've been coming here for weeks, making sure they didn't sell out."

As they walked slowly along, Barbie hugged David Epstein's right arm against her left breast as though they'd been dating for weeks. She was hoping they'd see Sandy and Scutaro, and before long they did. Barbie pulled David Epstein over to them.

"Hey, Sandy, Frankie," she said. "I'd like you to meet my new friend, David Epstein."

Sandy and Frank Scutaro looked at Barbie as though she'd gone mad, but said nothing.

After a few awkward seconds, Barbie said, "Well, gotta go! We gotta go buy God of War III."

As it happened, Frank Scutaro was a big fan of God of War II.

"Oh, man," he said. "That game is so wicked. Fucking blood looks totally real! It even shines and everything. I've got II. The blood is good, but I hear it's not as good as in III."

At that, David Epstein lit up.

"Awesome!" he said. "What level did you get to?"

"I've only gotten to the Cliffs of Madness," Scutaro said. "Fucking football practice takes all my time, and by the time it's over, I'm totally destroyed."

"I know how that can be," David said. "I've always got too much homework to play much. I still managed to kill Ares the second time through the Temple of Oracle, though. When you get there, remember that the secret is to be patient and counter-attack. Keep playing, it gets really gross! Those game designers are sick."

"Yeah they are," Scutaro said.

The two girls began to realize the boys were losing interest in them.

"Come on, Frankie," Sandy said. "We've got business to take care of."

"Yeah, OK," Scutaro said. "See ya around, David."

"Later," David said.

Barbie pulled him away toward the video game store.

"He seems like a nice guy," David said. "But I've never talked to him before. Football players don't hang around with nerds like me."

"You're not a nerd, Davey," Barbie said. "You're smart. That's sexy. Scutaro's OK. But Sandy's a fucking slut. Stay away from her. I think she's got the crabs."

"Ew!" David said. "Hey, there's GameStop. Let's go!"

The two new friends hurried into the store, easily found God of War III, and took a copy to the register. David pulled out a wad of fives and ones that smelled of motor oil and lawn clippings, but Barbie looked at him and said, "Put your money away, Davey. My treat."

Then she pulled out her Visa card and snapped it on the glass countertop. David Epstein picked up the card and handed it back to her.

"Thanks just the same, Barbie, but you don't have to buy my friendship. Besides, I've been saving for months to buy this game. If you buy it, it just won't be the same."

"Let me buy you something else then," Barbie said. "How about a new controller?"

"Stop!" David Epstein said. "I told you. You don't have to buy my friendship. We can be friends without you buying me anything."

"Damn!" Barbie said. "I was just trying to be nice! Let me at least buy you a Coke at the food court. We can sit down and talk for a while."

"OK," David said, handing the clerk his wad of hard-earned bills. "But I've only got about a half an hour. I've got a ton of calculus homework tonight."

"OK," Barbie said.

After they bought the game, the new friends walked to the food court. Barbie bought a couple of extra-large Cokes and a super-sized order of French fries and the two spent an hour-and-a-half talking. David talked mostly about God of War III, but he also told Barbie his mother and his father were both high school teachers, but not at their school. He said he had two younger brothers and lived in a modest middle-class home that didn't have a swimming pool, not even a small one.

When the conversation started to wane, Barbie asked, "Who's that on your tee-shirt?"

"It's Alan Turing," David said, looking down at the shirt. "He was an English mathematician, a really smart guy. During World War II he helped crack the encrypted messages used by the Germans. You've heard of the Enigma machine?"

"Not really," Barbie said.

"It was a teletype machine the Germans invented after World War I to encrypt secret messages. Hitler used it during World War II. Turing figured out a way to decrypt the messages, which of course gave the good guys a major advantage, since it meant they usually knew what the Germans were up to. Lots of people say the war would have been lost without him."

"He sounds like a hell of a guy."

"He was. But after the war they discovered he was gay, which was illegal."

"Illegal?"

"Yeah. Back then, being gay was a crime. Instead of going to prison, though, Turing agreed to be given female hormones. They called it 'chemical castration.' Lovely term, huh? Anyway, a couple years later he committed suicide. Lots of people said it was the hormones that drove him to do it."

"That fucking sucks!" Barbie said. "How could people be such assholes!"

"Yeah, heck of way to thank a guy for saving your ass, huh? Anyway, that's why I wear his tee-shirt."

Finally, David said, "I'm sorry, Barbie. I really gotta go. I actually do have a ton of homework tonight."

"That's too bad. Maybe we can go out sometime," Barbie said. "I really like you. I mean I really like you. You're cool!"

"That would be nice," David said. He pulled out his cell phone.

"What's your number?" Barbie told him her number and he punched it into his phone.

"I'll walk you to your car," Barbie said.

"I don't have a car," David said. "My parents are teachers, remember? I rode my bike. It's just outside."

Barbie considered offering to throw David's bike in the trunk of her Mercedes and drive him home, but she thought he'd probably just turn her down again. He seemed proud of being able to take

care of himself.

"OK," she said. "I'll walk you to your bike. I was leaving anyway."

Later that night, with David at home in his bed and Barbie at home in hers, they talked for two hours, until David fell asleep with his phone still on.

16
POTALA PALACE

T he morning of August fourteenth, Bailey awoke in her room at the Lhasa Commercial Hotel and meditated for thirty minutes, just as she'd done every day since she'd arrived in Tibet. Then she started getting ready to go to Potala Palace.

She pulled on the loose-fitting beige uniform the Dalai Lama had given her and strapped on the sandals she'd bought at Zuxia Shenghi. She lifted the round amulet over her head and fingered the lion's head on its lid. She prayed the lion would bring her luck.

Then she pulled the wig of straight black hair out of its shopping bag, put a fist inside of it, and shook it out. Her hope was that the wig would make her look more like the women she'd seen sweeping the walkways and washing the walls when Kama had taken her to see the Potala Palace. That had to be the reason behind the loose clothes Tenzin had given her – to help her blend in with the palace staff. It would be impossible to blend in with blonde hair. Why hadn't Tenzin thought of that? For that matter, why hadn't he been clearer about his plan in the first place, so she'd know what to expect?

"Expectations are the source of all unhappiness," she said to herself in the mirror.

Bailey pinned up her blonde hair and pulled the black wig on over it. She brushed and tugged at the wig until it looked as natural as it was ever going to. Then she used a mascara wand to paint her blonde eyebrows and eyelashes black.

Looking at herself in the mirror, she hoped that whoever was supposed to meet her at the Potala Palace would not be thrown off by her impromptu disguise. She worried that Tenzin might have told them to look for a blonde.

She turned to leave, then stopped. Her purse was on the bed. She hurried over to it, dug for her visa and passport, and slipped them into a pocket. She didn't want to be caught without travel documents. Make no mistake about it: Tibet was now China. It was no longer the land of the happy Buddha. Then she remembered the ticket she needed to get into Potala Palace. The number of visitors to the palace each day was strictly limited, so tickets were not easy to get on short notice. The Dalai Lama had wisely included one. She found the ticket and shoved it into a pocket of the loose-fitting uniform.

Bailey strolled out of the hotel and into a perfect Lhasa day. The green mountains to the north and to the south rose into a sharp blue sky. As much as she tried to look inconspicuous, she couldn't help feeling uncomfortable in her disguise. But there was little time to second-guess herself now.

The little city was wide awake. A gentle breeze made its clothed buildings flutter like the hem of a frilly Easter frock. Small cars whizzed by on Kang'angduo Road, whose cobblestone surface made the tires buzz. The sound reminded Bailey of a summer day long ago when she and her friends decided to attach playing cards to the front forks of their bikes with clothespins so that the spokes would slap at the cards noisily and make the bikes sound motorized. The memory brought a smile to her face.

Her mother, an early advocate of the nascent green movement, had been the only person in the neighborhood who didn't use an electric clothes dryer, at least not when it wasn't raining. When her mother had discovered her clothespins were half gone, she'd told Bailey to go get them back. Bailey knew it was impossible. Most of the clothespins had been destroyed after getting tangled in the spinning bicycle spokes.

"They're all broken," she told her mother.

"You go try anyway, young lady," her mother said. "I don't care if you have to glue them back together with Elmer's. I want my clothespins back!"

"Why don't we just buy more?" Bailey said, but the look on her

mother's face told her not to wait for an answer.

Bailey spent a long Sunday afternoon scrounging around in the neighborhood for unbroken clothespins. In the end, she was able to rebuild three and find five still attached to her friends' bikes. She went to deliver the eight clothespins to her mother and was surprised to find her in the backyard, hanging up the last of a clothesline full of clothes. Her mother had, after all, bought new clothespins.

"If you knew you were going to buy more," Bailey said, "why did you make me spend all day looking for them?"

"Why do you think?" her mother said, wiping her brow with her forearm.

Of course Bailey knew. She never used her mother's clothespins again.

As usual in Lhasa, the sidewalks were full of pedestrians. The people there seemed to walk everywhere. Bailey reached the Bank of China branch at the corner of Kang'angduo and Beijing Middle roads. As she waited for the signal to turn, she saw Kama ride by on his rickshaw. At first, he didn't seem to recognize her in the black wig, but then he made a sudden U-turn and pulled up next to her on the sidewalk. He cocked his head to one side and peered into her eyes.

"Bailey?" he said.

"Hi, Kama," Bailey said. "I can't talk now. Please go."

Kama smiled. He thought she was playing some sort of strange game.

"What's with the black wig, Bailey?" he said. "You look funny, like an American trying to look like a Chinese. But I could tell it was you. Chinese women aren't so tall."

Bailey looked around at the people on the street and saw that it was true. The women were all much shorter than her five-feet-ten-inches. Her impromptu disguise had failed miserably. Instead of making her invisible, she now realized, it was more likely to attract the attention of people who would be understandably amazed to see such a tall Chinese woman. She looked at her watch. It was ten thirty. She jumped into the rickshaw.

"Take me back to the hotel, Kama," she said.

"OK, Bailey Foster," Kama said.

A couple minutes later, they pulled up to the entrance of Lhasa

Commercial Hotel. Bailey hopped out of the rickshaw and turned to Kama.

"Can you wait for me here? I'll be right back. I need you to take me to the palace. I'll pay you," she said. She stuck a hand into her pocket, then remembered she had not brought any money with her.

"When I come back down."

"OK, Bailey," Kama said. "No problem. I'll take you for free. It's just up the road."

Bailey raced back up to her room, tore off the black wig in a single motion and threw it on the floor. She unpinned her blonde hair and brushed it hurriedly, then washed the mascara out of her eyes. She was Bailey Foster again. She went to her purse and pulled out a wad of money.

When she got back downstairs, Kama was waiting patiently, listening to his ear buds and dancing on his bicycle seat. Bailey shoved a wad of bills into his shirt pocket and said, "Potala Palace, please."

Kama took the bills out of his pocket, looked at them and said, "This is too much." He took one bill and handed the rest back to Bailey. Bailey shoved the bills into her pocket.

"OK fine Kama. Just please get me to the palace! Hurry!"

Kama's strong legs carried them up Kang'angduo road. They pulled up to the main gate of the palace at five minutes before eleven. Bailey hopped out of the rickshaw.

"Thank you, Kama! You're a lifesaver!"

She gave him a kiss on the cheek and noticed him blush.

"Do you need me to pick you up?" he asked, touching the place she had kissed.

"No thanks, Kama, you've been helpful enough. Thank you!"

She hurried to the main gate to the palace and gave her ticket to a man standing next to a table holding an array of guide books and maps for sale. She considered buying one of each, but Tenzin hadn't mentioned them, so she let the urge pass. She'd already done enough ad-libbing, she thought.

She looked at the man who took her ticket and said, "When does the third tour begin?"

"Third tour?" the man said. He looked confused.

"Yes, the third tour," Bailey said. "Am I too late? Did I miss it?"

"No tour," the man said. "You can watch video about Potala

there."

He pointed toward a circular kiosk where several people were watching video screens. Then group of Chinese tourists came through the gate and the man turned away from Bailey to take their tickets.

"This is not going very well," Bailey thought. "First that stupid black wig, and now I'm supposed to go on a tour that doesn't exist! Why did Tenzin think there'd be a tour? Maybe there were tours once. But now what? If I just wander around the palace, how will whoever is supposed to help me get inside the stupas ever find me?"

Suddenly she was glad she'd taken off the disguise. There weren't many blondes visiting the palace, at least not that she could see. Most of the visitors appeared to be either pilgrims who had come to repeatedly prostrate themselves or Chinese tourists on vacation. As a blonde, she stuck out like, well, like a blonde in China. She decided to behave as normally as possible and see what happened. She wondered if she should have brought a camera.

She walked over to the kiosk and looked over the shoulders of a couple watching a video. It was in Chinese. They glanced back at her with an uncomfortable look that reminded her of the Chinese family who'd been upset with her for taking a picture of their son in the Beijing train station. She circled around to an unoccupied screen and touched a green button on it that read "English."

"Welcome to Potala Palace," a voice with a thick Chinese accent said as the slide show started.

"The palace is perched atop Marpo Ri Hill in the center of Lhasa. It is the primary destination of most visitors to Tibet. Visitors have never failed to be humbled by the amazing structure. Its simple but grand exterior hides the exquisite interiors, which are covered with beautiful frescos and priceless works of art.

"Potala Palace is the former residence of the Dalai Lama, Tenzin Gyatso. The huge structure was originally built in the year 637 for the new bride of Emperor Songtsän Gampo, the founder of the Tibetan Empire and the one who introduced Buddhism to the culture. As you can see, the impressive palace looks like an ancient fortress.

"Over the centuries, much of the structure was destroyed by war and earthquakes. The building you see before you today was mostly

built by the fifth Dalai Lama, Ngawang Lobsand Gyatso, whose remains rest inside the most magnificent of the eight stupas housed in the Red Palace. The White Palace at the bottom was completed in 1645. The upper Red Palace was finished in 1694. Potala Palace remained unchanged until 1922, when the Thirteenth Dalai Lama, Thubten Gyatso, renovated many chapels and assembly halls and added two stories to the Red Palace.

"The building measures four-hundred meters by three-hundred-fifty meters and has sloping stone walls up to five meters thick. Molten copper was poured into the foundation to protect it from earthquakes. The entire structure has thirteen stories and contains over one-thousand rooms and ten-thousand shrines."

Bailey looked around to see if anyone was looking at her. She saw no one. Determined to behave like a normal tourist, she turned her attention back toward the video presentation.

"The White Palace was the living quarters of the Dalai Lama. It was used for secular purposes and contained offices, the seminary, and a printing house. The Red Palace was devoted to religious study and prayer. It is easy to get lost in its labyrinth of halls, which are built on several different levels.

"The tombs of the Dalai Lamas can only be visited in the company of a monk or other official. The giant white stupa of the Thirteenth Dalai Lama contains one ton of solid gold and other valuables including ivory, porcelain and elaborate murals. Welcome again to Potala Palace. Enjoy your visit!"

When the video ended, Bailey continued into the palace. One-thousand rooms! How was anyone going to find her?

Even with most of the precious artifacts removed, the palace was as spectacular as the video had claimed. Every inch seemed to be covered with intricate artwork that looked almost psychedelic, like those Peter Max posters her mother used to like. Huge frescos that told of the history of Tibet covered massive plaster walls.

Like the outside of the palace, many of the architectural features inside – pillars, door jambs and railings – were clothed in colorful textiles. Some were dyed a solid color, but others were woven with geometric shapes like those she'd seen at Jokhang Temple. Colorful streamers hung everywhere, as did other dangling decorations of every shape and size. The interior designer must have smoked a ton of pot, Bailey thought, and it brought a smile to her face.

Displays of artifacts had been set up nearly everywhere. There were the sculptures of the Buddha and also several of the Dalai Lamas. A portrait of the thirteenth Dalai Lama was set in a gold frame. Golden deer and antelopes seemed to be a favorite of the Tibetans. So were colorful lions, which were furious and funny in the fashion of those paper parade dragons used during the celebration of the Chinese New Year. Perfectly balanced and lubricated prayer wheels, some of them still spinning from the hand of someone no longer there, lined several hallways and balconies.

After wandering up and down through the maze of halls and stairways for what seemed like an hour, Bailey wished she'd brought her smart phone. She also started to wish she'd eaten breakfast. She wondered if the palace had a snack bar, or maybe some vending machines, but she hadn't seen any.

She found herself standing in front of a huge wooden doorway that looked unlike any other she'd seen in the palace. It was covered with intricate carvings and knockers in the shapes of deer, antelopes and yaks. Colorful tassels hung from the heavy knockers. A long row of fierce lions with oversized teeth stood guard above the entire width of the wide doorway. Bailey tried the door. It was locked.

What was this room? She wasn't sure where she was, or where she should go next. Was this the Red Palace? The palace's one thousand rooms and thirteen levels were indeed arranged as if in a maze. Much of it was poorly lighted, usually by the natural sunlight that managed to shine through small imperfect windows that appeared to have been made by early glassmakers, sometimes by the occasional and incongruent lighting fixtures placed, she supposed, where people were apt to trip and fall.

"Lawyers!" she thought. "They've even infected China!"

She turned and leaned her back against the ornate doorway. She was alone, and heard no one else in her vicinity. It made her uncomfortable. Was she somewhere she should not be?

Just as she was about to leave, she felt the door open quickly behind her. The palm of a strong hand covered her mouth and pulled her into the room. She resisted the urge to scream.

The door closed and she was plunged into darkness. She heard the door lock. She was breathing fast.

"I advise you not to hyperventilate in Lhasa's thin air," a man's

voice whispered. "Apologies for alarming you."

"Was that really necessary?" Bailey said in an annoyed whisper.

Her assailant ignored her.

"What color was the wrapper on the cookie?" he said.

"Excuse me?" Bailey said.

Her eyes were starting to adjust to the darkness. She turned to look at the man. He towered maybe eight inches above her and was dressed in the brick red robe of a Tibetan monk.

"The cookie," he repeated. "What color was the wrapper?"

Bailey remembered the cookie the Dalai Lama had given to her at the Biltmore Hotel.

"Gold," she said. "It was wrapped in gold cellophane."

"Is that all?"

"No," Bailey said. "It had a red ribbon tied around it."

"What kind of cookie was it?"

"What is this, twenty questions?" Bailey teased.

"What kind?" the big monk insisted.

Bailey adopted her best Dalai Lama accent and said, "Oatmeal raisin. Organic! Vegan! Delicious!"

The monk reached for something on the wall next to the door and the room filled with soft light.

"Hello, Bailey Foster," he said. "Welcome to the Red Palace. In this room are the stupas of eight Dalai Lamas: Five, Seven, Eight, Nine, Ten, Eleven, Twelve, and Thirteen. We'll visit them in order."

He handed her a pair of small stainless steel scissors.

"Follow me," he said. "You must work quickly. I would have done this for you, but His Holiness insisted that you would want to do this for yourself."

Bailey smiled as the big lama led her to the first stupa, a magnificent one holding the fifth Dalai Lama.

"Inside each stupa you will see a plain wooden coffin. I have loosened the tops to make it easier for you. Lift the top, get your sample, replace the top and then return immediately."

"OK," Bailey said.

She entered the stupa. It was poorly lit, but she immediately saw the simple casket and pushed its lid aside. Why was the casket so plain when everything else was so ornate? Inside the coffin she saw a mummified body wrapped in a soft fabric except for the arms and

head, which were exposed just as the Dalai Lama had said they would be. Steeling herself against the gruesome sight, she snipped a small piece of leathery skin from the head, placed it into the amulet in the compartment numbered 5, and snapped it shut. Then she replaced the coffin's lid and walked out of the stupa.

"Done!" she whispered.

The big monk led her to the stupa of the seventh Dalai Lama. Inside, she discovered that she couldn't snip a sample of skin from the head because it had dried too completely and so was stretched tightly over the skull. She moved around to the side of the coffin and used the sharp little scissors to cut off a tiny piece of leathery skin from the long-dead lama's left elbow. She snapped open the amulet and placed the bit of mummified skin into the compartment numbered 7.

Bailey continued from stupa to stupa until she had reached the thirteenth Dalai Lama. Just as she was about to snip a bit of skin from the shriveled skull, she heard an insistent and loud knock on the big door outside. She quietly replaced the lid to the casket and hid behind it. She felt her heart pounding. Had she not worked fast enough?

She heard the big door outside open. Several people entered the room. They spoke in Chinese. She didn't understand what was being said, but it was clear they were not happy about the monk being inside the sacred room. The monk's voice sounded calm and serene. It reminded her of Thipor Dulip's voice. Then the talking stopped and the room fell completely silent. Bailey tried to control her excited breathing so it would not be heard in the extraordinarily quiet room. Then she saw the beam of a flashlight enter the stupa where she was hiding. She heard footsteps enter the stupa and saw the flashlight beam scanning the inside.

She closed her eyes and prayed silently, "Please God. Please don't let them find me."

The man who had entered the stupa where she was hiding called out to the others. Bailey held her breath. Had he seen her? One of the others called back to him. The flashlight made three or four more passes around the room and then was gone. A few seconds later, she heard the large door close. Then it was quiet for several minutes. Finally, a whisper came from the entrance of the stupa. It said, "Hurry Bailey Foster!"

Assuming it was the monk, she rose out of her crouch, pushed the coffin lid aside and snipped a piece of skin from the thirteenth Dalai Lama's skull. She pushed it into the last tiny compartment inside the amulet and went outside.

"OK, done!" Bailey said.

She looked up to find a monk standing outside the stupa, but it was not the one who had been there before.

"Who are you?" Bailey Foster said.

"They removed my friend away," the monk said, his voice urgent and dire. "I am to take his place."

The monk hurried to a corner of the room and returned with a small soldering iron of some kind. "Give me the amulet," he said.

Bailey obeyed.

The new monk put the amulet on the flat surface of a wide wooden railing and started to seal it carefully shut with the glowing tip of the iron. The monk applied the tip of the hot iron to the edge of the amulet's cover until it glowed orange. Then he blew on it until it cooled. He patiently repeated the process on each spot around the entire circumference of the amulet. Bailey thought he would never finish. She feared the Chinese would return.

Recognizing Bailey's distress with a single glance, the new monk returned to his work and said, "I'm sorry this is taking some time. I must not damage the contents, but I must make the seal strong. To discourage thieves. There are many thieves in China. Sometimes they steal entire countries."

When he was done, he kept blowing at the amulet until it was cool to the touch and then handed it back to Bailey. Bailey returned it to around her neck and wondered how all that blowing hadn't made the monk pass out.

"I will leave first," he said. "If you hear a single knock on the door, come quickly. If you do not hear a knock, hide!"

The new monk stepped outside and closed the door behind him. Bailey waited for what felt like several minutes. There was no knock. She pressed her ear to the thick wooden door, but heard nothing over her own heartbeat. Had she misunderstood? Had he said to hide if there was a knock or if there was no knock? She decided the safest thing to do was to hide. She looked around and decided to return to her hiding place behind the thirteenth Dalai Lama's coffin.

She stayed crouched behind the coffin for more than an hour. Her legs were cramping from squatting for so long. Twice, she dared to stand up, to give her poor legs a rest, but then quickly returned to a crouch.

Finally, she heard the door open and saw the lights go out. It was pitch black inside the stupa. Again, she tried not to breathe, but it was difficult in the thin air. Some time later, the door opened again and the lights came back on. Then she heard the voice whisper from the opening of the stupa, "Come Bailey Foster! Come with me!"

She emerged from behind the casket. Her knees felt like they would break. When she got outside, she found yet another monk.

"I will complete our mission," he said.

The third monk grabbed Bailey by the hand and hurriedly pulled her out of the room, then shut the door quickly behind them. Then he released her hand and began strolling casually and talking to her as calmly as if he were giving a tour.

"Compassion is to provide food to those without food," he said as he led her along. "It is to provide clothes to those without clothes. It is to be kind to all beings as if they were your own children, to keep focused on the betterment of others and not to think about one's own pleasure or one's own comfort."

They entered a narrow stairway, leading down.

"The steps are uneven," he told her. "Use the handrail."

Then he continued his lecture.

"As we focus on others and not on ourselves, our mind gets stronger and stronger and in time we develop a powerful motherly compassion. We meditate on our compassion to develop an enlightened mind."

They reached the end of the stairway and continued on down a hallway lined with golden Mani Wheels, some of them still spinning from hands long since gone. Their pace remained casual, as though they were in no danger at all, like lovers walking blissfully beside a lake, aware of no one in the world but themselves. Bailey suppressed the urge to break into a run, or a least a brisk walk. The monk continued talking passively, giving no clue of their shared subterfuge.

"Many who come to Potala Palace are here for dharma. In Buddhism, dharma means helping other sentient beings. It means

to help others and free one's self from the three poisons. The first poison is attachment, or desire. The second poison is ignorance. The third, and the worst, is hatred. These are the poisons that control all of us. They produce fighting and killing of other beings, and hatred towards them. When others are being hurt, that is not Buddhist dharma."

They'd been walking for maybe fifteen minutes when they passed through a small doorway. Bailey saw that they were downstairs, in the White Palace. She could see the main gate and started toward it. The third monk stopped her, looked around casually to make sure he could not be heard, and then said, "Enlightenment is something you can't see with your eyes or feel with your hands, Bailey Foster. It is something we can only understand through practice."

Then the third monk removed a simple white scarf from around his neck and placed it around hers. He touched his forehead to hers. She could smell his breath. It had a pleasant earthy odor without being artificial or minty.

"Good luck, Bailey Foster," he said. "May the Buddha's wisdom soften your path and protect your every step."

Then he turned and was gone.

Bailey left Potala Palace. Her heart was racing with excitement. She struggled to walk as casually as she could back to the Lhasa Commercial Hotel. Once there, she immediately went to her room. She changed clothes, shoved the amulet into a pocket and went downstairs to eat. It was six o'clock. She was famished.

After dinner, she returned to her room. She had to get to bed early. The train back to Beijing left at eight the next morning.

17
TOO LUCRATIVE TO CURE

The day after taking Jane Whitmire to Morton's, Max did some preliminary research on Bayner Genetics. He learned that it had been started by the current owner's parents, who'd handed it over to their daughter a year or two before each of them had died of Huntington's disease. He confirmed that the daughter's name was Gwendolyn and saw that she had filed for divorce eleven years earlier, in the year 2000. (Unfortunately, the details of the settlement were sealed and her ex-husband refused to talk.) He also learned that Bayner was housed in a building on the beach. Property tax records showed that the property was assessed at twenty-four-million dollars, which meant it was probably worth a million or two more than that. The company's website said it focused on finding cures for exceptionally rare diseases, confirming what Clinton had said. Also on the website was a press release that announced the anti-cavity project.

Just after noon, Max drove over to the Bayner Genetics building to have a look. It was a non-descript glass-and-steel structure sitting on a plot of land that looked to be about eight acres, or twelve, if you counted the beach. The cars in the parking lot were mostly late-model imports. About twenty parking spaces near the front entrance were covered with a canvas awning. Below the awning, in the space nearest the front entrance, he saw a gleaming Bentley and next to it a small table where a black man was sitting on a folding chair, eating his lunch. He was wearing what could have been a chauffeur's uniform, the jacket slung over the back of the chair and

the cap on a corner of the table. Max pulled up next to him and got out of his car.

"Beautiful car," he said. "What is it?"

"Who's askin'?"

"Just a car lover," Max said. He started to walk around the impressive automobile. "You the chauffeur?"

The man looked at Max's four-year-old Toyota Celica with suspicion, but he was more than happy to chat. Most of his job entailed waiting around in the heat for his boss to order him to take her somewhere, usually just home or, on Fridays, to a fancy restaurant he'd never been to. Both the home and the restaurant were less than ten minutes away.

"What else would I be? If you wanna know, it's a Bentley. A Continental Flying Spur. Don't get too close. The owner raises hell when she sees fingerprints."

"I can imagine. The damn thing must be worth a couple hundred thou."

"I suppose. I don't much think about that, though. I don't expect I'll be making that much money in my whole life."

The chauffeur, a smallish man with close-cut graying hair and a pencil-thin moustache, stuffed the trash from his lunch into the brown paper bag he'd apparently brought it in, rose from his chair, and pushed the bag through the swinging door of a nearby trash receptacle. Then he took a chamois cloth from his back pocket and circled the car, checking for spots to buff out.

"All I know is, it drives like a dream, a magic carpet. You never drove a car so smooth. Only gets about five miles a gallon, though. Twelve cylinders, you know."

"The rich are different from you and me, my friend," Max said. "Very different."

"Uh huh."

"You know much about what goes on inside?"

"Under the hood? I told you. Twelve cylinders."

"No, inside the building there."

"They make pills is all I know. They're all smarter than I am. I'm a simple man, as you can see. I just drive here and drive there."

"I heard they're working on some kind of pill to prevent cavities. You know, tooth decay."

"I wouldn't know nothing about that. As I said, I just drive the

car."

"You must hear the owner talking on her cell phone now and then."

The chauffeur looked Max in the eye.

"And I'd be a damned fool to go jawing to you about it, now wouldn't I? I don't know you from Adam, sir. Why're you asking all these questions anyway? You some kind of spy?"

Max laughed. "Me? No way. I'm a simple man like you, just out for an afternoon drive after lunch. I'm an insurance agent."

"An insurance man, huh? Only people I hate worse is attorneys."

Max knew when he'd had a door slammed in his face. He looked at his watch and said, "Oops! I gotta get back to work. Nice talking with you."

"Uh huh."

Max got into his Toyota and drove off.

"Well, it was a good try, anyway," he thought. Sometimes chauffeurs know a lot about what's going on, like secretaries and janitors. Luckily, there was more than one way to skin an extortionist.

Later that night, after midnight, he drove by the Bayner Genetics building again and found only one car in the parking lot, a blue Toyota Prius. There was a light on the third floor, but there didn't appear to be any security in the parking lot. He parked his car and took a casual stroll around the sidewalk that circled the building. The property was landscaped immaculately. In the back there were three gazebos where he guessed the employees sometimes ate lunch or took smoke breaks. The dumpster was tucked in the northeast corner.

He made his way back to his Toyota, pulled it up to the dumpster, then popped the trunk. He flipped open the dumpster's lid. It was surprisingly heavy and made a loud bang as it crashed into the back wall of the concrete slot into which the dumpster had been placed.

"Shit!" he muttered.

He looked around. Seeing no one, he took a small step stool out of his trunk, set it beside the dumpster, and looked inside. There were several plastic bags, all neatly closed with twist ties.

"Nice and clean," he said to himself.

He'd dug around in strip mall dumpsters in his early days, garbage bins shared by several businesses, including restaurants whose foul-smelling bags of garbage, even if originally tied tight, were later ripped open by hungry rats and clever raccoons. This dumpster contained small white bags that appeared to be mostly full of shredded paper and large black bags like the one into which the chauffeur had deposited his lunch trash.

He looked around again, again saw no one, then climbed into the exceptionally clean dumpster. He started grabbing white bags and tossing them into the open trunk of his car. Then he climbed out of the dumpster, closed the lid – careful this time not to let it slam – and pushed his trunk stealthily shut. As he was about to slip back into the driver's seat, he looked up at the third floor, the one that was lit, and saw someone standing at the window. They'd probably seen him, but there was nothing he could do about that now. He jumped into his car and drove quickly away.

Once home, he carried the garbage bags onto his back porch and went to bed.

The next morning, he spent several hours digging through the bags. All of the documents in the bags had been shredded into strips no wider than a single character of type, about an eighth of an inch wide. All of the shreds were eleven-and-a-half inches long, which meant that the documents hadn't been folded before being shredded, which was good. They were also perfectly clean. No garbage had been mixed in with them. Moreover, the likelihood was that the shreds had been tossed into the bags straight from the shredders, so that a single garbage bag most likely held entire documents, albeit sliced into spaghetti-like strands. People thought if they shredded something no one would ever be able to read it. Of course, people were not only often as loony as tunes, they were also often wrong about things they were sure of.

A couple of years earlier, Max had been hired by a woman to investigate whether her husband was having an affair with his secretary. The man and his secretary were very discreet, and so Max was never able to snap a photo of them together. Fortunately, they had a bad habit of slipping love letters to one another at work, letters that talked in no uncertain terms about what they planned to do to one another once they were in a private motel room. The

man thought he was being clever by shredding the letters, but he always dumped the shreds in the same garbage bag together – one that held nothing but shredded documents. On a whim, Max went dumpster diving at the guy's office, found the shredded documents and – much to the adulterer's amazement – was able to reconstruct them.

Max worked this magic by hiring a local high-school kid to write computer software that inspected scanned images of the shreds and reassembled the thin strips back into full documents. The kid was a fucking genius. Even if the program took some time to run – days, in fact, depending on the number of scanned images it needed to reassemble – it worked like a charm.

Bayner Genetics shredded a lot more documents than the cheating husband, but with enough patience and perseverance, Max thought the job could be done. There was a lot of pasting and scanning to be done, though, so he decided to call the kid and ask him if he wanted to make a little extra money.

"David Epstein," the kid answered.

"David, this is Max Dubois. Remember me?"

"Hey, Mr. Dubois. How's the gumshoe biz?"

David Epstein was one of a very few people who pronounced Dubois correctly. It was one of the things Max liked best about him.

"Good. Really good. That's why I'm calling. I've got a few bags of shredded docs that I need someone to paste and scan so I can feed it into your software. You want to make a little extra money?"

"You bet!"

"I can pay you five bucks for every page you scan, and if your software helps me find what I'm looking for, there's a thousand-dollar bonus in it for you."

"No shit?"

"No shit."

"Excellent!"

"There's one hitch," Max said. "I need it done quickly, by the end of the week."

"No problemo, Max. I can get my friends to help. Can you bring the bags to my house later tonight? I'm in the middle of mowing a lawn right now."

"Sure," Max said, impressed with the kid's work ethic. "Give me

the address."

David Epstein gave Max his home address. Max dropped off the bags of shreds later that night.

A few days later, on a Sunday afternoon, he got a call from David.

"Mr. Dubois, I've got all the documents pasted and scanned. There's three-hundred-two of them. That's fifteen-hundred and ten bucks. You sure you want to pay me that much?"

"A deal's a deal," Max said, thinking it was a small price to pay. "And don't forget, if I find what I'm looking for, you get another grand."

"Cool beans!" David Epstein said. "I'll bring the disc over right away."

"I'm making the check out as we speak," Max said.

David Epstein threw the disc containing the scanned shreds into his backpack and pedaled his bicycle to Max Dubois' house as fast as he could.

"Fifteen-hundred clams!" he thought.

He'd had two friends help him do the pasting, but they'd only done fifty pages each before getting bored, and David had offered to pay them only a dollar per page. That was only a hundred bucks, so even after paying them he'd have more than fourteen-hundred dollars – and possibly another grand on top of that if Mr. Dubois found whatever it was he was looking for.

David was ringing Max's doorbell within ten minutes.

Max opened the door.

"Here's the disc," David said.

"Here's your check," Max said.

David took the check, folded it in half, stuffed it into his pocket and said, "Let me know if you need any more done."

"I will, David, and I might. So stay tuned."

"Thanks Mr. Dubois!" David said. He got back on his bike and pedaled away.

Max took the disc and loaded it into his computer, then fed the images on it into David Epstein's software. It would likely take several days to finish, so he let it run.

A few days later, he checked the computer and found that one-hundred-seventy-two pages had been reassembled. Some of them

appeared to be software code of some kind, which made no sense to him at all and would be useless in any case, since there was precious little in-code documentation. Luckily, there were also meeting minutes at which each of the research directors at Bayner Genetics gave progress reports. The last of these, which came after the announcement of the tooth-decay pill, had no mention of the project at all.

"Bingo!" Max said aloud, although there was no one there to hear him. "David Epstein, you are fucking genius."

He called Wallace Clinton immediately and got his answering machine.

"You've reached the office of Wallace Clinton. Please leave a message."

"Mr. Clinton. Max Dubois here. I have possession of the minutes from a recent meeting of the research directors at Bayner Genetics – one that took place after the tooth-decay announcement. Your suspicions appear to be correct. There is no mention of the project."

At precisely eight o'clock Monday morning, Max got a call from Wallace Clinton.

"Email me a copy of the minutes," he said.

"To be precise, I can't send you an actual copy. I can only give you a copy I reassembled from shredded documents."

"That's a hell of a jigsaw puzzle, Mr. Dubois. How did you manage that?"

"Trade secret, Mr. Clinton. What's your email address? I'll send the document to you immediately."

Armed with Max's reconstructed meeting minutes, Wallace Clinton decided to visit Gwendolyn Bayner personally. He wanted to be able to look her in the eye when he sprang the document on her. He called to make an appointment.

"Bayner Genetics," the receptionist said.

"Gwendolyn Bayner, please."

"Please hold."

"Bayner Genetics, office of the president. How may we help you today?"

"My name is Wallace Clinton. I am a vice president at Jones Industries. I'd like to schedule a meeting with Ms. Bayner regarding the tooth-decay project."

"Please hold, Mr. Clinton."

A few seconds later, Gwendolyn came on the line.

"Mr. Clinton, Gwendolyn Bayner here. How nice of you to call. Have you decided to accept our offer?"

"Perhaps, Ms. Bayner. But there are a few details I need to discuss with you in person before a final decision is made. Can we set up a meeting?"

"Most certainly, Mr. Clinton. I'll give you back to my secretary."

"Fine."

Gwendolyn put the call on hold and called out the door to her secretary. "Move whatever you need to move to make this happen as soon as possible," she told her secretary. "Tell him I'll take him to lunch."

The meeting was scheduled for two days later, a Wednesday, to give Clinton time to fly in from the company headquarters in Dallas. He showed up at noon and strolled into Gwendolyn's office wearing a business suit accented with a ten-gallon hat and expensive cowboy boots that had never seen dirt, no less a stirrup. When Gwendolyn saw he was taken aback by the stuffed alligator, she laughed and said, "I assure you he's quite dead, Mr. Clinton. You ready for lunch?"

"Whenever you are," Wallace Clinton said, not taking his eyes off the alligator.

Gwendolyn called out the door, "Charlene, please call down to Charlie and tell him we're going to Chez Paris."

"That's quite a specimen you have there, Ms. Bayner. I hope it doesn't say anything about how you treat your business partners."

"It's a gift from a grateful customer, Mr. Clinton. I couldn't turn it down without hurting the poor man's feelings."

"Of course not."

The two strolled downstairs, climbed into the back seat of the Bentley and chatted on the way to Chez Paris.

"Beautiful office location," Clinton said. "Right on the beach. Rather extravagant."

"We're a small company, Mr. Clinton. I like to keep my employees happy. Many of them are sun worshipers, and those who aren't enjoy the sea breeze. It's significantly cooler here than it is inland, and the bugs aren't as bad."

"That's very thoughtful of you."

"We think so."

"Speaking of thoughtful, I also understand that you concentrate on very rare diseases that other companies shy away from. How do you manage it?"

"Despite what you may assume, we're a thrifty company. We're small and nimble and do not fritter away money on private jets and expensive executive junkets as some of our larger competitors do. We also do no advertising. Our customers already know who we are. This car is one of my sole extravagances, and I consider it mostly an investment."

The chauffeur, hearing this, thought of the other four Bentleys, but of course said nothing.

"Quite wise of you," Clinton said, although he had utilized one of his company's five corporate jets to fly in the night before.

"Ah! We're here," Gwendolyn said as the car pulled in.

The two got out of the Bentley and took an elevator up to Chez Paris. They were seated immediately on the ocean side and given menus.

"Nice view," Clinton said. "Shall we get down to business?"

"I usually like to wait until after I've eaten," Gwendolyn said. "But if you insist."

Clinton considered how Gwendolyn would react to the accusation that she was trying to extort his company and said, "Maybe you're right. Let's eat first."

As if on cue, a waiter appeared.

"Good afternoon, Ms. Bayner, Sir. May I take your orders?"

Gwendolyn ordered a Cobb salad and an iced tea. Clinton ordered a club sandwich.

"Iced tea is fine for me as well," he said.

The waiter took their menus and left.

"I understand both of your parents have passed on," Clinton said.

"Yes. Huntington's disease. It's neurological, a dreadful way to go. Like being hit by a bus in slow motion. Sadly, because both of them carried the gene, I had a seventy-five-percent chance of contracting it myself, which tests back in ninety-three say I did. I'm happy to say that my daughter does not have it, however. That's the one bright spot in my life."

"I understand Huntington's is quite rare."

"Yes. That's the main reason my parents started Bayner Genetics. They realized that there were damn few companies pursuing a cure because there just wasn't enough money in it. It continues to be the reason I have focused our research primarily on curing diseases too rare for anyone else to care about. I have a natural empathy for people with such diseases, as you might imagine."

"How does an anti-tooth-decay drug fit into that philosophy?"

"Oh, Mr. Clinton! I thought you wanted to wait until after lunch to get down to business!"

"Quite right, Ms. Bayner. My apologies."

"None are necessary, Mr. Clinton."

Just then, the food came.

As they began eating, Gwendolyn said, "I've told you much about myself, Mr. Clinton, but I'm afraid I know next to nothing about you."

"There's not much to tell, really. I've had a rather typical career. MBA from Harvard…"

"My parents went to Harvard Medical, you know. I myself was a music major at the University of Florida. Not exactly Juilliard, but it was good enough for me."

"Yes, well, after I graduated from Harvard, I went to work for DOW Chemical as a middle manager in Indonesia and then was offered a position at Jones' headquarters in Dallas. I'd been hankering to get back to the states, so I jumped at the chance. I've been there ever since. It's quite a large company, as you know, with a wide diversity of affiliated sister companies. They've been very good to me."

"And I'm sure you've been very good for them as well."

"I suppose so."

"Any children?"

"Yes. I have a lovely wife and two children, a boy and a girl, six and eight."

"I think some people call that a millionaire's dream, Mr. Clinton. You're a lucky man."

Gwendolyn ate her fill of Cobb salad and saw that the club sandwich was gone.

"It appears that it's time to get down to business," she said.

"Yes."

"You asked me how the tooth-decay drug fit into our corporate philosophy."

"Yes."

"It's quite simple, really. Like any other business, we need to maintain enough revenue to meet payroll and keep the lights on. Otherwise, it won't matter how altruistic we are. We know our research into rare diseases is a loser right out of the box, so we are constantly on the lookout for other things that will have relatively low R & D costs and, therefore, are sure to reap profits we can then use to balance things out, to finance the unprofitable projects we deem worthwhile even if they're not big moneymakers."

"Have you actually taken any of these products to market?" Clinton asked.

"Well, actually, no," Gwendolyn said, taking a sip of iced tea.

Clinton felt a surge of confidence. He felt as though he was playing a game of chess with the woman, and imagined his knights and bishops pushing her king into a corner where she'd have to admit to the extortion he was so sure she was committing.

Gwendolyn detected the subtle smirk on his face and continued.

"As it has happened, each time we've announced our plans for ancillary products, there have been corporations such as yours who have recognized that they would be unfortunately harmed by them. We have no interest in harming anyone. Our business is healing. But we have to survive, of course. We worked hard to reach mutually beneficial agreements with the companies who felt threatened – agreements that have allowed them to continue to thrive and have allowed us to continue our important work. Personally, I consider them partners in our altruistic mission. I have offered to give them due credit publicly, but all of them have graciously declined. Apparently, being good corporate citizens was enough for them."

"I see," Clinton said. He felt like he'd just been ensnared by a clever gambit he'd been too stupid, or too cocksure, to see.

"You seem like a nice man, Mr. Clinton, and I want to make it absolutely clear that if your company feels it is not in its best interest to join our little family, there will be no hard feelings. It's business. I understand business. We will be more than happy to pursue the anti-cavity project. My researchers, who discovered the possibility of the drug while doing other work, tell me we're about

eighty percent of the way there. Everyone hates getting their teeth drilled, so I expect the drug will reap much more than the amount we would to receive in any settlement with you and the others. Still, I'd rather have my people working on diseases. Therefore, I'm willing to be reasonable, and I do think that it would be in your best interest to join us. Don't forget that you would be helping a great many sick people who would be otherwise totally neglected. Also, be aware that there's no telling if one of your own family or a close friend might come down with one of the awful maladies that only we are fighting against."

Clinton was twice as taken aback as he'd been by the stuffed alligator in Gwendolyn's office. He had expected the woman to be less forthcoming about the products he considered extortive, to be more evasive and secretive. Could she actually be telling the truth? He struggled to find a reason not to believe her, but came up empty.

"As long as we're apparently being honest and open, Ms. Bayner…"

"Please, call me Gwen."

"OK, Gwen. As long as we're being honest, I must tell you that I came here expecting to confront you with this."

He dug into the pocket inside his suit coat, pulled out the minutes Max Dubois had emailed to him, and slid them across the table.

Gwendolyn immediately recognized the minutes and said, "Where on earth did you get this? It's our policy to shred all corporate documents. I fear I may have a spy in my company!"

"Rest assured that you have nothing of the sort, Gwen. We hired a private investigator to look into your anti-cavity program, to determine if it was real. We had our doubts, naturally. He's quite a talented investigator, you see, and was able to reconstruct the document from the shredded bits. Don't ask me how. He wouldn't tell me. But when I saw no mention of the program in these minutes, I assumed that the anti-cavity program was not real and came here intending to accuse you of extortion. I intended to threaten to go to the FBI unless you backed off."

"Extortion! Why, Mr. Clinton! I assure you that Bayner Genetics would never be involved in any such skullduggery! We have not discussed the anti-cavity project simply because of our respect for

your company and the others the project would necessarily harm. As I said, we have no interest in harming you or any other company. We'd much rather have you join us in our charitable endeavors. That's why the anti-cavity project doesn't appear in these minutes, and that's the only reason."

Gwendolyn took a sip of iced tea and continued.

"Now that you mention it, Mr. Clinton, one of my employees – a particularly hardworking woman who has been burning the midnight oil on a special project of mine – told me last week that she saw someone taking bags of trash out of our dumpster well after midnight. I checked into it with the police. As it turns out, even though it's garbage, it is nonetheless illegal to trespass onto our property in order to take it. You should let your devious investigator know that we have ordered security cameras installed in order to prosecute future intrusions. As for you, Mr. Clinton, I am surprised that someone willing to engage in corporate espionage would have the temerity to accuse me of extortion. Shame on you!"

Wallace Clinton felt like he was a boy being scolded.

"Under the circumstances, Gwen. I am ashamed for having suspected you of such a thing. You're obviously not that sort of a woman. You have my word that I will report back to my company that I think it would be a fine gesture of corporate citizenship to help your company continue its fine work."

Gwendolyn held out her hand and Clinton shook it.

"That is certainly good to hear, Mr. Clinton. I'm sure you'll be able to convince your company that it is in the best interest of everyone concerned, especially the woefully sick people we're trying so hard to help."

Wallace Clinton returned to Dallas that night and the next morning convinced the corporation's board of directors to cooperate with Bayner Genetics.

"It's quite selfless work they're doing," he said.

Seven of the twelve board members voted to make the payment, which they noted could be written off as a charitable donation.

The five others accused Wallace Clinton of being gullible.

18
ZHENBANG IN BEIJING

The Qinghai-Tibet Railway ride back to the Chinese capitol was as spectacular as the ride to Lhasa had been, and just as uneventful. After disembarking from the modern train, Bailey easily found the shuttle that ran from Beijing West station to the Beijing International Airport. Once there, she was thrilled to find that there was a vacancy at the airport Hilton. Her China Air flight to Los Angeles did not leave until the next morning, and she was happy she didn't have to spend another night sleeping on the depot floor, however clean it might be.

She checked in, went to her room, and called room service for dinner – a spicy Hunan dish called Dong'an chicken, simple stir-fried vegetables and tea. The woman on the phone said the meal would take an hour to arrive, so Bailey hopped into the shower for the first time in days (she'd been advised to limit her bathing in the dry Lhasa air) and luxuriated in the hot water. Once out of the shower, she brushed her hair, left it wet, and slipped into a pair of cozy cotton pajamas.

When the food arrived, she arranged the meal on a small table and turned on the television. A Chinese Central Television newswoman named Luli Tan was broadcasting news from China in English. She looked Chinese, but sounded like she was from America, maybe California. Her first story was about two coal mine disasters said to be caused by heavy rain. (No mention was made of the central government's three-year-old promise to make the mines

safer.)

"Rescuers are racing against time to save forty workers trapped underground in two coal mine disasters in southwest China," the pretty Ms. Tan read as hardworking firefighters and paramedics dressed in fluorescent orange and green appeared on the screen.

"Workers at Guizhou Province's Niupeng coal mine are trying to release water before sending rescuers into the flooded pit," the newswoman continued. "The flood occurred on Saturday morning when twenty-nine miners were working at the shafts. Eight workers managed to escape to safety.

"In a separate mining disaster, three people were killed while nineteen others remain trapped after part of a coal mine in the Guangxi Zhuang Autonomous Region collapsed. Rescuers say it is difficult to reach the miners, who are trapped almost four-hundred meters underground. Days of heavy rain were blamed for the cave-in. This is Luli Tan, reporting for CCTV News."

"Sounds like coal mining in China is not so different from coal mining in America, Luli," Bailey said to the TV.

The next story was about the millions of young Chinese who had recently joined the Communist Party of China, a political juggernaut that had outgrown its name and now boasted eighty-million members, which was to say eighty-million people who vowed to support the power structure and reap the concomitant benefits of conformity.

Then Bailey heard about how party employers were humanely attentive to the health needs of their workers. Another story praised the party for implementing the socialist market economy that had transformed China into the second largest economy in the world and raised hundreds of millions of people out of poverty in three scant decades.

"Millions more where they came from," Bailey said.

As Ms. Tan's broadcast continued, Bailey heard a knock at the door. She froze and listened. She heard nothing over the sound of the television. She tiptoed to the door and looked through the peephole. Peering through it, she saw a well-groomed Chinese man in a business suit. He was waiting patiently.

Who was this? A salesman? Someone from the hotel? Whoever it was, she prayed he would give up and go away. Maybe he would figure she was sound asleep, or perhaps not there at all, gone to

take a walk or have a few drinks downstairs.

The knock came again, this time louder. Bang! Bang! Bang! Was he using a nightstick?

Whoever this man is, she thought, *he probably hears the television. Or maybe he even noticed that room service was just here. Maybe he even smells the food.*

She ran to the phone, picked it up and punched the button labeled "security."

"Jiǔdiàn bǎo'ān," a man's voice said. "Hotel Security."

"There's a man at my door. I don't know who it is," Bailey said. "I'm frightened."

"We'll send security right up, Ms. Foster."

"Thank you," Bailey said.

She hung up the phone and returned to the peephole.

"Who is there?" she asked. "I am expecting no visitors. I have called security. They're on their way!"

The man was smiling and unfazed.

"Hello, Bailey Foster! How unfriendly of you to call the hotel security! I am Zhenbang Zhao, minister of the Ministry of Science and Technology of the People's Republic of China. Please. Open the door."

"Do you have identification?" Bailey asked.

A smiling Zhenbang Zhao stood in front of the peephole and held his photo ID under his chin so she could compare the photo to his face. It looked like the same man.

"How do I know you're not using a fake ID?" Bailey said.

The man returned his wallet to his coat pocket, then said, "You are Bailey Foster of Bayner Genetics in Boca Raton, Florida, United States. You wrote a letter to me several months ago asking for permission to extract DNA samples from the eight Dalai Lamas at Potala Palace in Lhasa. You said computer software you had written had discovered what seems to be a unique, non-contiguous sequence of base pairs in DNA, spread across all twenty-three chromosomes. You said you were a student of Buddhism and that you theorized the sequence might be related to the soul or spirit. You said you knew how to extract DNA even from cremated ashes. You said you were willing to pay. I wrote back to you explaining that we could not help you because what you were doing seemed like religion, not science."

Zhenbang Zhao paused and smiled into the peephole.

"Is that enough, Bailey Foster?" he said.

Bailey was convinced.

"What do you want?"

"I simply want to talk to you, Bailey Foster," Zhenbang Zhao said. "Please. Open the door."

"What do you want to talk about?"

Just then, a hotel security guard arrived. Through the peephole, Bailey saw him chatting politely with Zhenbang Zhao. Then the security guard looked into the peephole and said, "He is Zhenbang Zhao, Ms. Foster. He is an influential member of the party. You must open the door. I assure you there is no danger."

Bailey thought it would be unwise to arouse Zhenbang Zhao's suspicion any further.

"OK," she said. "Let me go throw on a robe."

She had noticed a white terrycloth Hilton robe hanging in the bathroom. She went to get it and slipped it on over her pajamas. Then she returned to the door, unlocked it and began to swing it open.

Suddenly, two huge men Bailey hadn't seen through the peephole pushed the door open violently. The edge of it barely missed hitting her in the face. Terrified, she fled into the room. Luli Tan was talking about a visit to the Beijing Zoo.

"I thought you said you just wanted to talk!" she complained. She was short of breath.

Zhenbang Zhao ignored her. Bailey looked for the security guard, but he was gone. Behind Zhenbang Zhao she saw the two large men who had forced open the door. They looked to weigh at least three-hundred pounds each. They wore all black, like the Dalai Lama's protectors at the Biltmore, but Bailey knew that these big men were different. They were not there to protect anyone.

"Ah! Smells good!" Zhenbang Zhao said. He walked to the table where Bailey had been eating. "Dong'an chicken? My favorite dish!"

He ran his finger through some of the sauce on the plate and tasted it. Then Zhenbang Zhao noticed Luli Tan reading the news on the TV.

"This is bullshit, Bailey Foster," he said. He grabbed the remote control that was next to Bailey's dinner plate and clicked it off. "As

a scientist, you should know better than to listen to propaganda."

Zhenbang Zhao turned to his two goons and said something in Chinese. One of them picked up Bailey's purse, dumped it out on the bed and started picking through its contents. The other one moved toward her. He grabbed her by the arms and pinned her face-first against the wall. The wallpaper was rough. She could feel it making an impression on her face.

She shivered as the big man's hands roamed her body. It was not a polite pat down. His strong hands started with her hair, then poked about inside her ears and her nose. Then the man grabbed her face with one huge hand and pressed on her cheeks with his thumb and ring finger in order to force her mouth open. He stuck a thick finger into her mouth to explore inside it. Bailey bit down hard. The man howled, removed his finger, and struck her in the face hard with the back of his other hand.

"Oh!" Zhenbang Zhao crowed. "You should not have done that, Bailey Foster! You do not want to make that man angry! He is always thorough, but he is less gentle when he is angry."

Bailey felt like she'd been hit in the head with a two-by-four. She fell to the floor and started to scream, but fear gripped her throat and allowed only a whimper. The big man followed her to the floor and sat on her, pinning her down. She thought his weight would crack her ribs. He opened the white Hilton robe and checked under her armpits and breasts. Then Bailey felt a thick finger exploring her labia.

"Hey!" she protested. She tried to squirm away, but the big man pushed her face hard against the carpet and said something in Chinese to Zhenbang Zhao, who laughed.

Bailey thought of Suze's abusive father. She began to cry.

"No worries, Bailey Foster!" Zhenbang Zhao said. "He is a professional! Very thorough!"

Bailey felt a fat finger enter her rectum.

"Why are you doing this to me!" she wailed.

Finally, the man was done. He shrugged at Zhenbang Zhao, said something in Chinese, and lifted his weight off of her. She crawled to a corner of the room and gathered the Hilton robe around her trembling body.

The big goon who'd just molested her disappeared into the bathroom, Bailey assumed to wash his finger.

"He tells me he remembers when his wife was as young as you, Bailey Foster," Zhenbang Zhao said. "He also assures me you are hiding nothing."

"I could have told you that," Bailey said through her tears.

"Ah, but we are scientists. We had to make sure ourselves. I'm sure you understand."

After a few minutes, the big man who had assaulted Bailey returned from the bathroom and joined his partner at the bed. They began digging into her suitcases, tossing her things aimlessly around the room once they were convinced they did not contain the item they sought. Zhenbang Zhao turned to Bailey as they worked.

"I am sure you will not be surprised to learn that we have been following you since you arrived in China," he said. "You are not dealing with fools, Bailey Foster. We know you took the train to Lhasa. It is a great engineering achievement, is it not? You have nothing like that in America, I am sorry to say. What has happened to the great America? It is a sad story of imperialism, often repeated throughout history. China itself was great long ago, then lost its way. I fear that is happening to your America. Your greed is getting the better of you."

Zhenbang Zhao took a bite of Bailey's Dong'an chicken and returned to his main thought as he chewed.

"We also know that you visited Potala Palace, where you met with a Tibetan monk. I assume you were successful in your mission?"

"No," Bailey said. "He told me the stupas are off limits."

"That they are, Bailey Foster, that they are. But you'll forgive me if I don't believe you."

Bailey wished she'd hidden the amulet. It was in her suitcase along with the clothes the Dalai Lama had given her. When the goons came across the clothes – which they noticed were different from all the others – they tossed them to Zhenbang Zhao.

"Interesting clothing selection," he said, holding up the baggy pants and shirt as if he were interesting in buying them. "I understand this is what you wore to the Potala Palace. Did you buy this in Lhasa?"

"No," Bailey said. She touched her cheek where the goon had struck her. It was sore. It made her angry, but she was able to discard the negative emotion.

"It was a gift from a friend."

"What friend?"

"My lab partner," Bailey said. She blew her nose into the terrycloth robe and saw blood. "She wanted to give me a present before I left on the trip."

"I see."

Then one of the goons found the amulet and tossed it to Zhenbang Zhao.

"What is this?" he asked.

"Also a gift."

"From the same friend, I presume?"

"Yes."

"Interesting piece," he said, inspecting the amulet. "I've never seen one like it. Where did she get it?"

"I have no idea. Somewhere in America I guess. Or maybe on the Internet."

Zhenbang Zhao inspected the amulet closely and tried to open it but found he could not. He took a small knife from his pocket and began digging at it. He got nowhere.

"What are you doing!" Bailey objected. "You'll scratch it!"

She hugged her knees to her chest. Zhenbang Zhao kept digging at the amulet.

"This trip has been a total disaster!" Bailey cried. "I came here trying to do important scientific research. I failed miserably. Now, just as I am returning home with my tail between my legs, you do this to me. You call yourself a scientist? You are no scientist. You are a monster! You and those two assholes have scared the shit out of me, manhandled me, thrown my shit all around the room. I'm sure the American Embassy will not be pleased."

"The American Embassy!" Zhenbang Zhao stopped digging at the amulet and bent over with laughter.

"You must be joking, Bailey Foster! China owns America. I assure you there is nothing your darling little embassy can do for you."

As the two goons continued to destroy Bailey's suitcases and the rest of the hotel room, Zhenbang Zhao walked to where she was sitting on the floor. She looked down at his polished shoes and neatly pressed slacks and prepared to be kicked. Instead, Zhenbang Zhao dangled the amulet in front of her, letting it swing gently

from its chain. She did not look up, but could see its shadow on the wall.

"You don't mind if we take this curious necklace with us, do you?" he said. "It doesn't look very expensive. We will return it to you, of course, when we are done with it."

She could not stop Zhenbang Zhao from taking the amulet, Bailey reasoned, so why bother objecting? For that matter, why was he even asking for her permission?

"Sure. Go ahead. I don't care," she said, wiping her tears. "Just leave me alone!"

Zhenbang Zhao dropped the amulet. It bounced on the carpet in front of Bailey. She didn't react to it, and left it where it came to rest. The two goons finished emptying Bailey's suitcases and slashed open the linings with knives. Finding nothing, they tossed the suitcases aside, stripped the linens from the bed and inspected the mattress. Then they tossed the mattress on the floor and inspected the box spring, upending it and slicing it open in several places.

Finally, they stopped and looked at Zhenbang Zhao, who barked at them in Chinese. They left the room. The amulet was still on the floor in front of Bailey.

"I'm sorry your long journey was a failure, Bailey Foster," Zhenbang Zhao said. "I advise you not to try again. If you reenter China you will be arrested and charged with espionage against the People's Republic. Furthermore, you should assume we will be watching to make sure you get on your flight tomorrow. China Air flight A-324, I believe it is. Do not miss it, Bailey Foster. Do not miss it."

"You can be sure of that," Bailey said.

Zhenbang Zhao walked out without closing the door behind him. Bailey remained on the floor for a few minutes, paralyzed and waiting to awaken from the bad dream. A fear rose in her that the goons would come back to put an exclamation mark on things.

Then Bailey heard talking and giggling coming from down the hallway. She stood up just as a man and a woman appeared in the doorway. They looked with amazement at the destroyed room and the blonde American in the thin cotton pajamas who looked like she'd been raped. The woman whispered something to the man and the man said something in Chinese to Bailey.

"I'm good," Bailey said. She waved the couple off and started toward the door. Her legs were weak. The couple went on their way, murmuring as they did, and Bailey reached the door and closed it. She didn't bother turning the deadbolt or sliding over the security latch. If Zhenbang Zhao wanted an encore, she knew no number of locks could stop him.

Bailey was shaken, and her face throbbed, but she was otherwise OK. She went to the bathroom and noticed that it, too, had been searched. The toilet tank lid had been tossed into the tub. The towels had been thrown about, too, and the shampoo bottles had been emptied onto the floor. Even the bars of soap had been opened and broken in two.

She shuddered and picked up a towel off of the floor. She splashed water on her face and dried it. She looked at herself in the mirror. She looked horrible. Her hair was a mess and her eyes were red. There was a crimson welt rising on her left cheek where the goon had struck her. Then she flashed a clever smile at her reflection. She looked like a bloodied boxer who nonetheless had won a grueling bout: Battered, but victorious.

"Good girl, Bailey!" she said.

Then she caught herself. Was the room bugged? It certainly might be. It may have been more than just dumb luck that the busy hotel had a vacancy available on such short notice. She would be careful about what she said until she was safely back in America.

Bailey returned to the room that just a few minutes ago had been so cozy and comfortable. Now it looked as though it had been picked up by a giant and shaken like a snow globe. All the furniture was upended, including the little table holding her dinner, which was now on the floor, the Dong'an sauce soaking into the carpet. Her clothes were strewn everywhere: on the floor, on an overturned chair, on the headboard, on the television, on the lamp shades.

She went immediately to the amulet on the floor and picked it up. It had been scratched by Zhenbang Zhao's pocket knife, but had otherwise not be damaged. The seal had held firm. She noticed her smart phone on the floor. She picked it up and returned it to her purse and then started to search for the rest of its contents, especially her travel documents and plane tickets.

She found the hotel telephone on the floor, picked it up and

punched the button marked "security."

"Jiǔdiàn bǎo'ān," a man's voice said. "Hotel Security."

"That man you insisted I let into my room just assaulted me and completely destroyed my room," Bailey said. "I need to move to a new room."

"Yes ma'am. I'm sorry for your inconvenience," the man said as though Bailey were asking for extra pillows. "I'll send someone right up."

After a few minutes, there was a knock on the door. Bailey looked through the peephole and saw two maids. She opened the door and let them in.

"No more room," one of them said. She looked at Bailey's bruised cheekbone and gave a sympathetic look. "You should put some ice," she said, touching her own cheek.

The maids started helping Bailey put the room back together. The one who had not spoken went directly to the overturned plate of Dong'an chicken, tossed it into a plastic garbage bag and did her best to wipe up the stain it had left on the carpet. The other one returned the drawers to their slots in the dresser, the end table, and the desk, then replaced the two lamp shades. Then she helped her partner lift the shredded bed back onto its frame and dress it with fresh linens and a bedspread.

Bailey lifted her empty suitcases onto the bed, threw them open, then began to gather up her clothes from around the room and toss them into haphazard pile on the bed. One of the maids disappeared into the bathroom, where Bailey guessed she was restoring it with new toiletries and towels. The other vacuumed the floor and dusted the furniture, Bailey supposed out of habit. Bailey took an inventory of the contents of her purse. Everything was there. Then she began folding her clothes so that they would all fit inside the suitcases.

As the maids were leaving, Bailey tried to give them a tip, but the maid who knew English said, "It appears that you have paid enough, Bailey Foster."

The next morning, after a fitful night's sleep during which she was revisited in her dreams by the Chinese goon with the thick fingers, Bailey skipped her meditation and immediately dressed to leave. She thought about packing the amulet in a suitcase or stowing it in her purse, but decided to wear it instead. It seemed

smarter to hide it in plain sight.

She went immediately to the gate where China Air flight A-324 was scheduled to leave at 9:14 AM. Chinese customs officials again rifled through her suitcases and her purse. She half expected Zhenbang Zhao to show up, but he didn't.

"What happened to your suit case?" the customs agent asked, noticing the torn lining.

"A little accident," Bailey said.

"And your cheek? Was that also an accident?"

"Yes," Bailey said. Her eyes pleaded with the agent not to pry further.

Then the agent noticed the amulet around her neck.

"Lovely necklace," she said. "I've never seen one like it. What is that, a lion?"

"Yes, I think so," Bailey said. She started to remove the necklace. "Would you like to see it?"

"No, no," the agent said. "I just thought it was unusual."

Then the agent closed her suitcases and said, "You may go now."

"Thank you," Bailey said, "I've had a wonderful time in your country."

She boarded the plane and, although she did not drink, ordered a cocktail. A double.

19

NINE CHERRIES

As Bailey waited for her flight from Los Angeles to Miami, she called Suze on her smart phone.

"Griffin," Suze answered.

"The eagle has landed."

Suze recognized Bailey's voice immediately.

"You got the samples?"

Bailey touched the amulet hanging around her neck, then she touched her tender cheek.

"All eight of them," Bailey said. "And a mouse on my cheek for my trouble."

"A mouse?"

"I had a little tussle in Beijing. Some goon smacked me in the face after I almost bit his finger off. I'm OK. I'll be home tonight around nine. Can you pick me up in Miami? It's American Airlines. Flight 436."

"Sure, Foster. It sounds like you'll have some stories to tell."

Flight 436 from Los Angeles to Miami enjoyed a tail wind and arrived fifteen minutes early. Bailey was waiting at the curb with her two suitcases when Suze pulled up in her blue Prius. Suze hopped out and helped Bailey lift one of the suitcases into the trunk and the other into the back seat.

"So, Bailey. Nice shiner you got brewing there," Suze said.

"You shoulda seen the other guy," Bailey said.

They laughed.

As the Prius pulled away, Suze asked, "So, how was China?"

Bailey recounted her adventure as the little Toyota sped along. She told Suze about sleeping on the train station floor and the family who didn't want their boy's picture taken, about the spectacular train ride from Beijing to Lhasa, about the prayer wheels and Buddhists prostrating themselves, about the charming and helpful Kama, about the monks at the Potala Palace who'd loosened the coffin lids and helped her avoid the Chinese security guards, about Zhenbang Zhao's intrusion into her Beijing hotel room, about how he'd almost taken the amulet, about how she'd bitten the goon's finger and how he'd retaliated.

"When he was sticking his fingers in me, I thought about you and what your father did to you," Bailey said. "It wasn't the same, I know, but I can understand why you still don't talk to him. It was worse than I'd ever dared to think. I can't imagine having my father…"

"That's enough, Foster," Suze said, keeping her eyes on the road.

After a few silent seconds, Bailey said, "It's just good to be home. That's all I'm saying."

"It's good to have you back, girlfriend," Suze agreed. "I've missed you!"

"Aw, you're gonna make me cry!" Bailey said, only half joking.

Bailey put a loving hand on Suze's shoulder. Suze looked at her.

"Keep your eyes on the road!" Bailey said.

Suze looked back at the roadway.

"Listen," Bailey said. "I think I'm still kinda freaked by the goons that attacked me. You wanna spend the night?"

"Slumber party? Sure, Foster! You got any wine?"

"I think so."

"OK, I'm in."

When they arrived at Bailey's apartment, Bailey said, "The wine's in the living room. I'm going to take a quick shower. Be right with you, OK?"

"OK," Suze said. "I need a shower, too."

"You want to go first?" Bailey said.

"No, no," Suze said. "I'll wait."

After ten minutes, Suze heard the shower stop.

"OK, Suze, it's all yours," Bailey called to her.

Suze entered the bathroom and saw Bailey wrapped in a towel

and brushing her hair in the mirror. Suze peeled her clothes off and jumped into the shower. She saw Bailey looking at her naked body in the mirror.

When Suze got out of the shower, Bailey was gone and clean towels had been placed on the bathroom countertop.

"I put out some jammies for you," Bailey called from the living room.

"OK, thanks Foster," Suze called back.

Suze dried off, ran her fingers briskly through her short hair and walked out of the bathroom. The pajamas were on the bed. She shed her towel and put them on. Bailey was a couple inches taller than she was, so the sleeves and the pant legs were too long. She shuffled into the living room where her friend was waiting.

"I didn't realize how big you were!" Suze said.

She stood with her arms and one foot held out to show Bailey how loose the pajamas were on her. Bailey laughed.

"I think those might be a little big on me even" she said. "Here, let me help you."

She got up, handed Suze a glass of wine, and rolled up Suze's pajama pants as Suze took a sip.

After the two friends had enjoyed each other's company and two bottles of wine, Bailey said, "You don't have to sleep on the couch, you know. I have a queen. It's big enough for two."

"OK, Foster," Suze said. "That's great."

The two friends got into Bailey's bed together.

After five minutes, Suze whispered, "Ya wanna spoon? Just as friends?"

"Sure, Suze," Bailey said.

Bailey rolled onto her right side and offered her back to her friend. Suze crawled next to her and hugged her from behind. She kissed Bailey's shoulder and ran her left hand under her pajama top so she could feel the smooth skin of her flat stomach. Then she let her hand wander further under the pajama top, until it was touching Bailey's left breast.

"I love you, Suze," Bailey said. "But I don't know if I can do that."

"I love you, too, Bailey," Suze said. "See you in the morning."

She kissed Bailey's shoulder again and slid her hand out from under her pajama top.

A few seconds later, Bailey flipped over onto her left side so that she was facing Suze. She kissed her gently on the lips.

"What's going on, Foster?" Suze said.

"I said I didn't know if I could," Bailey cooed as she pet Suze's short hair. "I didn't say I don't want to try."

That night, the two friends made love for the first and last time, then fell asleep in each other's arms.

The next morning, Suze was gone before Bailey woke up. Bailey wore the amulet to work and handed it to Suze as soon as she arrived. Like Zhenbang Zhao, Suze had some trouble opening it, but eventually got into it by using a tiny diamond saw to cut through the tight seal that had been patiently welded by the monk.

Inside, she saw tiny black bits in each of the eight small compartments.

"Skin," Bailey told her. "The hair was so old I didn't think it would work. And I didn't want to have to go back and try again. It's a good thing, too, because the welding would have burned the hair."

"It might have destroyed the skin, too," Suze said. "But I think we can probably work with this."

Over the next two months, Suze carefully processed the Dalai Lama DNA samples. First, she extracted the DNA molecules hidden inside them. Then she replicated the DNA so she'd have enough to sequence. Then she fed the DNA strands into an automatic sequencer that was about the size of a refrigerator. The machine took about a month to create the list of three billion A's, G's, T's and C's.

When all eight Dalai Lama samples were sequenced, she fed them to her software. In about an hour, the report was ready. Bailey looked over her shoulder as she read it.

"What's it say?" Bailey said.

"Stop standing over me and let me look at it!" Suze said.

It only took Suze a few minutes to flip through the small report. Bailey watched as she made red checkmarks here and there. When Suze was done, she leaned back in her chair and looked up at Bailey.

"Well?" Bailey asked.

"We have nine cherries," Suze said. "The IDs are all the same."

"Every one of them?" Bailey asked.

"Every one."

"Holy shit!" Bailey said.

"Precisely," Suze answered.

It took Suze and Bailey six weeks to agree on the exact wording of the article they planned to send to Science magazine. At least part of the reason they lingered over the details was that they feared how Gwendolyn would react when she caught wind of the reason Bayner Genetics had hit the pages of Science, as she surely would.

Their fears were allayed when Gwendolyn called Suze into her office less than a week before the article was completed. When she walked into the chilly office, Suze saw that Gwendolyn was looking over a report from the company's finance director. It had a lot of red circles and exclamation marks on it.

"I think we've spent enough money on the lesbian project, Susan," Gwendolyn said. "I'm convinced there's no such thing as a human lesbian gene. In any case, I know we've spent enough money looking for one."

Gwendolyn did not share with Suze that her daughter had announced that she was no longer gay and, in fact, had started dating a boy named David Epstein. The boy was poor, but at least he was male. Even better, he seemed to be having a beneficial effect on Barbie, who had stopped wearing all black and was letting her blonde hair grow out. She'd even begun bringing David Epstein to Chez Paris every Friday night.

Suze pretended to be disappointed, but she recognized immediately that Gwendolyn had just handed her a solution to her dilemma.

"I'm sorry we were unable to reach our goal," Suze said. "We worked as hard as we could."

"I know you did," Gwendolyn said. "But sometimes it's just time to pull the plug."

"Perhaps we should just redirect the project's focus," Suze said.

"In what way, Ms. Griffin?"

Suze took a deep breath.

"As it turns out, in our hunt for the lesbian gene we discovered a non-contiguous sequence of base pairs that appears to be unique across a large number of DNA samples. We did some empirical

testing and found that the sequence is related to the body's soul – however unbelievable that sounds."

"A soul gene?" Gwendolyn said. "Why haven't you mentioned this to me, Ms. Griffin?"

"I didn't want to waste your time with a half-baked theory," Suze said. "But since all nine Dalai Lama IDs matched, I think it's pretty solid evidence that we have something. In fact, Bailey and I have just about finished writing an article explaining our findings. Of course we were going to get your approval before…"

"The Dalai Lama?" Gwendolyn interrupted. "The Dalai Lama has something to do with this?"

"Yes," Suze said. "To her credit, Bailey was the one who suggested that the identifier we found might be related to the soul. More than that, her interest in Buddhism led her to the idea of comparing the living Dalai Lama's DNA with the DNA of eight of his antecedents. Remarkably, her hypothesis held up. The sequences matched in each of the nine samples and did not match any of the twenty-six-million samples in our database."

"My goodness!" Gwendolyn said. "How in the world did you get hold of the DNA from the dead Dalai Lamas?" A horrified look crossed her face. "You didn't rob their graves, did you?"

"Oh no, Gwen! The mummified bodies of the Dalai Lamas are entombed inside an old palace in Tibet. It's where the Dalai Lama used to live before he was exiled. Bailey convinced the current Dalai Lama to help her get the DNA samples from the mummies."

"I'm not sure tomb raiding is any better than grave robbing," Gwendolyn said. "In any case, how the hell did she do that? She didn't beak any laws, did she?"

"She's quite a resourceful woman, Gwen. That last vacation she took was to Lhasa. It's in Tibet, where the palace is. She met up with a helpful monk still loyal to the Dalai Lama. Three of them, in fact."

"And the Chinese let her? I understand they're not too fond of the Dalai Lama."

"Well, she did have to slink around a bit, I guess," Suze said. "Sometimes science calls for a little subterfuge."

"I hope that subterfuge doesn't come back to bite us in the ass," Gwendolyn said.

"Yes ma'am."

Gwendolyn glanced at the DNA model on her desktop, then at the stuffed alligator on the floor. She pushed the financial report into a wastebasket marked SHRED.

"Where do we go from here?" she said, folding her hands on her desk.

"Well, there's lots more research to be done," Suze said. "For one thing, I need to figure out how the ID gets created in the first place. As you know, your DNA is a combination of both your mother's and your father's DNA. Each of the twenty-three chromosomes has two halves: one from the mother and one from the father. When the DNA is copied during reproduction, small mutations occur during meiosis. It is these random mistakes that must be responsible for creating…what did you call it, the soul gene? But it makes no sense that something supposedly random could be so unique and precise. It's as though something purposefully makes the mutations, like a computer programmer tweaks software."

Suze could see that Gwendolyn was confused. She was giving too much detail. She pushed on.

"Also, we need to start collecting DNA samples from people all over the planet. There are almost seven billion at this point, so it could take a while."

"Good Lord! Seven billion!" Gwendolyn said. "I'll be long dead before that's done."

Suze had noticed Gwendolyn's Huntington's tremors increasing, but considered it impolite to mention it. The Bayer Genetics team assigned to find the cure for Huntington's disease – a team that had existed since the company was founded – had made some progress, but were nowhere close to finding a cure.

"It's not as bad as it sounds, Gwen," Suze said. "At first, we need to focus on collecting DNA from elderly people and babies. The theory, of course, says that the ID will find its way, somehow, from a dead person's DNA to the DNA of a newborn. Our collection strategy can begin by creating a coalition of hospitals, obstetricians, midwives, funeral homes, crematoria and others around the world. Once a body is buried it will be much harder to get at the DNA, of course. And once it's cremated, well, you can just forget it.

"With each new batch of data that arrives, we can compare

newborn IDs to the IDs of the deceased in our database. If we find a match, we can tell the baby's family and the family of the deceased person that the two are related – albeit in an entirely new and dramatic way."

"What good would that be?" Gwendolyn asked. "I would think people would be more interested to know if they have the soul of Beethoven or Mozart or some other famous person."

"Yes, I agree, and we may be able to do some of that. But do you remember your idea a few years back to make everyone look the same in an effort to eradicate racial prejudice?"

"Sure," Gwendolyn said. "It was a crazy idea, I guess. But I still think it could work. What does that have to do with this?"

"Well, imagine the effect of discovering that the soul of a dead Israeli now lives inside the body of a Palestinian child. Or that the soul of a dead American now lives in a member of the Taliban in Afghanistan. Or that the soul of a dead white supremacist now lives in the body of a black man. I imagine human beings, on the whole, would be less apt to kill one another if they knew they might be killing the reincarnation of their own countrymen – or even a relative."

"I guess I see your point, Susan, but I don't have much hope that human beings would be so enlightened. We Americans, especially, seem to like killing as much as we like apple pie."

"Maybe," Suze said, "but there's also karma to consider. People who believe in reincarnation believe their deeds in this life determine the amount of comfort and happiness they will be granted in their next life. This belief might encourage people to be less hard-hearted, more enlightened. Better, in a word."

"I imagine you'll be expecting the company to pick up the tab for all this work?" Gwendolyn said.

"Actually, I expect that after our article is published that we'll have plenty of other genetics companies willing to join the effort, to say nothing of churches."

Gwendolyn began to see that the consequences of the girls' discovery might turn out to be more far-reaching than she'd imagined. After reviewing the financial report, she'd been fretting over having wasted millions chasing after the lesbian gene. Now she saw that the soul gene discovery might well change the world and secure Bayner Genetics' place in history, a concern she'd

developed after her Huntington's symptoms had begun to escalate. She was elated.

"Will you find me if I come back?" she said.

"We will do our best, Gwen," Suze said. "And when we do, we will use all of Bayner Genetics' assets to make sure your new life is as enjoyable as possible."

"Susan Griffin, you are a goddamn genius," Gwendolyn said.

Just then, a tear welled up in Gwendolyn Bayner's eye. It was the first tender emotion Suze had ever seen in her. (Suze had never attended a meeting with the victims of ultra-rare diseases.)

"That's very kind of you, Gwen. But Bailey is the one to be commended. She is the one who discovered the meaning of the ID. I thought she was crazy."

The following month, Science magazine ran a photo of the Dalai Lama on its cover with a headline that read, "Is Reincarnation Real?" When the issue hit, Suze's prediction came true. Bayner Genetics was inundated with phone calls, and the calls came not just from interested scientists around the globe, but from religious leaders as well.

Everyone seemed to want to get in on the discovery. Even Zhenbang Zhao – who after seeing the Science article had fired off a scathing letter to the National Institutes of Health criticizing Bailey Foster for "violating the sovereignty of the People's Republic of China" – eventually offered to supervise the collection of DNA in China.

Media outlets from around the world immediately began clamoring for interviews with the two geneticists. Suze passed. She wasn't interested in becoming any more famous than she'd already become. Besides, there was more work to do.

And so it was left to Bailey to travel to New York, London, Paris, Canberra, Tokyo, Buenos Aires, Brasilia, New Delhi, Seoul, Rome, Moscow, Madrid, Bern, Berlin, and even Beijing to publicize the discovery. (In Beijing, she made no mention of Zhenbang Zhao, except to thank him and the People's Republic for their kind cooperation.)

Using government grants and donations from several thousand sources, Bayner Genetics organized a global army of doctors, morticians and others who began feeding them DNA samples from newborns, the elderly and the recently deceased. To collect DNA

from other people, the company opened Soul Gene Clinics that charged a nominal fee designed to discourage people from visiting twice. As part of the deal, Soul Gene Clinic customers were told they could type in their ID at a web site called soulgene.com and see if any of their antecedents had been found.

Soul gene clinic customers also were required to complete a survey. The questions included such things as whether they considered themselves happy, whether they considered themselves to be spiritual, and whether they had ever been in trouble with the law. As the data rolled in, Suze started to compare the survey answers with the IDs. She discovered that if she converted the IDs to a base-four number – where an A equaled 0, a T equaled 1, a G equaled 2 and a C equaled 3 – people with large IDs tended to have stormier lives and people with lower numbers tended to have calmer, happier lives and also seemed to possess a greater capacity for compassion. The fourteenth Dalai Lama, whose ID computed to 174,491, was counted among this latter group. It was hypothesized that if the IDs were assigned sequentially, people with smaller IDs had lived more lives than people with larger IDs. This further bolstered the idea that reincarnation was real, since souls with more past lives were thought to have had a greater number of opportunities to mature and achieve enlightenment.

Suze also investigated a list of unusual children that had been compiled by Dr. Ian Stevenson of the University of Virginia, who had himself died just a few years earlier. The list, which was created toward the end of the twentieth century, included more than twenty-five hundred people who as children had claimed to have lived before. Many of them had even given the names of the people they'd previously been, along with the places they'd lived, including specific details. The children, all of whom were now adults, were located living in several places around the world. Two-thousand-three-hundred of the cases were discovered to have IDs that matched the people who they identified as their former selves.

There were yet more developments. The Masonic Lodge – descendants of the Knights of Templar, who had been rumored for centuries to possess the head of Jesus Christ – admitted that they did, indeed, have the head. They offered to have it tested. No living human was found to have the same ID as the DNA extracted from the head. Although far fewer than seven billion samples had been

collected, Christians around the world took this as proof that Jesus had, indeed, ascended into heaven.

Adam and Eve, who were assumed to have IDs one and two, respectively, similarly were never found. Devout Christians said this was proof that Adam and Eve both had lived enough lives to become enlightened and so, like Jesus Christ, had ascended to heaven, or nirvana, as most people now called it.

The lowest ID in the database was 144,444. It belonged to a vegan woman who had used her substantial inheritance to open an orphanage in Bangladesh.

Four years after the Science article appeared, the fourteenth Dalai Lama died. The monks charged with finding his successor turned to Bayner Genetics, who soon identified a child born to a dirt-poor family in Raj Nandgaon, India. The monks' confidence in the finding was bolstered by Tenzin Gyatso's pre-death prediction that he would be reincarnated in India. When the boy identified by Bayner Genetics as the reincarnated Dalai Lama was old enough to identify the possessions of the prior Dalai Lama as his own, he was immediately granted the title, although because China still occupied Tibet he attended his lessons in the City of Ten Thousand Buddhas in northern California.

As the years passed, other dramatic changes emerged. Violent crime – murder, assault, rape, child abuse and the like – dropped dramatically in every corner of the globe. Empty prison beds became so common that many prisons were converted into schools, homeless shelters and hospitals. In addition, because criminals invariably had relatively large soul gene numbers, the assumption was that they'd had fewer lives during which to achieve enlightenment. Thus, more attention was paid to their rehabilitation. Recidivism dropped from around eighty percent to ten percent, meaning only one in ten criminals returned to prison after they'd been there the first time. This, in turn, had a dramatic effect on the economies around the world, since governments had to spend so much less on prisons and police.

As Suze predicted, people also became less willing to kill. Nations reliant upon volunteer militaries found it increasingly difficult to find citizens willing to enlist. Those countries with mandatory military service found that most people were willing to

be imprisoned rather than become soldiers. Most of the countries with conscientious-objector exceptions extended these to people who chose not to serve because of reincarnation.

The drastic reduction in the numbers of citizens willing to enlist for military service turned out not to be much of a problem in practice because conflict throughout the world declined to the point that only a few African nations that had been warring for centuries (anthropologists argued that they had developed a psychological need for war) still had an occasional skirmish, but even those battles ended quickly and without the usual carnage.

Reallocating the resources once spent on crime prevention, incarceration and defense, the world's nations improved social welfare programs. Spending on education, health care, infrastructure and support of the arts went up, while the budgets for police departments, jails, prisons, and security services of all kinds shrank to a tenth of their former size.

Moreover, it became obvious in everyday life that people generally were becoming more loving and humane. Donations to charitable organizations increased steadily with each year that passed. The lists of children waiting to be adopted shrank to the point that families wanting to adopt were placed on waiting lists, even if they wanted to adopt black children, who had traditionally been considered the least desirable except by a few rich starlets. The number of blood and organ donors skyrocketed.

Perhaps the soul gene's most ironic effect, given the fact that Bayner Genetics under Gwendolyn's direction had focused only tangentially on actually curing diseases, was that several diseases eventually were cured with the help of government funds and donations. These included Batten disease, cancer and diabetes.

"Human beings no longer have to suffer through multiple lives in order to achieve nirvana," Bailey was quoted as saying. "Nirvana has come to Earth."

Gwendolyn Bayner died in 2020. She was forty-nine. She did not pass the company on to her daughter, who had married David Epstein right out of high school and, with Gwendolyn's financial assistance, had helped him start a video-game development company. Instead, Gwendolyn handed the reins to Susan Griffin, with whom she'd developed the closest friendship she'd ever had.

Suze waited for Gwen's soul gene to show up in the database, but it never did.

"Maybe she's decided not to come back," Bailey theorized.

As even more years passed, Griffin and Foster grew to be as famous and revered as any scientists in history. Their validation of religion and God, via the empirical proof of reincarnation, had transformed the human condition worldwide.

Schoolchildren learned their names alongside Newton, Einstein, Bohr, Galileo, Pasteur, Kepler, Copernicus, Mendel, Darwin, Faraday, Hawking, Feynman, Schrodinger, Pauling, Planck, Salk, Heisenberg, Dirac, and Watson and Crick. There was scarcely a university anywhere that hadn't named at least one building for them. Statues and monuments were erected in their honor in every city with the means to do it. The projects were all approved by unanimous votes. In poorer places, graffiti artists decorated walls and hilltop crosses with "God Bless Griffin and Foster."

Their praises were sung in churches, synagogues, temples, mosques and every other place where people came together to worship.

The Oxford English Dictionary included an entry for each of them that read: "One of two geneticists who showed in the early 21st Century that reincarnation is real."

Songwriters wrote songs about them. Poets wrote poems about them. Posters of their portraits were sold in gift shops, along with little plastic busts that only loosely resembled them. "New Baby" greeting cards showed a famous dead person on the cover and on the inside read, "Congratulations! We're keeping our fingers crossed!"

May 24th – the day their article appeared in Science – was established by the United Nations as Griffin-Foster Day.

Not satisfied to rest on her laurels, Suze continued working well into her sixties. In her search for how the soul gene got inserted into a baby's DNA, she found that it was not, in fact, a product of the random mutations that occurred during reproductive meiosis.

Tests of fetal DNA – even if performed mere hours before birth – showed that the ID in it was different from the ID in the newborn's DNA, although nothing else about the molecule had changed. This seemed to indicate that it was during the actual birth process that the new soul gene was somehow copied into the

baby's trillions of cells.

This new discovery was taken as proof that the soul entered a baby's body just before it was born. Religious leaders agreed that this last-minute alteration of trillions of DNA molecules was something that could only be accomplished by the hand of God. Certainly Suze had no other explanation. She would spend the rest of her life trying to figure out how the ID – which was absent before the final moments of labor – was nonetheless there when the baby emerged. She never would.

In her sixties, Suze lived in a luxury hi-rise condo on the beach in Boca Raton. Well aware of the Sun's danger, especially for someone her age, she never sunbathed, but she enjoyed the sea breeze that washed over her penthouse balcony on the thirty-second floor.

For her part, Bailey wholly abandoned genetics and focused on her study of Buddhism. She wrote several books on the religion, including the best-selling "What Did the Buddha Say When He was Asked, 'Is there a God?'" and lectured around the world about the Four Noble Truths and the Eight-Fold Path. By the time she reached her sixties, she had lived in the City of Ten Thousand Buddhas for twenty years.

Neither Suze nor Bailey had ever married. Suze said it was because she was already married to science. Bailey said it was because she'd never loved a man as much as she loved freedom.

They were both lying.

20
REPENTANCE

Father Jim and Jesus

When Father Jim read about the discovery of the soul gene, his heart sank. Modern Catholics didn't believe in reincarnation, but he knew repeated rebirth had been a part of the doctrine until it had been banished during The Inquisition.

Could reincarnation really be true? Certainly those two smart scientists from Bayner Genetics thought it was. Scientists had been right so many times about so many other things that the church had been wrong about, Father Jim figured they probably were right about reincarnation, too.

Father Jim also reasoned that reincarnation being true meant it also was undoubtedly true that he would be doomed in his next life, and perhaps for many lives after that. For if reincarnation were true, karma certainly was true as well – and he'd done horrible damage to his karma. Realizing this, he spent countless hours scouring the Bible for evidence that Jesus Christ immunized believers from bad karma as well as original sin. Finding none, he became plagued by a recurring nightmare.

In the dream, which he suffered repeatedly for months on end, he was visited by Jesus Christ in a botanical garden.

***

Jesus takes Father Jim by the hand and leads him silently down a gravel walkway that winds through plants and trees of every sort and size. Every now and then, Jesus pulls back on Father Jim's sleeve and asks him to stop as an insect of some kind makes its way across the stony path.

The path ends at a small pond. At the center of the pond is a fountain that shoots water ten feet into the air. Beside the pond, a picnic has been prearranged on a red checkered cloth. They sit. Jesus opens a bottle of red wine, pours two glasses, and offers one to Father Jim. Father Jim takes a sip. It tastes salty and thick. He looks down and sees that the wine has been turned into blood.

"Very funny," Father Jim says to Jesus.

"Sorry," Jesus says. "I couldn't resist. Try again."

Father Jim sees the blood has been changed back into wine. He raises the glass to his lips, then quickly moves it away to see if Jesus has changed it into blood again. He hasn't.

"You don't trust *me*?" Jesus says.

"You just did it once, why wouldn't you do it again?"

"I said I was sorry," Jesus says, and He takes a sip of his own wine.

"Why have you brought me here?" Father Jim says.

"You need special help. I'm here to offer it to you."

"Thank you, Jesus! I know I have sinned. I am ashamed what I have done to all those boys."

"The boys? Oh, that's nothing. It's already been handled," Jesus says. "Sodomizing twelve year olds is nothing new. You're hardly the first and you won't be the last. It's been going on for millennia. The ancient Romans were famous for it. I didn't even break a sweat on that one. It's your other problem I'm here to help you with."

"My other problem?"

"Yes. Look around you, my child. What do you see?"

"I see a pond with a fountain and a beautiful garden with plants and trees of every sort and size. And Jesus Christ sitting on a checkered picnic cloth, drinking red wine."

"Look closer. Open your heart."

Father Jim tries to do as Jesus says, but he still sees only the things he has listed.

"I'm sorry Jesus. I guess I don't know what you're getting at."

"See that old tree over there?"

Jesus points to a tree behind Father Jim. Father Jim turns and sees a wizened old oak. It's mostly leafless, but is holding on to a few sparse sprigs of green.

"It looks almost dead," Father Jim says.

"It is almost dead," Jesus says. "In fact, it will be dead by the end of the year. It looks awful compared to what it looked like when it was a young and vibrant oak with strong bark and a canopy of shiny leaves and roots that gripped the earth twenty feet down. Yet the oak nonetheless stands, proud of its gnarls and broken branches, and grateful that it lives yet another day."

"What does an old tree have to do with me?"

"You, my son, could learn something from that old oak. You look at your gnarls and your broken branches and you feel dismay, when you should feel gratitude that you still have life."

"Of course you're right, Jesus. I just hate growing old."

"Exactly. And that's what I'm here to help you with."

"You're going to make me young again! Thank you, Jesus!"

Jesus takes sip of wine and shakes his head.

"I'm not going to make you young," He says. "In fact, I'm going to do quite the opposite. But hopefully this change will help you see that beauty truly is only skin deep and that the real treasure lies within."

Then Jesus is gone. In his place on the checkered cloth is a small mirror. Father Jim picks it up and looks into it.

"No!" he howls. "Jesus! No! Come back! Don't do this!"

In the mirror, Father Jim sees that the gerbil-sized tuft of hair has been replaced by a bald pate with no more than ten thin hairs spouting from it. His eyebrows have grown bushy and wild, and his splotched face is creased and cracked like a desert floor. The bags beneath his eyes have dried up and deflated. He paws at them with his free hand and notices that the fingers are gnarled and bent and the joints are swollen and painful. There is a black mole on the tip of his nose. He parts his lips he sees that his teeth are all but gone.

*****

Each time Father Jim suffered the nightmare, he always awoke at exactly this moment. Then he would rush into bathroom, flip on the light and be relieved to find that he was his old self again and

not the craggy old gnome in his awful dream. As the months wore on, Father Jim grew more and more terrified of sleep, and the less sleep he got, the worse he looked. Everyone at the church started to notice his sad state.

"Father Jim, are you feeling OK?" they would ask, and he would always answer, "Fine, fine. I'm just having a little insomnia."

Then one night, desperate and without hope, he kneeled at his bedside, clasped his hands in prayer and bowed his head as he'd done when he was a boy.

"Forgive me, Lord Father, for I have sinned," he said aloud as the tears rolled down his face. "I have been having sexual relations with young boys entrusted to my care by their loving parents. I have betrayed that trust in ways most heinous. I have sinned against you, my Lord. I have sinned against these young boys. I will atone, my Lord. I must atone. Amen."

Then Father Jim counted the Oxycontin pills he had on hand. Thirty two. He went to the bathroom and got a large glass of tap water, then returned to the bed, swallowed all of the pills, and laid back to die.

After a few minutes, the drugs began to take effect and Father Jim heard a voice say: "This is not what I had in mind, Jimmy."

Father Jim sat up with a start and saw Jesus at the foot of his bed. He was surrounded by a golden glow and looked nothing like the Jesus in his dream.

"You better hurry into the bathroom, my son," Jesus said. "Those pills are going to come up any second."

Father Jim felt his stomach turn a flip and knew Jesus was right. He ran into the bathroom and vomited violently into the bowl.

When he came back into the bedroom, Jesus was gone.

"Jesus?" he said. "Are you there?"

"I am always here," he heard a voice in his head say.

That night, Father Jim slept without dreams. In the morning, he awoke refreshed. With his mind cleared and his supply of Oxycontin exhausted, he realized what he must do.

That very day, he volunteered to leave the posh St. Paul in Chains church and join the staff of a Catholic orphanage in Dhaka, Bangladesh, where he vowed to spend the rest of his life caring for the parentless children.

He had never worked so hard for so little money in his entire

life. Nor had he ever been so happy. What money he did earn he spent entirely to improve the orphanage. He also campaigned to improve the education offered to the children, many of whom went on to live fulfilling lives of helping others.

Father Jim grew to look exactly like the haggard old man he'd been in his nightmare, but it no longer bothered him. His hair fell out, as did his teeth, and a big black mole rose on the tip of his nose.

He died at eighty-nine years old, when his heart gave out one Sunday during mass. They found him sitting in the front pew and thought at first he had merely gone to sleep. He was smiling subtly, but was unresponsive.

"Call a doctor!" someone finally said.

When the doctor arrived, he listened to Father Jim's chest and announced, "He's dead."

When Father Jim was reincarnated, he came back as a poor Bangladeshi child whose parents subsequently died in a flash flood. After discovering that the child's antecedent was the great Father James O'Toole, child welfare workers took him to live in the very orphanage he'd helped create.

Rocco Retires

The day Rocco Magnano read about the soul gene, he felt like every guy he'd ever done had cast a hex on him from beyond the grave. It was obvious to him that there was no such thing as "instant karma." He'd proven that himself, hadn't he? His life was grand, despite all the poor schmucks he'd done. But his next life? Rocco thought he'd suffer bad unless he did something, and quick.

You could tell he was seriously concerned, because he even risked sharing his fears with the boss.

"You heard about that soul gene thing, right boss?" Rocco said.

The boss blew a cloud of cigar smoke into Rocco's face.

"Yeah, what about it? Sounds like a load of crap to me. Don't worry about it."

"You know what they're saying, right? That what you do in this life comes back to haunt you in your next life?"

"You're a fucking Catholic, Rocco. Catholics don't believe in reincarnation."

"Yeah, but here's the thing, boss. Once upon a time they did. The Grand Inquisitor even had this guy done for believing in it. Bruno, I think his name was. Something like that. Anyways, they burned the poor bastard at the stake."

"OK," the boss said. "So the Grand Wizard says there's no reincarnation. I'm with him."

"Grand Inquisitor, boss."

"Whatever."

"But boss, these scientists say it's true. They did experiments. Scientific experiments. There's this number in your body. Every cell of your body. And it stays with your soul even after you're reborn, so God knows what you did in your past lives. Why else would God want to know such a thing unless He wanted to punish you for being bad?"

"Why you bothering me with this shit Rocco? Can't you see I'm busy?"

"Because I gotta quit, boss. I gotta quit being a bad man. I've been bad enough for ten guys. Shit, a hundred guys. I gotta stop. I gotta make amends."

"OK, Rocco," the boss said. "OK. You can quit. That's fine. Now get outta my sight. I never want to see you again."

When Rocco turned to go, the boss looked at a big goon standing near the door, raised his right eyebrow and gave a little cough. Rocco turned in horror and looked at the boss.

"It's these damn cigars, Rocco," the boss said. "No worries! I'd never do anything to hurt you. You're my favorite. You know that."

But when Rocco turned away a second time, the boss's right eyebrow went up again and the goon followed Rocco out the door.

The goon's name was Paul Simone. He followed Rocco to his house and confronted him in the driveway.

"Hey Rocco," Paul Simone said.

Rocco turned around and saw the barrel of a gun pointed at his forehead.

"Hey Paulie," Rocco said. "Still in the business, I see."

"Yeah."

"You heard about the soul gene?"

"Yeah, the boss says it's a load of shit."

"Yeah? Well a lot of smart scientists say it's so. You know about scientists, right Paulie? They're the Einsteins who flew us to the moon and invented computers and microwave ovens," Rocco said. "So if they say reincarnation is real, reincarnation is fucking real."

Then Rocco looked into Paul Simone's eyes.

"How old are you, Paulie?" he asked.

"I'm forty-five," Paul Simone said. "Why?"

"Here's why: If you shoot me in the head now, those smart scientists say I will be reincarnated. At first, of course, I'll be a helpless baby. But I'll grow, Paulie. And when I am a strong young bull of twenty and you're a sixty-five-year-old geezer with a bad back and shriveling nuts, I promise you as I stand here today that I will hunt you down like the heartless gutter rat you are and pay you back for being such a stupid shit. And trust me, I will make it hurt. Don't be a schmuck, Paulie."

Paul Simone thought about what Rocco said. He'd always imagined himself retiring in a few years to some sleepy Florida town. Maybe he'd open a strip club and play a little golf. You know, enjoy life. He certainly didn't want to have to be constantly looking over his shoulder and wondering whether every twenty-year-old bullethead was Rocco come back to do him.

Then Paul Simone remembered the boss's order and reset his sights on Rocco's forehead.

"I gotta do you, Rocco. If I don't, what I am gonna tell the boss? He'll be fucking pissed, and he won't wait no twenty years to do something about it."

Rocco thought about that. The boss would definitely be livid, and when he ordered Paulie done, he'd more than likely say "make it hurt."

"You got a good point there, Paulie. But here's the deal. You tell the boss you did me and dumped me in the river. I'll get the fuck out of town tonight and disappear for good. Right? Then everybody's happy. You, because you won't have to worry about being done in your old age, and the boss because he'll never see me again."

Paul Simone thought about Rocco's offer. He envied the big moose. Rocco was about to free himself from the sociopathic and violent life in which Paul Simone was still hopelessly mired.

"Let me go with you then," he said.

"What the fuck, Paulie! You can't come with me. You gotta tell the boss you did me. If we both disappear, the boss will hunt us down and we'll both get done."

"I guess you're right, Rocco," Paul Simone said.

He returned his gun to the waistband behind his back.

"Sorry about that, Paulie," Rocco said. "If I could, I'd take you along. Maybe you can come along later, if you figure out some way to do it."

"OK, Rocco. But how am I gonna find you?"

"You're not such a dumb schmuck after all, Paulie," Rocco said.

He spread his big arms wide, took a step toward Paulie and gave him a bear hug. Paulie hugged back, and as he did Rocco quickly slipped the pistol from Paulie's waistband, took a step back and pointed the barrel at Paulie's head.

"Jesus, Rocco! I thought you were quitting!"

Rocco smiled, lowered the gun, took a step toward Paulie and slipped the gun back into the stupid shit's waistband.

"I am," he said. "And by the looks of it, you'd better, too, if you don't want to wind up with a fucking slug in your head."

With that, Rocco started walking toward his house and Paulie started to get back into his car. Then Paulie called out to Rocco.

"Hey Rocco!"

Rocco turned and looked at Paulie.

"Yeah, Paulie?"

Paulie paused while he considered pulling his gun back out and finishing the job.

Then Rocco said, "Paulie! I gotta get outta here!"

"Have a nice life you fat fuck," Paul Simone said.

Rocco Magnano left that night. He drove non-stop to a small town in New Mexico, where he opened a bakery specializing in banana cream pies.

Lolly Turns Over a New Leaf

Shirl walked into Lolly Webster's office and dropped a copy of the Miami Herald on his desk.

"Look at that," she said.

A headline screaming across the top of the front page read,

Boca Geneticists Discover Reincarnation is Real.

"What's this about?" Lolly said.

"These two smart scientists up in Boca say reincarnation is a fact. When you die you just don't go away, you come back as another person."

"Very interesting," Lolly said. "How much money have you made today?"

"Lolly, this is serious! You know about karma, right?"

"Heard of it."

"Karma is like your scorecard. You get good karma if you do good things and bad karma if you do bad things."

"I've got some fucking shit-ass bad karma then." Lolly smiled, showing his gold-inlaid teeth.

"Go ahead and laugh," Shirl said. "People who believe in reincarnation say that what you do in this life affects your next life. Like God keeps score. And if you're an evil bastard this time around, He's gonna hammer you in your next life."

"Fuck!" Lolly said. "You think this is really true?"

"The scientists say it is," Shirl said, "and they're a lot smarter than I am. They say every cell in your body has a number in it that God uses to keep track of you from one life to the next."

"A number?"

"Yeah, it's in the DNA."

"Like the DNA cops use?"

"The one and the same."

"Well, if you're a bad person, why doesn't God hammer you while you're still in this life?" Lolly said. "He could if He wanted to. He can do anything."

"I've been talking to the girls about it and they think it's because your life is like a single game. Until it's over, God doesn't know the final score. Like you could rack up a lot of bad karma in the beginning, but make up for it in the end. Or vice-versa. One of the girls told me this story about a bad man who killed nine-hundred-and-ninety-nine people and strung their finger bones around his neck like they were jewelry or something. But then he had a change of heart and spent the rest of his life improving his bad karma, and it worked! He was able to do it."

"You told the bitches about this?"

"They saw the paper, Lol. One of the customers brought it in."

"Help me Jesus," Lolly said.

He got up to go see what the girls were up to, but when he opened his office door he found a bunch of them standing right there. They looked at him like children about to beg for ice cream money.

"Help me Jesus," Lolly said again.

He returned to his office and said, "Come on in. All of you."

Lolly sat back down in his chair and the girls formed an arc around him. His office took on the flowery aroma of a department store perfume counter.

"Out with it," Lolly said.

"We all want out, Lolly," Shirl said. "Every one of us."

"That true?" Lolly asked the assembled girls.

Some of the girls shook their head yes, some of them just looked at Lolly with sad eyes.

"What the fuck you bitches gonna do?" Lolly said. "Get jobs as waitresses? You can't live on that money, bitches. You are fine bitches! You need shit!"

"Actually Lol, we were thinking we could convert the club," Shirl said.

"To what? A Chuck E Cheese?"

"Yeah, and you get to be the big rat."

Lolly glared at Shirl. She continued anyway.

"Listen, Lol. We got this all worked out. We want to convert the place into a sexy sports bar. We'll call it 'Pop Lolly's At the Buzzer.' We'll still need some money from you – it's your place, after all – but the girls have pooled their savings and have enough to buy eight big-screen TVs to show the games on. All of us have already worked as waitresses, so you don't need to train anybody. The girls have volunteered to redecorate the place. Chelsea majored in art until she had to drop out, so I'm sure she can come up with all kinds of neat ideas. Debbie's boyfriend is in construction, so he can help out with changing the lighting and anything else we need done. Red even worked up some uniforms for the waitresses."

A redheaded girl pulled a piece of paper out of her garter, unfolded it and handed it to Shirl, who put it in front of Lolly.

"Damn, Red! I gotta say, that is one sexy waitress! But who's gonna cook? Sports bars need a full kitchen."

"Just so happens," Shirl said, "Carly's boyfriend is an out-of-

work cook."

Lolly rubbed his chin and smiled his gold-plated smile.

"I still get my sugar?" he said.

"Sure Lolly!" Little Lila said. She hopped into his lap and gave him a kiss.

The other girls agreed, too, that Lolly would get his sugar. They held their collective breath as they waited for his answer. Just then, the phone rang. Lolly picked it up.

"Pop Lolly's."

"Yeah, Lolly, this is Joey Loco," said the voice on the line.

"Hey, Joey, what gives? How's the bitches?"

"They all say they don't wanna dance no more! They wanna turn my place into a roller derby!"

"Crazy bitches!" Lolly said. "Wonder what got into them?"

"Shit, I don't know. They keep talking about something they call the soul gene, but you know bitches. They're fucking crazy!"

"That's what I said."

"Your bitches all right?"

"Oh sure, Joey. Everything's fine here."

"I told 'em I'd fire 'em all if that's what they wanted, and I'll be goddamned if they held firm. I can't whoop all their asses. Shit, the way they were acting they'd probably all gang up on me. I could just fire them, I s'pose, but how the fuck am I gonna find another twenty girls?"

"Damn, Joey. I don't know. Maybe you should go with it."

"What the fuck do I know about the roller derby?"

"What the fuck do you know about keeping bitches in line?"

"Yeah? Fuck you Lolly!"

Lolly heard the phone hang up.

"Have a nice day, Senior Loco," he said.

He punched the phone off and started to laugh until he lost his breath.

"What's up Lolly?" Little Lila asked. "What's going on with Joey Loco's girls?"

Lolly struggled to compose himself. It took a few seconds, but finally he managed to talk.

"I'm in. Let's do it!" he said. "At least you bitches don't want to turn my shit into a fucking roller derby!"

The girls were all elated. They each kissed Lolly before leaving

his office and then started to redecorate the place immediately. Lolly called the sign company and ordered a new flashing neon sign that would say "Pop Lolly's At the Buzzer" one second and show a basketball going through a hoop the next.

Over the next few months, Lolly noticed that a lot of the regulars of Pop Lolly's Peek-A-Boo kept coming to Pop Lolly's At the Buzzer. More than that, they brought their friends and families, too. The place had never been so profitable. He'd never made so much money, and neither had the girls, since he'd made them partners in the venture in an effort to rehabilitate his karma.

Eventually, Lolly started to think that maybe his karma needed even more help, and so he started a scholarship fund that sent several of his girls to college. One became a businesswoman who was named chief executive officer of a large computer manufacturing firm. Another became a dentist. Still another became a lawyer.

Little Lila, who had studied piano as a child, became a jazz pianist and traveled the world. Once a year, she played at Pop Lolly's At the Buzzer and packed them in so much they had to set up tables and loudspeakers in the parking lot. After one of the concerts ended, Lolly went to Little Lila and told her that her father was in the audience. Little Lila went to see him. He was in a wheelchair and had plastic tubes in his nose.

"Hi daddy," Little Lila said. She bent down and kissed him on the cheek.

"Hi sweetie. Looks like you've done well for yourself. I'm proud of you."

Little Lila bent down again and gave her dying father a hug.

"Thanks daddy. I love you."

"I love you, too, sweetheart," her father said. "I love you too."

21
SUZE'S SOUL

I t had taken a bottle and a half of wine for Susan Griffin to work up the nerve, or maybe it was to dull her nerves, but here she finally was, poised for a third time on the edge of her thirty-second-floor balcony.

"Third time's a charm," she said.

The night was sublime. A familiar sea breeze washed over the balcony, carrying with it the briny and organic odor of the Atlantic. It smelled of life, but also of death, of creatures left half-devoured by predators who had eaten their fill and then abandoned the watery carcasses to be furiously picked over by fastidious crabs and small fish who in all likelihood would themselves soon become some other creature's dinner.

A full moon hovered on the distant horizon, big as an orange at arm's length. Its peaceful glow reflected off the rippling Atlantic, revealing ghostly seabirds night fishing near the shore. A flickering necklace of party boats bobbed beyond the point at which the waves began to break. Farther out still, solitary shrimpers, their spotlight lures aimed downward, took advantage of the gentle surf.

Below the balcony, not more than a block away, a calypso band played an old Alan Cherry song.

Enjoy yourself, the years are flying by!
Enjoy yourself, it makes no sense to cry!
Enjoy yourself, don't stop to wonder why!
Enjoy yourself, enjoy yourself, the years are flying by!

Suze turned away from the nocturnal seascape and pressed the small of her back against the aluminum railing. After careful consideration – having rejected taking a running start from the door of her condo and leaping over the railing like an Olympic hurdler, or simply diving over it head-first as if the balcony was a high platform and the concrete below a swimming pool – she'd settled on gradually leaning backwards against the rail and flopping over it, as someone who has had too much to drink might do by accident.

She imagined passersby discovering her body on the courtyard below.

"Is that Susan Griffin?" they would say. "The Susan Griffin? Oh my God! She must have had a few too many and lost her balance. Poor thing! What a shame! And after all the good she's done…"

Little did they know.

She took a step forward, back toward the condo, grabbed the half-empty bottle of wine from the little table and drank directly from it. Like a pirate, she thought. Or a wino.

Suze returned the bottle to the table, wiped her sweaty palms against the front of her shirt, stepped back again against the railing, and began again to battle her instinctive will to live. Alarms screamed in every corner of her mind. She felt her heart race. Beads of sweat popped out of her forehead. She brushed them away with a shirt sleeve. Did she really want to do this? Really?

"Shut up!" she said to herself. "Just do it!"

She lifted her trembling arms above her head as if she were preparing to fall luxuriously backwards onto her bed, her wonderfully soft and safe bed with the pillow-top mattress and the down comforter, where she could go right now and end this insanity. Frozen in this position, she recalled the fanatical Buddhists Bailey had told her about, the crazy ones who prostrated themselves again and again on their painstaking thousand-mile journeys from wherever they had decided to start to Lhasa, where they would continue to prostrate themselves ad nauseam – not for their own sakes, mind you, but for the greater good of humanity.

Who's crazy now? she thought.

The band played on.

"Come on, Susan," she said to herself. "Easy as pie. It's fucking thirty-two floors. Once you hit the sidewalk you won't feel a thing.

It will be all over."

Suze bent her back and felt the soles of her Nikes grip against the concrete floor of the balcony. All she had to do is lift her toe and . . .

Then she was falling.

She had imagined she might scream, but she didn't. Instead, she was rendered speechless by how slowly she seemed to be falling. Time appeared to stretch out, so that each second took five. It was if she were falling through an invisible and viscous liquid that she could not feel. She worried she would not land hard enough to kill herself, but quickly dismissed the thought, for surely she must actually be falling faster than she seemed to be. She had calculated that it would take only about five seconds to hit the sidewalk, at which time she would be falling at about one-hundred miles per hour, plenty enough to kill her, especially if she landed on her head.

As she fell past the column of thirty-one condos below her own, she noticed that she had time to glance at each one. Three floors below hers, she saw a couple who had pulled a mattress out onto the balcony and were too busy making love in the beautiful moonlight to notice her. The next few condos all had their blinds closed, and then she saw a couple cuddled on a couch, illuminated by the glow of a television. A few more floors passed by and Suze passed a couple enjoying a bottle of wine on their balcony, just as she'd been doing just a few seconds before. As she floated by, she felt as if she could reach out and touch them. They saw her as she flew by, then looked over the railing after she had passed. Suze clearly saw their shocked faces.

How many floors had gone by? She'd lost count. Anyway, it would all be over soon. Five seconds wasn't long. She heard the calypso band winding up their number.

Enjoy yourself, the years are flying by!
Enjoy yourself, it makes no sense to c...

When she hit the sidewalk, she was pleased to discover that it didn't hurt at all. Instead, she found herself floating twenty feet in the air, as if she was in one of those flying dreams she used to have as a child. She looked down and saw her broken body lying on the

sidewalk. It had created a deep impression in the concrete, which had cracked as if it were made of plate glass. Her arms and legs were splayed awkwardly like a marionette that had been carelessly tossed on the floor of some naughty child's untidy bedroom. Blood pooled around her head.

Then everything went black.

Suze looked around, blinking her eyes, and saw a single dot of light appear in the distance. At first, it was no bigger than a pin prick, a single distant star on a moonless night, so small she wasn't sure on first glance that it was even there. Gradually, almost imperceptibly, it began to grow larger, as if it were far away and she was growing nearer to it, or it was growing nearer to her. As it approached, she saw that it was not a star, but a swirling eddy of light. It seemed to beckon her as if it were a lighthouse and she a ship caught out on a storm-tossed sea.

She yearned to hurry toward the light. The urge was strong, as if the swirling glow were a loved one returning home after a long, treacherous journey. Or maybe it was she who was returning. She tried to run toward the light, but when she looked down she saw that she had no legs. She tried to swim or to fly toward the light, but saw that she had no arms. She closed her eyes, thinking she might will herself closer to it, but found that she could still see the light. She looked away from it, but it followed her gaze. Wherever she looked, it was there, swirling, growing gradually nearer, filling her heart with tranquility one droplet at a time.

She waited for some time for it to come. Maybe it is some sort of supernatural being, she thought, like the good witch in the Wizard of Oz. Maybe it will float up next to me and Glinda will materialize as the ball of light fades away.

Suddenly, the swirling light exploded and engulfed her, and she was inside it. Everything that once was black now was white.

"Hello!" she tried to say, but found that she had no voice, or perhaps there was nothing through which the sound might propagate. She looked around, but there was nothing to see. There was only white, pure white, as featureless as an arctic blizzard.

She felt something rising within her and soon was overcome with an emotion so powerful that her first impulse was to run from it. But of course she could not run. The feeling was so strong she feared it might take her breath away, but then she realized she was

not breathing, and had no urge to breathe.

A few more seconds passed and she felt an infinite joy begin to fill her heart as warm water from a faucet fills a sink. She felt like crying, but realized she had no eyes. *What is this place?* she wondered. Then she realized that she had asked the wrong question. *What am I?* she asked, she supposed to whomever might be listening. But there was only her.

A second later, she felt the answer pop into her mind, as if she'd known it all along, as if the question she had asked was as elementary as *What is my name?*

The answer was: God.

But there is no God, she thought. *There can't be, because no God would* …

Would what? She searched the recesses of her mind for the thing that had kept her from believing in God, the thing that she had relied on her whole life to help her easily reject any thought that God might exist. She dug through the life she'd just left behind, searching the far reaches of her memory, but she could find nothing there but peace, love and understanding.

And Bailey Foster.

"Bailey!" she called. "I love you! I love you! I love you!"

Then Susan Griffin prayed. She prayed she would be able to hold Bailey Foster once again, to feel her warm and tanned body next to her own, to tell her that she loved her, and to hear her say the powerful words back to her: "I love you."

And then, just as suddenly as the swirling glow had enveloped her, turning everything white, everything was black again.

Floating.

Warm.

Safe.

Joy.

Bliss.

Love.

Love.

Love.

"Push!" she heard a voice say. It was far away, like the light had been, and muffled, as though someone was yelling into a feather pillow.

"Push!" the voice said again, this time more urgently.

She felt the blackness collapsing around her, pressing against her. She could not breathe and yet she did not feel like she was suffocating. She noticed that she could not open her eyes. Eyes! She had eyes! And arms! And legs, too! She tried to move, but was held fast by the pulsating blackness.

"Here it comes!" the muffled voice said.

Suze sensed fingers feeling around on the top of her head, which felt as soft as an ripe cantaloupe.

"One more push!" the voice said, and this time it sounded as though the pillow had been removed.

She heard a woman scream in a final crescendo of ecstatic pain, and then the darkness was gone and a harsh artificial light filled her world. She clamped her eyes shut. Cold! She cried out and heard a baby's wail. Cold! Stop the cold! She shivered as though she'd been dropped into a bucket of ice. She felt someone wiping her body with a cool cloth. Cold! Cold! She shivered again and felt something poking into her nostrils and then into her ears and mouth. She felt something hard and metallic on her back. It was cold, too. Why were they making her so cold? Why wouldn't they make it stop? She wailed and wailed. Stop the cold! She tried to open her eyes, but the light was too bright. She closed them back shut.

Then she heard a woman's voice say, "Congratulations, Mrs. Hanford, it's a girl!"

Suze felt someone gently take hold of her legs and cross them, like a Buddha, and wrap her body tightly in a warm blanket. Then someone slipped a soft sock onto her head. The cold started to subside.

Then she was being lifted again. She was placed in the embrace of someone who was crying, a woman. Why was she crying? Not from sadness. It wasn't sadness. It was joy. Everything was fine, everything was perfect.

Suze started nursing at her new mother's full breast.

Joy.

Bliss.

Love.

Love.

Love.

22
BAILEY BURNS THE EVIDENCE

The morning after Susan Griffin's suicide, a sixty-eight-year-old Bailey Foster awoke before sunrise, donned her robes, and walked to the center of the City of Ten Thousand Buddhas. Once there, she sat beneath a Banyan tree that had stood in the same spot for centuries. Looking east, she saw the morning star appear from behind a cloud. It was Venus, she knew, named for the goddess of love and beauty. As the moment of sunrise grew nearer, the sky began to lighten and overwhelm the other stars, but Venus remained bright and beautiful. Then it, too, faded into the power of the rising sun.

An unexpected feeling of dread filled Bailey's heart. Something horrible had happened, the feeling said. She pushed the emotion away and concentrated on clearing her mind, on being in the moment. The dread kept returning, kept floating up through the placid pond of her mind like a murder victim who had been poorly anchored to the bottom. Bailey hadn't had so much trouble meditating in years. She forced herself to continue for thirty minutes – half of her normal routine – and then hurried back to her room.

The City of Ten Thousand Buddhas was alive with activity. She saw several friends as she walked briskly along.

"Is everything OK?" she asked them, and they all answered, "Yes, sister. Everything is perfect."

Bailey wasn't convinced.

When she got to her room, she went inside and looked around,

half expecting the place to be in flames. She made a cup of tea with honey and sat down at her computer. She opened a web browser and navigated to the news of the day. Then she knew why she'd been feeling such dread. As she read, she began to cry.

Discoverer of Soul Gene Falls to Her Death
By International News Services

Famed Geneticist Susan Griffin died yesterday after she apparently leapt from the balcony of her apartment on the thirty-second floor of a beachfront condo in Boca Raton and hit a concrete sidewalk below. She was 66.

Police called it an apparent suicide. Paramedics said Griffin died immediately upon impact.

Griffin was one of two geneticists who discovered the soul gene shortly after the turn of the century. The other is Bailey Foster, who lives in a Buddhist settlement in northern California. Foster could not be reached for comment.

The soul gene, which has been accepted by the science community as proof that reincarnation exists, has been credited with subsequently transforming civilization on Earth. Conflict between nations has ended and cooperation among people has increased notably. Sociologists say the resources saved by not having to fight wars and maintain large prison populations, once the norm, has helped the transformation take place.

Griffin began her career as a young geneticist at Bayner Genetics in Boca Raton, Florida. Shortly after she began working for the company, which focused on finding cures for exceedingly rare diseases, the scientist discovered a non-contiguous sequence of DNA base pairs that appeared to be unique across a surprising number of samples.

Her partner, Foster, who had been a student of Buddhism since college, suggested the sequence was an identifier for a person's soul as it passed from body to body. Foster's hypothesis was supported when the soul gene of the living Dalai Lama was found to match all eight dead former Dalai Lamas, who Tibetan tradition said were reincarnations of the same soul. Later, the soul genes of children who claimed to have past lives matched the soul genes of the people the children identified as their former selves.

The two scientists were awarded the Nobel Prize for their work and became famous the world over.

Griffin never married and is not known to have any living relatives.

Bailey cried. Why would Suze do such a thing? Why hadn't she called first?

"She was afraid I'd talk some sense into her, that's why," Bailey told herself.

Bailey collected herself and called Bayner Genetics.

"Bayner Genetics," the receptionist said. "How may I help you?"

"This is Bailey Foster. I just read about Susan Griffin."

"Oh! Ms. Foster! I'm so sorry. I'm sure you were very close."

"Yes we were. Does anyone know why she did it?"

"No one that I know of," the receptionist said. "But we just heard about it today. I understand the cops didn't find a suicide note, and there were no signs of a struggle. Her condo door was locked, so I think it was an accident, despite what the newspapers are saying. I don't think Ms. Griffin would kill herself. She seemed fine to me, and to everyone else too. They found a couple bottles of wine on the balcony. One was completely gone and the other only had about an inch left in it. I think she probably lost her balance and fell."

"I see," Bailey said.

Four days later, Bailey received a letter in the mail from Suze. As she read it, she could hear Suze's voice in her head. Tears again ran down her face.

```
Dear Foster,
    I hope this letter finds you happy and healthy.
    Let me cut right to the chase.
    It has taken me more than thirty years, but I've
finally found the error in my software. Can you imagine?
I'm the smart one, right? Ha! I don't feel so smart right
now.
    As a scientist -- someone supposedly dedicated to the
truth -- I can't tell you how utterly devastated I am to
finally realize that my whole life has been based on a
lie.
    It began with that foolish lie I told to Gwen. You
tried to stop me, bless your heart, but I was too
bullheaded and too full of myself to listen. I just wanted
to be a big shot, and I just knew that researching Junk
DNA would yield something fantastic. Which it did.
Literally.
    As small lies often do, mine mushroomed into a giant
mess. Now the lie has grown so pervasive I can't possibly
correct it.
    I know full well how important belief in the soul
gene is to every human being on this planet. I know how it
has transformed our world. Shit, even little kids know
that. I know that disclosing it as a mistake would likely
return the planet to what it was before: a violent,
greedy, inhumane shithole plagued by war, pestilence and
fear. I have no interest in helping that happen.
    I could maybe handle being branded as the biggest
fraud since those evil bastards who convinced everyone
```

that climate change was a hoax back at the beginning of the century. Their lie only resulted in the flooding of a few coastal cities, a few million deaths. Can you imagine the utter havoc revealing my lie would bring? I don't even want to think about it.

And yet I DO think about it. With every breath I think about it. It makes me feel like a fugitive. People on the street are always waving and smiling at me, thanking me for the soul gene. But I expect at any moment some smart young scientist, probably one at Bayner, will find what I have found: that my software, the very foundation of the soul gene, is horribly flawed.

You know the scientist in me desperately wants to tell the truth, Bailey. You know that! But in my heart and, yes, even in my soul I know that that's the wrong thing to do. I'm literally between a rock and a hard place. There's no way out. I've thought about it, trust me. God how I've cried! I've even prayed, if you can believe it!

My greatest fear is that the day will come when I WILL tell. The scientist in me will defeat the human being, and I will come out with the truth and scream it from the highest mountain, publish it on the Internet, take it to the media, write a correcting article for Science.

I can't let that happen.

I've left all the details of my findings about the error on my computer at Bayner Genetics. Of course you know I'm using Gwen's old office. The password to my computer is the same as it's always been. You can find the file at My Documents\Bailey\SoulGene.zip. The file is protected with the password sG+lOvEs+Bf.

In case the computer is cleaned out for some reason before you get to it, I've also printed a hard copy of the file and jammed it in the mouth of that stupid alligator.

I'm sorry for dumping this on you, but I couldn't go to my grave without telling someone, and you're the only one I could trust. I know you'll do the right thing.

If you return to South Florida, I'm sure the board of directors will name you as my replacement, if that's what you want.

By the way, I knew you would ask and so I've turned it over and over again in my head, but I still can't explain why the DNA of an infant is not the same as the DNA of the fetus, how it gets changed somehow during childbirth. But this is a detail unrelated to the soul gene, and the soul gene is predicated on the software. The software is the foundation of it all, and it is wrong, damn it. Wrong!

As for me, as soon as I mail this letter, I'm going to have a good stiff drink (maybe three!) and enjoy one

last evening on my balcony. Then it's goodbye Susan
Griffin. It's time to get off the bus, Bailey! I simply
can't go on living like this, and I can't trust myself not
to tell the truth and bring all of nirvana crashing down
just because of my own selfishness.

    It was a great life except for the beginning and the
very end. So no hard feelings, OK?

    Too bad you didn't turn out to be gay! I may not have
always shown it, but I loved you dearly, more than any
human being I ever met. We made a great team. We would
have made an even greater couple!

    Well, I've rambled on long enough. Peace and love to
you.

    Suze OXOXOXOX

    PS: I left a key to my condo in the top drawer of my
desk at Bayner. On the kitchen table inside the condo, you
will find all the necessary paperwork to take possession
of my stuff. You're all I have in the world, Bailey
Foster! Good luck. I love you!

Bailey was devastated anew. It had not been an accident. She asked herself again why Suze hadn't called her. She might have done something, said something, talked some sense into her, gotten her to stop and think.

Now, nothing could be done.

"God damn it, Suze!" she said through her tears. "How do you know you weren't wrong when you thought you found a mistake? Maybe thinking there was a mistake was the mistake! God damn you!"

Bailey booked the first flight to Fort Lauderdale. She drove a rented car directly to Bayner Genetics. When she arrived, she was greeted by the employees with a reverence to which she had never grown accustomed. It was one of the reasons she'd sought refuge in the City of Ten Thousand Buddhas. Everyone there treated her with equanimity, as if she were just a person, like them.

"Ms. Foster!" the Bayner employees exclaimed. "May I have your autograph?"

"Later," she told them.

They respectfully backed away from her with worried looks on their faces.

Then Bailey went to Suze's office, which she still thought of as Gwen's office. She said hello to the secretary, then went into the

office and closed the door behind her. She logged into Suze's computer. It had the same password she'd been using since they were lab assistants: 5865362, which Bailey had recognized years ago was JUNKDNA on the telephone keypad. She opened the SoulGene.zip file using the password Suze had given her: sG+lOvEs+bF.

The file contained a long explanation of how the code worked and how the error had produced the erroneous output. Bailey understood none of it. She deleted the file anyway. She found the key to the condo in the top drawer and threaded it onto the rental car's key ring. Then she went to the alligator and found the printed version of Suze's supposed mistake in its scary mouth. She stuck it in her pocket.

On her way out of the building, she ran into one of the members of the board of Bayner Genetics. He could see she had been crying.

"I guess you've heard," he said.

"Yes," Bailey said. "It's why I'm here."

"I pray you're interested in taking over for Ms. Griffin."

"I'd be honored," Bailey said.

"That's fine, Ms. Foster. The board meets the first Tuesday of next month. I'm sure you'll be confirmed."

"OK," Bailey said. "Thank you."

"My condolences, Ms. Foster. I'm sure the two of you were close."

"Yes we were," Bailey said. "Very close."

Bailey drove to Suze's building, took the elevator to the thirty-second floor, found Suze's apartment, and let herself in. The apartment was beautifully decorated with wicker furniture and abstract paintings that evoked the DNA double helix. There was a pedestal in one corner with a bust of Charles Darwin resting on it and another holding a bust of Gregor Mendel.

Bailey went to the kitchen, opened a bottle of wine and poured herself a glass. She went to the balcony from which Suze had jumped and looked over the railing. Below, far below, she saw the sidewalk where Suze had landed. It had not yet been repaired. Bailey could see where the body of her lifelong friend had impacted in the concrete. She imagined herself jumping, too, then turned away in horror.

She set her wine glass on the little balcony table, then returned to the kitchen and dug around in the cabinets until she found a large roasting pan, one that might have been used to cook a Thanksgiving turkey. She opened a few drawers until she found a book of matches. Then she took the roasting pan and the matches outside to the balcony, set them on the table and began crying again. She pulled the printed copy of Suze's paper from her pocket and looked at it one last time.

"Soul Gene Does Not Exist," the title said.

Bailey crumpled the paper into a ball, then dropped it into the roasting pan. Then she lit a match, cupped it with her hand to protect the little flame from the ocean breeze, lowered it into the roasting pan and lit the paper on fire. In thirty seconds, it was reduced to ash.

"You were wrong, Suze," she said, looking out over the Atlantic. "The soul gene does exist."

23
LITTLE DOT

T he move back to Boca Raton was a breeze. Everything Bailey owned – a few clothes, a smart phone, a laptop computer – she was able to shove into a single suitcase and a shoulder bag. Her friends at the City of Ten Thousand Buddhas threw her a going away party. There was plenty of wine and vegetarian hors d'oeuvres, and several of her closest friends gave little going-away speeches in her honor. One said simply, "See what needs to be done and do it."

Bailey boarded the high-speed AmeRail train at eight in the morning on a Monday. The sleek train, which ran solely on electricity generated by the sun and raced along on a cushion of electromagnetism, arrived in Boca Raton in ten hours. She took a cab from the train station to Suze's condo building on the beach. The cabbie refused to be paid for the ride, and Bailey naturally remembered Kama, lovely Kama in Lhasa, who'd been similarly generous so many years ago.

The small stack of legal papers Suze had prepared and left on her kitchen table allowed Bailey to easily take possession of the condo and the car, an experimental Ford Future that, like the high-speed train, also ran entirely on sunlight. Bailey knew less about how the Future worked than she had even known about her old yellow Bug. Then again, she also didn't understand most of what was going on at Bayner Genetics, either. The whole world, it seemed, had sped far ahead of her, like that black Mercedes on the expressway, and, like the universe itself, it was racing away from her

faster and faster each day.

Bailey smiled and let it go. Suze's suicide had been sudden and unnecessarily tragic, but Bailey soon accepted it. Some of her old friends in Boca Raton suggested she sell the condo, put the past behind her. While it was true that the condo (and the Ford Future as well) reminded her of Suze, the memories filled her heart not with the sadness of her death but with the joy of having known her at all, of having loved her.

"All things must pass," she said, remembering the enlightened Beatle, the one named George.

As she settled into her new home, the one in which she expected she too would die, Bailey meditated for an hour each morning on the balcony Suze had leapt from, and could feel Suze's powerful spirit still there. It seemed to have permeated the space and everything in it, like a lady's perfume that lingers long after she has left the room.

Shoulder high on the painted white frame of the bedroom door was the light gray handprint Suze had made over the years by swinging through the doorway a thousand times like a playful chimp. On the couch was the indented place where she sat to read or watch TV. On the carpet leading from the bedroom to the balcony was a vague path she'd made, a worn swath not unlike the body-sized patches of polished stone put there by generations of believers prostrating themselves on the courtyard outside Jokhang Temple.

Bailey loved the beachfront condo. Why should she leave? At sixty-eight, she was much too old to lie in the sun safely, but she enjoyed sitting on the balcony in the steady ocean breeze, just as Suze had. Someday she would buy a telescope and spend hours peering through it at the big ships as they sailed over the edge of the horizon and the little catamarans as they zipped over the waves.

Bailey Foster found joy in her work at Bayner Genetics as well, but the science had advanced so far since her departure that she was relieved to be just managing and not actually doing the technical work. She was, if the truth be told, quite unnecessary. There were a few papers to sign each day, which she did without reading them closely. People never tried to defraud you anymore, so contracts were mere formalities meant to limit misunderstandings, not obscurely clever documents meant to give

unfair advantage to one party or the other. Her favorite task at work was the occasional pep talk she gave to employees, usually to announce a new discovery she barely understood.

The soul gene and soulgene.com were still the pride of Bayner Genetics, but Suze also had steered the company back toward its original goal of curing diseases. Revenues to keep the company alive came from government grants and donations from corporations who no longer needed to be extorted into being altruistic. The smart young Bayner geneticists had even finally conquered Huntington's, which turned out to be triggered by mutations in any one of twenty-five different segments of DNA. Huntington's victims were cured as if by magic, by taking a pill that contained billions of microscopic biobots that visited each cell in the body and fixed the flaws in the DNA, just as God apparently imprinted each copy of a baby's DNA with the soul gene as it exited the birth canal.

To Bailey's relief, the young researchers at Bayner soon realized that they knew much more than she did, so they stopped treating her like a deity. She imagined it was how young scientists must have treated Albert Einstein in his later years, as an old man worthy of great respect, but one whose time had inevitably, if not sadly, passed.

The first thing Bailey did every day at work was check soulgene.com to see if Suze's ID had appeared in a newborn's DNA record. It showed up one day in the DNA of an infant named Dorothy Hanford, the first child born to a couple who had a small organic farm in Kansas. Bailey immediately sent an email to the new parents:

```
Dear Mr. and Mrs. Hanford,

    Congratulations on the birth of your new baby girl!
My name is Bailey Foster. You've probably heard of
me. I am one of the two geneticists who discovered the
soul gene and am now serving as president of Bayner
Genetics.
    You may also be aware that your new baby daughter has
been identified as the reincarnated soul of my former lab
partner, Susan Griffin, who died a few weeks ago.
```

The purpose of this letter is to ask your permission to visit your daughter once she has learned to talk -- say about three or four years from now.

In the intervening years, I invite you to investigate the research of Dr. Ian Stevenson.

Dr. Stevenson was a professor of psychology at the University of Virginia during the latter half of the twentieth century. A serious scientist obviously ahead of his time, Stevenson found that some children in the first five years or so of life are often aware of their past life, especially if that life ended traumatically. The memories usually are innocently expressed. The children simply start talking about a life in another place and time.

Please don't say anything about this to little Dorothy, even if you think she's too young to understand. It may spoil my purpose.

I would be forever indebted to you if you would allow me just a single visit.

Sincerely Yours,
Bailey Foster,
President, Bayner Genetics

A response came that night.

Dear Ms. Foster,
How exciting to learn that our precious little girl is the reincarnated soul of the great Susan Griffin!

We would be more than pleased to have you visit us when she is old enough to communicate -- or at any other time, for that matter.

We will contact you as soon as she begins to talk, especially if she seems to be talking about her former life.

We can already tell you that she is a bright little baby. She opened her eyes prematurely and is always looking around at everything. It almost seems that she'll be talking any day now!

God Bless you and your research. I'm sure you're tired of hearing it, but it has truly transformed the world.

Jack Hanford

In addition to searching for Suze's soul gene upon her return to Bayner Genetics, Bailey had also restarted the search for Gwendolyn Bayner's ID – a search Suze herself had given up on several months after Gwendolyn's death. Bailey knew about Suze's

promise to help Gwendolyn's reincarnated successor. She was also quite sure Gwendolyn hadn't been enlightened enough not to be reincarnated. After three years, Bailey's persistence paid off.

Gwendolyn's soul had, in fact, been reborn soon after her death thirty-three years earlier, the way it normally happened. Bailey discovered a thirty-three-year-old man in Kenya by the name of Fadhili Abasi, whose ID matched Gwendolyn's. Although he was middle-aged, Mr. Abasi's DNA had just been added to the database.

Fadhili Abasi had been born in a grass hut near Kirimiri in 2020, the year Gwendolyn died. Because the tribe he belonged to lived in a remote village (Kirimiri was about fifty miles northeast of Nairobi), his DNA had not been submitted at his birth. As a young man, he had worked as a potter. When he turned thirty, however, he began to feel restless and dissatisfied and decided to move to the big city to seek his fame and fortune.

He worked as a Nairobi taxi driver for a year and then as a short-order cook for another two. Neither job was as fulfilling as being a potter, making useful things with his hands for appreciative people. Finding the urban life and the work distasteful, he decided to move back to his home village. Before he left Nairobi, though, his friends implored him to register his DNA. There was no Soul Gene Clinic in Kirimiri, they noted, so this might be his last chance to do it. The day he left, he stopped into the Nairobi Soul Gene Clinic to have his cheek swabbed.

Bailey found Fadhili Abasi's soul gene the very next day and set up a trust immediately. The trust would give the astonished man $5,000 a month for the rest of his life, which worked out to about 500,000 Kenyan shillings – plenty enough to live, quite literally, as a king. Rather than lavish the money entirely on himself – which he was, quite literally, unable to imagine – he donated most of the windfall to improve the living conditions of the people in his village, who thereafter did, in fact, treat him as a king.

One year after finding Gwendolyn's soul gene and four years after having contacted Jack Hanford for the first time, Bailey got the email for which she'd been waiting.

```
Dear Ms. Foster,
    I'm writing to let you know that our little Dot has
started talking.
```

She's turning into quite a little chatterbox, in fact, but we've not heard her talk about her previous life as of yet.

Please let us know when you'd like to visit. We'll be happy to have you stay with us in our modest home. (In fact, you'll have no other option, since we live quite far away from any suitable lodging.)

Jack Hanford

Bailey scheduled a visit and flew to Wichita, Kansas, the following Friday. She rented a car and drove north on Interstate 135 and then west on I-70 and north again on County Road 232 until she came to a little dirt road effortlessly named Avenue B. In the distance, to the west, she saw a small wooden house with a windmill next to it.

She turned onto Avenue B. It was not much of a road at all, and she prayed the car would not bottom out in one of the giant potholes. As Jack Hanford had warned, his home was in the middle of nowhere.

It took her half an hour to reach the little wooden house. Bailey pulled into the dirt driveway and got out of the car. She stretched, reaching toward the sky as if she were preparing to prostrate herself, then yawned luxuriously. To the right of the house, she saw a windmill erected beside a small garden. The windmill squeaked as it turned in the breeze. To the left of the house, a wooden pen held goats and their kids, who jumped about as if on springs. A pair of pigs luxuriated in a mud hole, and a dozen or so chickens strutted about the yard, pecking at the ground for seeds and insects. Beneath a lone tree, a languid milk cow peacefully chewed its cud. A big brass bell had been tied around its neck with a red ribbon.

Bailey got out of the car and began walking toward the little house. Just then, a girl with blonde hair came running out of the front door. She wore overalls with the legs rolled up, and had no shoes on her feet. Following close behind was her father, dressed in a farmer's overalls and a straw hat.

"Ms. Foster! I'm so glad you made it," Jack Hanford said. "This is our little Dot."

"Hi Dot!" Bailey said.

She patted the girl on the head and noticed that she had blue eyes. Dot was very excited. She jumped up and down and spun

around on one foot like a ballerina. Bailey figured she must not get very many visitors.

"Say hello to Ms. Foster, Dot," her father said.

"Pleased to meet you, Ms. Foster," Dot said. She gave a little bow. "My name is Dot Hanford. I'm four years old!"

"Well, good for you, Dot!" Bailey said.

"Won't you come inside, Ms. Foster?" Jack Hanford said. "We've made some iced tea and cookies for your arrival. I'm sure you must be tired."

"I'm feeling quite fine, actually," Bailey said, "but I'd be pleased to go inside."

Dot took Bailey by the hand and the pair followed Jack Hanford into the little wooden house. The pigs grunted as they passed, which made Dot laugh.

The front door opened into large room with a kitchen nestled to the left and, next to it, a big dining room table. To the right, a couch and an easy chair addressed a television. A hallway led to what was likely the bedrooms and, Bailey assumed, one bathroom. The home was plain, but clean and comfortable. The floor had been fashioned from simple wooden planks, as had the walls. Dot's toys littered the floor, and her artwork covered the refrigerator. One wall held several photographs of the girl as she'd grown from an infant to a toddler. In the center of the sea of Dot's photographs was a picture of Jesus Christ.

"Want to see my room?" Dot said.

"This room looks like it is your room," Bailey said.

"My room is down there," Dot said, pointing to the hallway entrance.

Jack Hanford put an arm around his wife and said, "This is my wife, Jill."

"You have lovely home, Mrs. Hanford," Bailey said, thinking how quaint it was that Dot's parents were named Jack and Jill.

"It's nice of you to say, Ms. Foster," Jill Hanford said. "Please, call me Jill. Won't you sit down and have a glass of tea and some cookies?"

"Thank you kindly, Jill," Bailey said, "but I really can't wait to see Dot's bedroom."

"Come on, then!" Dot said, and she dragged Bailey down the hallway.

Dot's room was as simple as the rest of the house. There was a bed, of course, and a dresser and a small desk above which there was a picture of Jesus. The window looked out on the vegetable garden and the windmill. On the bed, there was a collection of stuffed animals. Dot introduced Bailey to each one.

"This is Mr. El Elephante," she said, holding up a gray elephant. "He has crinkly ears and a rattle on his nose. I had him when I was a baby."

She tossed elephant aside and picked up a mouse.

"This is Ed Mouse," she said. "Daddy named him that. I don't know why. And this is Raggedy Ann. Everybody knows her. This is just a teddy bear. He doesn't have a name. And this is a snake. I call him 'Snakey,' but that's not really his name. Over there is my desk, where I color and read. That's my dresser, where I keep my clothes. And that's my closet, where I keep more of my clothes."

"You have a lovely room, Dot," Bailey said. "And it's so tidy!"

"Mommy told me to clean it up before you got here," Dot admitted.

"Well, you did a fine job. Come on, let's go have a cookie!"

Bailey and Dot returned to the dining room table and Jill Hanford poured Dot a glass of milk and everyone else a glass of iced tea. Then she gave each of them a single cookie on a paper napkin. Bailey saw the cookie was oatmeal raisin.

Dot ate her cookie quickly, wiped off her milk moustache with a napkin, and then got up from the table and went to where Bailey was sitting. She held her arms out, tacitly asking to be picked up.

"Dot!" her mother said. "I'm sure Ms. Foster is tired after her long trip."

"Actually, I feel fine, Jill. It's OK," Bailey said. "And please, call me Bailey."

Bailey lifted Little Dot onto her lap. The girl ran her small fingers through Bailey's silver hair and gazed into her blue eyes. Then she reached for the amulet hanging around Bailey's neck and held it in her hand.

"Lion!" she said proudly.

"That's right!" Bailey said.

Then little Dot looked at the Dalai Lama's amulet closely and grew very serious.

"I know you," she said, looking up at Bailey.

Bailey looked at Jack Hanford, who pushed his straw hat back on his head.

"You do?" Bailey asked. "How do you know me?"

"We were friends!" Dot said, slightly irritated. "I love you."

Then little Dot buried her face in Bailey's breast and hugged her tight.

Bailey hugged back.

"I love you, too, Dot," she said. "I love you, too."

There was a knock at the door. Jack Hanford got up to answer it. Dot jumped down from Bailey's lap to go with him. Jack opened the door and a tall man walked into the house. He was dressed formally, in a suit and tie. His shoes had been shined with care and were remarkably clean, considering the dusty surroundings. He looked to be in his mid-fifties.

"Hi pops," Jack said.

"Hi daddy," Jill Hanford said.

"I just stopped by to see my little Dot," the man said.

Dot jumped into his arms and kissed him square on the lips.

"My Pop Pop!" she squealed. She threw her little arms around his neck and squeezed until his face turned red.

"My goodness we are full of love today!" he said.

"Come and meet my friend!" Dot said, pointing at Bailey.

Bailey rose from her chair and walked over to Jill's father, who put Dot down and extended his hand. Bailey reached out and shook it.

"It's a pleasure to meet you, sir. My name is Bailey Foster. You have a lovely family. I'm not sure you'll ever be able to convince me to leave."

"How nice of you to say, Ms. Foster. I am Jill's father, Will Chambers. Your reputation, of course, precedes you. Everyone in town has been quite excited about your visit. We have, in fact, been waiting years! I do hope you'll be coming to church on Sunday. It's a little early, just after sunrise, around seven. Most of the folks here are early risers. Farmers, you know. If you like, we can push it back a bit. I'm sure no one would object."

"Sunrise is fine," Bailey said. "I am an early riser myself. I like to see as much of each day as I can, especially the sunrise. At home, I usually begin my meditation while the morning star is still visible."

"In that case," Will said, "We will set up a sunrise service outside the church. Folks do love them, and the sight of the sun rising, turning the darkness into light, seems to bring out the Christian in them."

"That would be lovely," Bailey said, "but please don't go to any trouble on my account."

"Pshaw!" Will said. "It's no trouble at all. We just have the young ones pull the chairs out into the field and I stand on a little wood altar a kind carpenter built for the church. We often do it for weddings, since the church only seats a hundred or so."

"You're the minister?" Bailey said.

"That I am, and I have written a special sermon in honor of your visit!"

"Oh my," Bailey said. "You really..."

"Don't say another word, my dear! It's all done, and I don't have another one prepared, so it will have to do. I only hope it does you justice. One small minister could never hope to change the world as you have."

Bailey looked at Will Chambers. There was something familiar about him she couldn't quite put her finger on. She felt like she'd met him before.

"Daddy! Come have some iced tea and a cookie," Jill Hanford said. "I made them fresh this morning. They're oatmeal raisin. Your favorite!"

"Don't mind if I do, princess. But just one." Will Chambers patted his belly, reminding Bailey of the Dalai Lama. "Your old dad's pants aren't getting any looser these days."

The next day was Saturday. Jack Hanford rose early and looked out the window to find Bailey sitting in the front yard, among the chickens, facing east, meditating. He told Dot not to bother her until she stood up.

"She's meditating," he said.

"What's medicating?" Dot said.

"Medi-tat-ing. It's her special time, when she talks to God."

"Oh," Dot said. "Like praying."

"Yes. So leave her be until she stands up."

"OK, daddy."

"Come eat your breakfast, Dot," Jill Hanford said, and Dot

climbed up into her chair and began eating a bowl of warm oatmeal with cream and sugar. When she was done, she got down from her chair and went to the window. Bailey was still sitting among the chickens and appeared not to have moved.

"She prays for a long time," Dot said.

After a few more minutes, Bailey raised her arms into the air and stood up. Dot opened the front door and ran to her, hugging her legs.

"Good morning, Dot," Bailey said.

"Good morning, Foster," Dot said. It did not escape Bailey's notice that Suze, and only Suze, had ever called her Foster.

Jill appeared at the door and called out, "Dot! Tell Bailey her breakfast is ready!"

"Your breakfast is ready," Dot said. She took Bailey's hand and began dragging her toward the house. "Come on! It's yummy oatmeal!"

After breakfast, Dot again took Bailey's hand and began to show her around the little farm. First, she walked up to the cow, which Jill was busy milking.

"Her name is Gwendolyn," Dot said as her mother pulled rhythmically at the cow's teats and the jets of warm milk sang against the side of a stainless-steel bucket. Dot reached up and scratched the sedate cow under its chin.

"We named her after a queen," Dot said. "Isn't she cute?"

Bailey patted the cow on the head and looked into its big brown eyes. "She's lovely," she said. "And very generous to share her milk with you."

"Docile as a bunny, that's my Gwendolyn," Jill said as she lifted the milk bucket away. "I haven't been kicked once. Some people slaughter their milk cows after they grow too old to produce much milk, but I couldn't bear to do that to Gwendolyn. She's like part of the family. We'll put her out to pasture and let her enjoy a long retirement."

"That's nice to hear, Jill," Bailey said. "I'm sure Gwendolyn will be pleased."

Next, Dot pulled Bailey over to the pig pen.

"That's Pinky," she said, pointing to one of the pigs, "'cause she was pink when she was little, and that's Floppy, 'cause he has floppy ears."

Dot grabbed a stick that was wedged in the metal fencing and scratched Floppy between the ears. Seeing that, Pinky moved in to get her share and Dot scratched her as well.

"They love being scratched on the head," Dot said. "I wasn't going to name them, because daddy said when they get big we're going to have them made into sausage and pork chops. But he said they're God's creatures, and they will give their lives for us, so that we can eat. So he said I could name them anyway, and scratch them on the head every day."

"That's nice of you, Dot," Bailey said. "They sure seem to like it."

"Oh! They do! Watch when I stop!"

Dot pulled the stick away and the two pigs began begging for more, snorting and butting their noses against the metal fencing.

"You wanna try?" Dot said. She held the stick out to Bailey.

"Sure," Bailey said. She took the stick and scratched the happy pigs like Dot had, but not quite as vigorously.

"You can go ahead and do it hard," Dot said. "They like it."

Next, Dot took Bailey to the pen holding the goats.

"I haven't named any of them yet except that white one," she said.

"What's his name?" Bailey asked.

"Whitey! What else?" Dot said, and she laughed.

Then Dot showed Bailey the vegetable garden, pointing out the onions, garlic, potatoes, squash, peppers, corn, beets, carrots, peas, lettuce, celery and tomatoes.

"You know all of your vegetables," Bailey said.

"Sure I do," Dot said. "I live on a farm!"

The clouds had been building and finally it started to rain. Dot and Bailey ran into the house and spent the rest of the afternoon coloring and reading. For dinner, Jill made a mushroom quiche and a salad.

24
LET IT BE

The next morning was Sunday, the day Will Chambers planned to deliver his special sermon at sunrise. The Hanfords awoke at five o'clock and had a quick breakfast of cold corn flakes.

"Gwendolyn's milk is delicious," Bailey said. "I don't often drink it, but when in Rome…"

"I'm sorry, Bailey," Jill said. "Jack told me you were a Buddhist and a vegetarian. I'm just not much of a vegetarian cook. Most folks around here eat a lot of meat, including us. It's just the way we were raised."

Bailey touched Jill's hand. "Please don't take it as a criticism. You have been more kind to me than I had any right to expect. I am essentially a stranger to you, after all. You knew my peculiar diet would make things difficult for you, and yet you've taken me in and treated me with the utmost kindness. I am grateful. It's true that I don't often eat dairy or eggs, but every now and then I do, especially if I am sure the eggs have not been fertilized. Your quiche last night was delicious, by the way!

"Also, you know it's only Mahāyāna Buddhists who are vegetarians. We think it helps us be compassionate. Theravāda Buddhists – you know it's actually older than Mahāyāna, even though it doesn't have as many followers – don't teach vegetarianism at all. Anyway, how we respect other life is really a personal choice. There are some crazy Tibetan lamas who won't even swat a mosquito when they see it stealing a bellyful of blood from their arm. They just let it

suck and suck. Can you imagine? I've never had a problem swatting mosquitoes. Of course, I live in Florida, not Lhasa. If you don't swat them, they'll drain you dry!"

"Thank you for your understanding, Bailey. Just the same, I have vegetarian lasagna planned for tonight," Jill said. "I'll make it from the vegetables in our garden."

"Dot showed me the garden yesterday," Bailey said. "It was beautiful. I'm sure the lasagna will be delicious."

Jack looked at the clock on the wall and said, "Time to go."

The family piled into the rental car and Jack told Bailey how to get to the church. It was a small white building with a simple steeple topped by a modest wooden cross. "Church of God" was painted over the double-door entrance. A single spotlight that had been installed on the ground shone up at the church building, illuminating the steeple against the black sky.

To the left of the church, on the side opposite the parking area, was a freshly mowed field of hay where hundreds of chairs of varying kinds had been arranged in neat, if incongruous, rows. It appeared that most of the congregation had already arrived. Most of the chairs were taken, and several people were standing in the rear. Four soft chairs at the front had been reserved for Bailey and the Hanford family.

Bailey parked the car. As she and the others made their way toward the congregation, they heard the murmur of conversation stop and the singing commence.

> From the rising of the sun
> to the going down of the same,
> the name of the Lord shall be praised.
>
> From the rising of the sun
> to the going down of the same,
> the name of the Lord shall be praised.
>
> So praise ye the Lord.
> Praise ye the Lord.
>
> From the rising of the sun
> to the going down of the same,
> the name of the Lord shall be praised.

As the congregation sang, a teenaged girl with ribbons in her hair and dressed in a white Sunday dress and dainty ballet flats ran up to

241

Bailey and the Hanfords. She handed them each a small flashlight, and then began to lead them to front of the assembly. Bailey followed the girl across the rough hewn field and, out of the corner of her eye, saw people pointing at her in the darkness. She heard a few of them stop singing and exclaim "There she is!" and others beside them implore them to hush up and keep singing, to be polite.

Bailey and the Hanfords came to their seats just as the morning star appeared from behind a cloud in the eastern sky, which was to the assembly's left and had just begun to lighten. The singing came to a stop with the customary Amen cadence, and Pastor Will Chambers appeared from out of the gloom as if by magic. He stepped up onto the simple wooden altar, where he was lighted from either side by spotlights that had been erected on poles. He was dressed in a suit identical to the one Bailey had seen him wearing two days before.

Pastor Chambers raised his arms, looked at the dark blue sky, and announced, "Thank you Jesus for this beautiful day!"

"Thank you Jesus!" the throng of worshipers crowed, not in unison.

"Amen!" others said.

"Hosanna!" a few others said.

Just then, as if on cue – or perhaps because Will Chambers knew exactly what time the sun would rise that morning – the top of the sun peeked over the horizon to his right and graced the churchyard with the precious first light of day.

"As you all know, we are blessed today to have with us a very special guest who has come all the way from Miami, Florida, to be with us. Some of you younger folks may have learned about her in school. You older folks have no doubt read about her in the newspaper, or even seen her on TV, for she is among the most famous and most beloved people on the planet today. I'm certain you will give her your warmest welcome."

Then Will Chambers pointed all five fingers of his flattened left hand at Bailey and said, "Ladies and gentlemen, the discoverer of the soul gene, Miss Bailey Foster!"

With that, everyone in attendance – many of whom rarely attended church but would not have missed a chance to see the legendary Bailey Foster – rose from their seats and applauded and cheered and whistled as if they were at a rock concert. Will Chambers implored Bailey to stand and then began to applaud along with his

adoring congregation.

Bailey threw the smiling preacher a stern look, waggled a scolding index finger at him playfully, then stood up and turned toward the ebullient crowd, which upon seeing her erupted into an even louder ovation. Startled by the outburst, Bailey gave a small bow with the palms of her hands pressed together beneath her chin, in the fashion of the Dalai Lama, and then returned to her seat as the roaring continued.

Dot, who was standing and applauding with the rest, called out, "They love you like I do, Foster!"

After thirty seconds more, when the clamor did not appear to be fading on its own even with Bailey back in her seat, Will Chambers motioned for the congregation to calm themselves.

"Please, be seated," he said, holding his hands out to them with the palms down, as if quieting an orchestra. They sat. He waited a few seconds for the excited murmurs to cease, then continued.

"Now, you may or may not know that Miss Foster is a Buddhist. I imagine few of us, as followers of Christ, know very much about Buddhism. We know the Buddha only as that fat and jolly fellow on the menu at the Chinese restaurant in town. But with the exception of a few details here and there, the fact is that we Christians follow the same basic teachings as those who follow the Buddha.

"Most importantly, Jesus teaches us to be kind and compassionate. In Ephesians four-thirty-two, Paul the Apostle says, 'Be kind to one another, tenderhearted and forgiving of one another, just as God in Christ forgave you.'

"The Buddha, who lived five hundred years before our Lord, likewise espoused kindness and compassion. Among his followers, he is famous for having said, 'Thousands of candles can be lighted from a single candle, and the life of that candle will not be shortened. Happiness never decreases by being shared.'

"The power of human kindness, a power shared by Christians and Buddhists alike, a power not to be underestimated, is what I want to talk about today."

An infant far in the back cried out, as babies at church sometimes do. Will Chambers easily overlooked it.

"The first story I have to share with you happened after the end of a war – a dreadfully big war. We don't fight wars anymore, of course, but at one time the world was plagued by many wars. There

were two big ones in the first half of the last century that you probably have heard of, and several smaller ones you may not know anything about. This story is about a pilot who fought during the second big war, the one named World War Two. This pilot's name was Gail Halvorsen.

"World War Two was fought all around the globe, as its name implies, but it was started in Europe by a misguided tyrant by the name of Adolph Hitler, who came to power in Germany. This Mr. Hitler was a small and sickly man who had the devil in his heart and pure evil running through his veins. After the war, the people of Germany were starving because Mr. Hitler had spent all of the country's treasure on the war, even after it was clear that all was lost. When Gail Halvorsen visited Germany after its surrender, he was surrounded by German children who tugged at his shirtsleeves and begged him for a piece of bread. Mr. Halvorsen didn't have any food, but when he checked his pockets he found two pieces of gum. He gave the gum to the children, who tore each stick into small pieces so they could each have a tiny share. Gail Halvorsen had kindness in his heart, so he was touched by these hungry children. The next time he brought food to the war-ravaged country, he brought rations of gum and candy for the children as well.

"The bad news was that Halvorsen's immediate supervisors reprimanded him for distributing the unauthorized sweets. The good news was that a general with a warm heart heard of Halvorsen's impromptu charity and supported it. Within days, candy companies in America were donating tons of candy for Halvorsen to give to the devastated Germans, enough so that even the adults could enjoy some.

"It was just candy, you might say. But what Halvorsen and his enlightened general understood was that the candy was more than just treats for the children. First, it represented the hope that things would get better. Beyond that, it showed the defeated German people that their former enemies had charitable hearts and harbored no ill will toward them despite the ferocity with which they had mercilessly firebombed their country. In this way, a small act of kindness on the part of one man hastened the healing between the two countries, and Germany went on to become a great nation again."

Will Chambers continued to talk about several other examples of random kindness and how they had made the world a better place.

There was the young girl who had begun selling homemade hair clips in order to raise money to buy teddy bears for children afflicted with cancer. When others discovered her work, they donated money to her and the girl was able to give teddy bears to thousands of children.

Then there was the woman who'd kept three dollars in a special place in her purse and gave it instantly to the first person she saw who needed it more than she. One homeless man to whom she had given the money later established his own homeless shelter. Then there was the poor elderly man who thanked the checkout girl "just for being here" every time he bought food at the grocery store. Other shoppers heard the man and began doing it themselves, and not just at the grocery store.

"The last story about kindness I have for you concerns a newborn baby who someone left in a gymnasium bag in the back of a city bus in Orlando, Florida."

Bailey, who until this point had only been listening politely, now sat up in her chair and looked closely at Will Chambers as he spoke. As he continued, she became more and more certain that she now knew why Will Chambers had seemed so familiar to her.

"This infant, so new it was covered in *vernix caseosa* and had the umbilical cord still attached, was taken in by the bus driver and his wife," Pastor Chambers continued. "They raised the child as their own, gave him a room in their modest home, and although they were far from wealthy, provided for him in the best way they could. Most of all, they taught him to love Jesus, and so the infant grew up to be a Christian man.

"More than that, the infant grew up to be a minister, a man of the cloth. In fact, he grew up to be the minister you see standing before you today. I, your humble preacher, am the infant who someone left on the bus, the infant who went on to have a fulfilling life, all thanks to the bountiful kindness of a simple bus driver and his wife."

The congregation stirred. Bailey sensed that many of them were unaware of their pastor's humble beginnings until this very second.

"We all have many opportunities to be kind each day," Pastor Chambers said, "and whether they are big or small makes little difference, for each of them adds to the amount of kindness that exists in the world, and that makes Jesus smile. Let us pray. Every head bowed. Every eye closed."

Bailey looked around and saw that the Hanfords, including little Dot, had bowed their heads and closed their eyes reverently. Everyone else seemed to be doing it, too. She looked up at Will Chambers, who nodded and smiled to her. She closed her eyes and bowed her head.

"Dear Lord," Pastor Chambers said, "as we walk each day through the lives you have graciously given us, help us remember to be kind. Help us to think first of the needs of others, and not of our own needs and wants. Dear Lord, help us to be more like you. Help us to remember to help the needy, to comfort the sick and to show compassion for those who have lost their way. Help us to see ourselves in the eyes of our brothers and our sisters. Help us to remember, as Jesus implored us, to do unto each of them as we would have them do unto us. In Jesus' name we pray, Amen."

Then, just as the singing had begun upon Bailey's arrival, it began again, as if it had been preplanned.

Let us gather up the sunbeams,
Lying all around our path.
Let us keep the wheat and roses,
Casting out the thorns and chaff.
Let us find our sweetest comfort
In the blessings of today,
With a patient hand removing
All the briers from the way.

Then scatter seeds of kindness,
Then scatter seeds of kindness,
Then scatter seeds of kindness,
For our reaping by and by.

Strange we never prize the music
Till the sweet-voiced bird is flown!
Strange that we should slight the violets
Till the lovely flowers are gone!
Strange that summer skies and sunshine
Never seem one half so fair,
As when winter's snowy pinions
Shake the white down in the air.

Then scatter seeds of kindness,
Then scatter seeds of kindness,
Then scatter seeds of kindness,
For our reaping by and by.

If we knew the baby fingers

Pressed against the window pane,
Would be cold and stiff tomorrow –
Never trouble us again –
Would the bright eyes of our darling
Catch the frown upon our brow?
Would the prints of rosy fingers
Vex us then as they do now?

Then scatter seeds of kindness,
Then scatter seeds of kindness,
Then scatter seeds of kindness,
For our reaping by and by.

Ah! those little ice-cold fingers,
How they point our memories back
To the hasty words and actions
Strewn along our backward track!
How those little hands remind us,
As in snowy grace they lie,
Not to scatter thorns – but roses –
For our reaping by and by.

Then scatter seeds of kindness,
Then scatter seeds of kindness,
Then scatter seeds of kindness,
For our reaping by and by.

When the hymn was finished, Bailey looked back to see the assembled congregation rise from their chairs and spontaneously hug their neighbors and give them a kind word or two, as if immediately taking Will Chambers' sermon to heart.

"Thank you all for coming," Pastor Chambers announced. "We have cake and coffee for everyone in the church building, and sodas and milk for the young ones."

As the older folks made their way slowly toward the church, many of them were helped to navigate the coarsely mowed field by younger parishioners who graciously offered supportive arms and received thankful smiles for their kindness. Meanwhile, the men and the teenaged boys, whose bodies appeared to have been made strong by farm work or perhaps football, or both, worked hurriedly to move the chairs inside so that the old folks would have a place to sit.

Bailey climbed up on the wooden altar and pulled Will Chambers aside.

"You may find this difficult to believe, pastor, but I know who left you on that bus," she said. "I know who your natural mother was."

"You do?"

"Yes, I do. She was a very dear friend of mine. Many years ago, a short time after we'd met, she told me the story of how she left you on that bus. I even have the newspaper article about it. You may have seen it, I suppose. She carried it with her all her life."

Bailey pulled the laminated article from her purse and handed it to Will Chambers. As he read, his eyes welled with tears.

"Why is Pop Pop crying?" Little Dot asked.

"I don't know, Dot," Jack Hanford said. "Maybe he'll tell us later. For now, come with us and leave them be."

"That was my father," Will said. He did not wipe the tears from his face. "I was named after him. He was the best man I've ever known, a man who walked the walk. He died of cancer. How long has it been now? More than twenty years ago, I guess."

Will Chambers held out the laminated article so that Bailey could put it back into her purse.

"Please," she said. "You keep it."

"Who was my natural father?" Will Chambers asked. "Do you know that, too?"

Bailey paused. She considered telling the truth, but couldn't immediately see what purpose there would be in it.

"Oh, some boy, I guess." she said. "Your mother had you when she was only sixteen."

"I see," Will said. A clever smile came to his face. "I also see that you're lying. But why would you fib about such a thing?"

"Why would you think I'm lying?" Bailey said.

"Miss Foster, I am a minister. My stock in trade is people. Listening carefully to them, understanding them. I have learned over the years to sense when I'm being deceived. I don't mean to be critical, but you are the worst liar I've ever seen."

Bailey laughed. In truth, she was happy Will Chambers had caught her in the lie. She'd felt uncomfortable telling it in the first place.

"The truth is," she said, "that your mother's father was a lost soul, an alcoholic who was overcome by his basest instincts."

Will Chambers considered what Bailey said and easily read between the lines.

"You're telling me I am the product of incest," he said. "that my mother's father was my father as well, and my grandfather, too, I guess."

"I'm afraid so," Bailey said.

Will Chambers turned his tear-stained face toward the sky.

"I'm glad you told me," he said. "Thank you. I have wondered my whole life what drove my natural mother to leave me on the back of that bus. I guessed that it was because she was young and didn't want anyone to know she was pregnant. That part was easy. But even though I know child abuse was not uncommon when I was born, I guess I could not bring myself to imagine that I was myself a product of such a low sin."

Then Will Chambers looked back down at Bailey and said, "What was her name? My mother's name, I mean. This dear friend of yours. You haven't told me her name."

"It was Susan Griffin, Will. The same Susan Griffin whose soul now lives in little Dot."

Will Chambers laughed, then spoke in a soft voice, so as not to be heard.

"Please don't take any offense, Miss Foster, but I never have believed any of that soul gene hooey."

Bailey was taken aback. Hadn't Will Chambers just proudly introduced her as the discoverer of the soul gene? He'd given no hint that he himself didn't believe in it.

"Everyone in your congregation seems to believe in it," she said. "When you introduced me before the sermon they gave me an ovation that nearly broke my eardrums. Have you told them you don't believe it?"

"Why would I do such a hurtful thing?" Will Chambers said. "The soul gene, true or not, has brought peace and kindness to the world. I have seen personally the change it has made to many of the good people here today. It doesn't matter one whit to me whether it's true or it's not true. It's a good thing, and that's all that matters."

Bailey smiled. They stepped down off of the wooden altar together and Susan Griffin's grown son offered her his arm. She took it lovingly.

"Let's go have some cake and coffee," he said.

THE END

ABOUT THE AUTHOR

Lynn Demarest is a former newspaper reporter and a computer programmer. He lives near a toad pond with his wife, Diana, a cat, and a dog.